THE FLYING MOUNTAIN

THE
SEAGULL
LIBRARY OF
GERMAN
LITERATURE

THE FLYING MOUNTAIN

Christoph Ransmayr

TRANSLATED BY SIMON PARE

Seagull
BOOKS

LONDON NEW YORK CALCUTTA

This publication has been supported by a grant
from the Goethe-Institut India

Seagull Books, 2019

Originally published as Christoph Ransmayr, *Der fliegende Berg*
© S. Fischer Verlag GmbH, Frankfurt am Main, 2006

First published in English translation by Seagull Books, 2018
Translation © Simon Pare, 2018

ISBN 978 0 8574 2 720 5

British Library Cataloguing-in-Publication Data
A catalogue record for this book is available from the British Library

Typeset by Seagull Books, Calcutta, India
Printed and bound by WordsWorth India, New Delhi, India

Judith, for you

Contents

Aside

Since most poets have abandoned metrical language and now, instead of verses, use free rhythms and floating lines arranged in stanzas, here and there a misunderstanding has arisen that any text consisting of floating lines, i.e. lines of unequal length, is poetry. That is incorrect. A floating line—or better: a *flying line*—is free and does not belong to poets alone.

CR

The Flying Mountain

1.

Resurrection in Kham.
Eastern Tibet, twenty-first century.

I died
six thousand, eight hundred and forty metres above sea level
on the fourth of May in the Year of the Horse.

My deathplace
lay at the foot of an ice-armoured needle of rock
in whose lee I had survived the night.

The air temperature at the time of my death
was minus 30 degrees Celsius
and I saw the moisture
of my final breath crystallize
and disperse like smoke into the light of dawn.
I felt no cold. I was in no pain.
The pulsing of the wound in my left hand
was strangely dulled.
Through the bottomless chasms at my feet
fists of cloud came drifting from the south-east.

The ridge leading from my shelter
up and up
to the pyramidal peak
was lost in driving banners of ice,
but the sky above the highest heights
remained so deep a blue
that in it I thought I could make out the constellations
of Boötes, Serpens and Scorpio.

Neither did the stars vanish
when the sun rose over the plumes of ice
and sealed my eyes,
but appeared in my blindness,
even against the red of my closed lids,
as white pulsating sparks.

The readings on the altimeter,
which had somehow slipped
from my frozen glove
and bounced away into the clouds below,
were still branded on my retina:
atmospheric pressure, altitude, degrees Celsius . . .
the lost instrument's every measurement
a burning number.

Only when these numbers
and then the stars melted away
and finally vanished did I hear the sea.
I died high above the clouds
and heard the breakers,
thought I could feel the surf

foaming up out of the deep towards me,
carrying me once more up to the peak—
just a snow-covered rock on the beach
before it sank.

The crashing of the hail of stones
that had pulverized my hand,
the hissing of the wind, the beating of my heart—
all were drowned out by the tide.

Was I on the seabed?
Or at the summit?
In a painless peace,
which I know now
was indeed the end, my death,
and not mere exhaustion,
high-altitude hallucinations or a blackout,
I heard a voice, a laugh:
Get up!
It was my brother's voice.

We had lost each other
the previous night as the temperature plummeted.
I was dead.
He had found me.

I opened my eyes. He was kneeling by my side.
Holding me in his arms. I was alive.
My pulse was raging where the stones had crushed
my hand; my heart.

Now, when I recall
that moonlit night
as I climbed down with my brother
from the peaks of the mountain
the nomads of Kham call *Phur-Ri*,
the Flying Mountain,
staggering back to the valley below
along an ice-glazed ridge,
down gullies hollowed smooth by the wind, black
     chimneys in the rock,
and then through hip-high snow
across the saddle where we lost each other . . .

Thinking back to our stumbling progress through this
     labyrinth
of ice towards the world of men
that lay somewhere far below the towering clouds,
I always see Nyema,

hear her calming voice,
the jingling of the coral-and-shell necklaces she wore
and feel the warmth of her hands,

I see Nyema

as if her arms,
not my brother's,
had cradled me back then.

No one, I hear Nyema say,
no one dies on his path but once.

Nyema Dolma: how persistent she was
as she sought to explain a word of her language
or a simple gesture to me.
How warm her breath was
when she spelt out the name of a plant
into my ear.

Her plaited hair smelt of yak wool
and smoke, and as she spoke
she would sometimes draw
swift, fleeting figures with her index finger
on my arm or the back of my hand—
spirals, wavy lines, circles.

Get up!

I had lost my brother's tracks
in a blizzard
when the moon vanished,
as if doused by a wave of black water.
The storm had torn us apart
and driven me on through the darkness,
in which the beam of my headlamp,
splintered by crystals of ice, was the only light,
into the shelter of a rocky pinnacle.
There I survived until sunrise.

Get up!

My brother was kneeling beside me.
Holding me in his arms.

Then rose as if borne down by a leaden weight
and tried to drag me up with him.
Laughed.
Swore in helpless rage.
His face, his balaclava,
an icy grimace.

How much time had passed since we were separated?
The sun was riding high over the ridge to the peak.
The sky—cloudless.
And in the lee of the rocky needle,
in my leeward shelter—no breath of wind.

I was alive.
It was snowing.
Black snow?
Black snow.

Like charred,
shredded paper from an invisible fire,
black flakes came tumbling
out of the cloudless sky.

But when one of these flakes
settled on my brother's
ice-encrusted glove,
another on his shoulder,
on my chest, my forehead,
I saw antennae!
I saw insects' threadlike legs,

wings. Encased in hoar frost
that exaggerated and magnified
their compound eyes, proboscises and wing scales,
dead butterflies rained down
on me and my brother—
first one at a time, then in their hundreds,
and finally in a whirling swarm
that darkened the sky.

Many of these filigree corpses
appeared to shatter
as they struck my chest,
my brother's glove,
and I thought I heard a tinkling.

A tinkling?
No, there was silence.
Complete silence.

Out of a sky that at its zenith
seemed already to take on the blackness of space
fell frozen butterflies, Apollo butterflies,
like those we had seen weeks earlier in the valleys of Kham,
circling in huge swarms
above the prayer flags festooning
a ruined monastery,
above a glacier lake,
a rhododendron forest.

I was weary, unspeakably weary.
Yearned to lie there.

Lie there, sleep.
Sleep.

Get up!
My brother pulled and hauled me up,
sank back into the snow with me.

And I huddled in his arms,
six thousand, eight hundred and forty metres above the sea,
and stared through a thick flurry of flakes
at the plumes of ice above Phur-Ri,
at the dazzling peak of the Flying Mountain,
where I had carved
our names in the snow
with the handle of my ice-pick.
I was alive.
You think you were asleep,
I hear Nyema say, and see her
rocking Tashi, a sooty, bawling baby,
in her arms;

you think you were asleep, dreaming,
and yet you were dead, far from life.
Were dead and came back
because a hand fetched you back and
a voice called you.
Nyema often laughed as she spoke.
I believe it was her cheerfulness
that made me realize that that morning
under the pyramidal peak of Phur-Ri
it was not my brother's words

that ordered me back to life,
but his laughter.

He held me in his arms
and laughed, shouting through his laughter: *It's snowing!*
It's snowing butterflies! Get up!

It was as if this laughter alone
could free all other noises and words
from the silence as well—
the screech of a crampon
on the ice-glazed rock,
the roar of blood in my head,
the sound of our breathing,
which, in the rarefied air at this altitude,
was like the panting of animals.

Perhaps my brother read in my eyes
that it was above all his breathless speech
that captured my attention and
pulled me, phrase by phrase, back into our life.

He spoke so insistently, with such urgency,
as if words were his last hope
of reaching me
and I would disappear for ever
were he to fall silent.

From a gradually dwindling distance
I heard him say, *Do you remember . . .*

do you recall
you must remember, remember.

Whenever I closed my eyes
he'd call my name, again and again,
then the names of the porters
in Nyema's clan, the names of passes
we had crossed on our endless march
towards Phur-Ri's icy cliffs,
name after name, *Can you hear me,*
do you remember, get up!

During that march
we'd seen swarms of butterflies
in shimmering bands hundreds of metres long.
They fluttered over even the highest
snow-swept passes into uninhabited valleys
crisscrossed by streams of meltwater,
perhaps following a food chain
that linked flowering marshes to glaciers,
or perhaps simply
the errant trail
of a memory stretching back to an age
when no icy mountains had reared their heads
between their point of departure
and their destination,
only gentle, fertile hills.

Can you hear me?
Get up!

Once before, on the afternoon
when Phur-Ri's summit
first revealed itself to our eyes,
distant and cloud-free,
we had seen
one of these swarms of butterflies
trapped in seasonal turbulence and
sent spiralling up on columns of warm air
to invisible heights, into cold and death,
until, released at last by the exhausted thermals
and sheathed in frost,
they fell back onto the glaciers as snow.

Remember.

Nyema . . . It was Nyema who said
that, in the shelter of my final refuge,
my brother had *talked* me back from death
to life,
evoking with his litany of names
a shared memory
so indelible
that it could turn the past into the present
and call me back from the distant horizon
beyond which I'd already vanished.

I recall trying
to follow the tumbling butterflies
with my eyes,
but suddenly my head was reeling
and the first words I could force out

when in my brother's arms
were a question: *Are they dead?*

And I remember that my brother,
in his joy at my awakening
or at the tumbling corpses
in their frosted shells, could not stop laughing
and called to me through the cloud of breath
shrouding his face:
But they're flying! They're still flying!

My brother is dead.
For over a year now he has lain
buried in the ice
at the foot of the south face of Phur-Ri,
down which we had clambered for three days
and two nights, snow-blind,
repeatedly led astray by hallucinations,
towards the thundering cloud of the avalanche
that swept him away.

I think Nyema was the first,
weeks later, to express the full horror.
She was applying a thick ointment
to my bloody fingertips
and the slow-scarring wound on my battered hand
when she said, *Your brother is dead*.

Dead.
He had held me in his arms
among the swirling ice-encased butterflies.

He had warmed me
and talked me back to life,
and then preceded me
on the agonizing, interminable descent
of Phur-Ri's avalanche-torn south face
down a chasm through which no man had ever gone before.

I do not know how many hours I spent
burrowing for him in the debris of the avalanche cone.
I had no fingernails left
when a shepherd from Nyema's clan
searching for some lost yaks
came upon me near an abandoned camp.
My hands were black,
my toes black from frostbite—
but I was alive.

I remember the lancing pain
as the shepherd towed and dragged me
out of the high valley on a sled
made of branches, skins and leather straps
and, as he walked, occasionally lapsed
into a breathy, monotonous chant.

I tried to sit up,
to reach out to the singer, touch him,
reassure myself
that he was flesh, that he was *real*,
that he was not just another of the mirages
that had accompanied me down into the depths,
metamorphosing into snow,

stones and clouds
the moment I answered their questions or
groped for their outstretched arms.

I wanted to embrace this singer,
but I remained a groaning, immobile burden,
on his sled,
no longer even having the strength
to raise a wad of roasted barley,
tea and yak butter to my mouth.
The singer had to feed me.

Today,
as I walk around my brother's
sun-drenched house
on Horse Island,
from one empty, echoing room to the next,
and, through a window all but obscured
by the tracery of the salt spray, see the breakers,
the cliffs,
the Atlantic, whipped up by the gales
of recent days, I know
that a laugh may be able to fetch us back to life
but it cannot keep us there.

What keeps Nyema,
the people of her clan and me
and, no doubt, most of us alive
must be part of the sometimes-consoling,
sometimes-menacing mystery that
wherever we are
we are not alone.

Someone is always *there*
who at least knows of us, who will not let go of us
or of whom we cannot let go,
someone who pervades our memories,
our fears and our hopes,
who holds us in his arms, warms us, feeds us
or who drags us, puffing and chanting,
on a sled of branches and pelts
across the scree.
Sometimes the shepherd needed all his strength
to haul me across a stream of meltwater,
over a barrier of rocks or dead-ice moraine.
If a stone or even water
hit my black, nail-less hands
or my feet, I screamed in pain.

But he was not to be deterred
and wove every one of my screams
like a new motif into his chants
and repeated it until it melted
into the monotonous melody of his lament,
and thus he sang me into oblivion and into sleep.

I awoke
as he struggled to pull me up
from the sled before a black tent,
his face continually taking on
my brother's features.

Like some indestructible edifice, the tent towered
into the circular sky
streaked with cirrus clouds

and framed by human faces—
these were the laughing, inquisitive, distrustful
and frightened faces of my saviours.

They stooped over my wretched figure,
over a stranger
scorched by the sun and the frost
who lay with bleeding hands at their feet
and who, by the singer's account,

had fallen from the flying mountain,
out of the sky above
into the snow.

2.

Horse Island. The inheritance in West Cork.

My brother Liam
owned twelve Highland cattle,
more than a hundred Targhee sheep,
five sheepdogs
and two powerful computers
at whose screens he spent whole days
and even the occasional night.

Until we set off for Kham
Liam had made everything—almost everything—he owned
or that was of any import in his life
appear on, then disappear from
these liquid crystal screens—

the driveway, paved with dark slate,
to a farm that lay high up
on the cliffs of Horse Island;
digitized panoramas of glaciers
in the Himalaya and the Karakoram;

nautical, topographical and astronomical maps;
securities accounts, lonely-hearts ads,
letters from New Zealand and Pakistan,
and the mysterious migration routes
of the puffins
nesting at the western tip of Horse Island
on a pillar of rock covered in droppings as white as snow.

Sometimes, however, the only thing visible
on the five screens installed in the study,
in the living room and in the kitchen and bedroom
was pastureland sloping down towards the sea,
which a storm-proof electronic camera
surveyed day and night
and on which his animals grazed all year round
amid flocks of gulls.

I can no longer say today with any certainty
which of the invitations
that my brother had dispatched over the years
finally induced me
to return to Ireland
and to follow him to a near-uninhabited island
that was inaccessible on stormy days,
which of those postcards,
each offering a different view of the west coast,
which of the letters
he wrote on blank pages
from the logbook of Dunlough lighthouse,
in which he often enclosed photos.

Was it the letter from which
there slipped a photo of our masked father?
A colour photo
showing a heavily built man
wearing a blue balaclava.
He was brandishing a lobster
by its wide-open claws,
as if it were crucified.
(Every time I looked at this photo
I heard my father's muffled giggling
through the balaclava.)

Or was it the photo, scrawled with the names
of excursions undertaken,
of the rust-eaten Ford Galaxy
in which we had spent
so many childhood Sundays bouncing
towards the mountains of Kerry and Cork?

On this photo the wreck lay
in my parents' driveway,
without wheels or a bonnet,
engulfed by ivy and briars.
Ferns waved to us through the empty windows,
which we kept wound down on mountain roads
because Liam would get *seasick*
on the hairpin bends leading up
to Healy Pass or Moll's Gap.

Liam would occasionally embellish his letters
with sketches—drawings

of his astronomical observations
(such as the loop of Mercury),
plans for an extension to his boathouse
or the position of a ship
that had run aground and foundered
at Dunlough Head decades or centuries earlier.

Come home! You must get out of the water!
he would add between the drawings
and unfailingly sign off with an exclamation mark.

Although Liam insisted on keeping his computer connected
day and night to a worldwide web
that provided weather reports, satellite images,
details of disasters
and fighting somewhere or other,
stock markets, archives, libraries and electronic mail,
he never made use of this web
to exhort me to change my life.

Come home!
I would read on postcards
or on yellowed paper from Dunlough
(of which he had sheaves and sheaves),
but never on a computer screen.

Yet we had remained in touch for years
almost exclusively via the web—
he at the computers on his farm,
I at some shipping company's screen

or at the radio set of one of the freighters
on which homesickness would occasionally overwhelm me.

But when I wrote a digital message in a bottle
telling him of this homesickness,
he would ignore my complaints in his reply
and answer in his scurrying handwriting
only much later
at the anachronistic snail's pace of a courier service:
You must get out of the water!

My decision to give up my life in the machine rooms
and shaft alleys of freighters
or in drab, noisy harbourside hotels
and, like a castaway, to seek dry land
on Horse Island, a rock in the Atlantic,
touched on a longing that tied me
to many emigrant relatives,
scattered over three continents,
and also to my brother—

a longing for something
he invoked in one of his letters
as an *immovable place* beneath
an *immovable sky*.

Of course we both secretly knew
that such a place could not exist,
never and nowhere,
but even when he described Horse Island to me,
after a night at his telescope,

as a flying carpet, around which westerly winds
and rising and sinking constellations swirled
on their elliptical orbits
around the sun;
after all these reveries
it was this ruin-strewn island of all places
that always appeared from the Atlantic near Dunlough
as a haven—
a wave-beaten shelter
beyond time,
as distant and indestructible as Utopia.

I came to Horse Island.

And the signals of the beacon on Dunlough Head
(automated flashes in the darkness)
flitted night after night
across my bedroom wall
and kept me from sleeping
on my first nights on the island.

Living on Horse Island is like being on board
a ship lying far out in the roads,
connected to Ireland and all other land
by the Atlantic
—or separated by it from everything else.

During the winter storms,
even the 2-kilometre channel
we crossed two or three times a week
on the ferry or in our own cutter to reach Dunlough

would sometimes be impassable for days.
It was not only our trips for provisions that were cancelled,
but also our evenings at Eamon's Bar,
where the patrons' salty shoes
left scuffed marks on the sawdust-strewn floor
as if there'd been a brawl.

On the first day of clearing out our farm,
as I was rolling up the Tibetan carpet
my brother had bought from a Dublin trader
the year before we set out for Kham,
some sawdust from Eamon's Bar
trickled out of the finely knotted pattern
of white mountain ranges
guarded by mythical snow lions.

That carpet is now in storage with the computers
and the screens, the telescopes,
the books and all the furniture
in a shed behind the pub,
wrapped in plastic and up for sale.

I spent two weeks clearing
the bright and airy house
my brother had built from slate and teak and glass
on the foundations of a farm
(the building had been abandoned
during the disastrous nineteenth-century famines
and had subsequently fallen into ruin,
as had the other houses on Horse Island).

Four days of storms in those two weeks
hampered my crossings between the island
and the mainland, but finally all the livestock
—the cattle in pairs, the sheep in families
(their legs hobbled),
the turkeys, a couple of peacocks, the dogs,

my inheritance,

had been carried across in our cutter, my cutter,
to the breakwater in Dunlough.

There, the sheep, poultry and dogs were loaded
into the pickups of farmers
with whom Liam had shaken on deals.
The cows—Scottish Highland cattle
with Gaelic names—
disappeared on board a cattle truck
belonging to a livestock trader from Cork,
for, despite my brother's breeding for resilience,
Scots were as alien to our shores as Tibetan yaks,
and always a cause for headshaking
or merriment in pubs
from Dunlough to Skibbereen:
Those *horsemen*, those *cliffhangers*
and their Scottish buffalo!

On the mainland,
though they sometimes lifted
an appreciative glass to my brother
and the zeal with which

he had rekindled light after light
on Horse Island, the hunger island, the island of ruins
that had lain deserted
for over one hundred and fifty years—
still the agricultural experiment
on that distant rock
struck the coastal farmers as an expensive folly,
not back-breaking farmwork.

I had come from the merchant navy
to Horse Island,
my brother,
years before me,
from the programming departments
of the computer industry;
yet, however near, however visible
our parents' house
with its flimsy walls and acidic pastures
and peat fields might have been
(less than two hours' drive from Dunlough,
at the foot of the Caha Mountains),
we were presumably still too foreign
to be taken seriously in Eamon's Bar
when it came to cattle and sheep breeding.

The good-natured teasing at the bar
never bothered my brother:
Cliffhanger, Buffalo Liam . . .
But he could become rude, obscene even,
if anyone dared call him a drop-out.
He had never! dropped out of nowhere!

had only ever entered into things,
always moving forwards and upwards, step by step,
never back or down, arsehole!

It was true that on Horse Island we lived
amid an abundance of technical equipment
that enabled even island-dwellers
to do paid work at a computer screen,
to correspond, negotiate, do business
with the mainland or with transatlantic partners,
without setting foot out of doors,
while keeping sheep and cows on the side
or pursuing a passion for gardening,
breeding tree ferns, orchids
or shrub roses resistant to the salty air.

Horse Island was in step with its time,
and via the Net we kept
in touch with the world and with a life
that stretched further back into the past
and whose course was slower and wider
than any stream of information.

Now the island risks slipping back into its
former isolation. Although Liam had wired it
to the west coast of Ireland with a submarine cable,
of the sparse population it attracted
my brother and I alone
lived there all year round.

Our three neighbours
—summer and fair-weather guests
from Kerry, Cork and Dublin
(including Deirdre, a patent lawyer,
and Kieran, a publisher of illustrated books)—
lived in the slate-roofed houses
they too had built on ruins only for pleasure,
appreciated the isolation as a luxury
and, long before the winter storms arrived,
fled back to their homes.

Strangely, the emptiness
of our abandoned farm can be felt
most keenly out in the pastures
and not inside the vacant house,
whose sliding glass panels still frame
sections of a familiar panorama:

the Atlantic dotted with cloud shadows
(in broad spectrums of lead-grey, silver,
light green, midnight blue);
the black teeth of protruding reefs and rocky islets;
the jagged lines of the Irish cliffs stretching off to the west
of the picture; the flaring spray of the breakers
caught in the flashes from the Dunlough beacon . . .

Although the grass in the cow and sheep pastures,
surrounded by walls of moss-covered, unhewn stones
and a thorny mesh of wire and dry gorse,
now stands in such high waves that gusts of wind
can be seen running in silvery shadows across it

and, as ever, the gulls hang in the updraught
over the pylon of our windmill;
the pastures in particular look
as if they have been struck by disaster,
desolate for all their lushness.
Never in my years on Horse Island
have I seen them so empty.

If you break through or simply climb over
the hip-high boundary walls of these pastures
to reach the sea to their west, there is still a 3-
or 4-metre strip
of gentle grassland dotted with heather,
briars and ferns to cross
before you realize that you are standing above a chasm
on an overgrown terrace of rock
beneath which lies nothing but the roaring deep.

Black walls, sheer and overhanging in places,
with seabirds wheeling around them,
drop 200 metres down
into the waves rolling in from the Atlantic Ocean,
gouging and smashing everything in their path.

Up until the day we set out
for western China and Tibet,
I climbed these crumbling rock faces and cliffs
by dozens of routes
of vastly varying difficulty,
mainly with my brother for company,
secured by his rope,

sometimes without a safety line, close by his side,

and once only
—it was in a thunderstorm
that smoked up like a mushroom cloud
over Roaringwater Bay,
and then rushed towards Horse Island—
alone, ropeless
and as if numb with fear;
hailstones and rocks rattled down
on me from the dark sky while the gusts
threatened to tear me from the wall.
Way below me, the hailstones and rocks plunged
noiselessly into the breakers.

On summer days, when the ocean
in some bays fell so smooth and silent
that even the slap of the fin
of a seal sliding off a sunny rock into the water
was audible from afar,
we would approach these black walls
by boat, peer through our binoculars
for new starting places and ascents,
drop anchor a safe distance before the reef,
jump into the water, *swim* to the rock face
and then let the sea carry us up
to the first step of a path leading to the clouds
which we could see high above,
drifting serenely away
over the outermost edge of the pastures.

As I swam I sometimes had a sensation
of flying over chasms,
valleys and mountain peaks.
Far beneath me, floating fields of seaweed cascaded
into the submarine darkness
and sunken, shell-encrusted ribs of rock,
past which pebbles and stones,
white with bird droppings, dislodged
by the claws of flocks of launching gulls,
sank twisting through the water,
sank down
to the foot of a cliff, to depths
beyond reach of sounding lines.

As I swam I felt the gentle,
almost imperceptible breakers
carry me like a rising current
over every abyss,
raising me higher and higher
towards the top of a black mountain
that reared out of the sea
(and towards the clouds it reflected).

Should I finally find my footing
on a submerged rock
and catch a hold to pull myself
out of the mirror of clouds,

I would sometimes let myself
sink back into the weightlessness
with the disappointed sigh

of someone awaking from a dream of flying,
back into the sea;
and so I would begin my climb
a second or a third time.

On those summer days
we would always climb without a rope,
leap back into the sea
when faced with impassable sections
or become so absorbed in our games
that we were too high to jump
and were suddenly forced onwards
and upwards to that dark, jagged edge
that divided Horse Island from the sky.

But when at last we stood at the top,
and there was no more doubting that we'd reached our goal,
because the next step led no higher,
only into the void,

we found ourselves not on a summit
but gazing once more at grazing cows
across a summer pasture,
saw the boat far below us
rocking amid dazzling reflections
and, relieved, walked back
(along a winding path carved
from the rock) to sea level.
Each of our upward paths
began with a descent to the sea.

Mindful
that even the heights and peaks
of the barren mountains furthest from the sea
are measured in relation to sea level
and therefore that every ascent
equates to a path out of the sea,
we gave our routes the names of fish—
Turbot, Hake or Cod—
and avoided marking or signposting them,
but kept an exact log of the course,
difficulty and length of each ascent.

The only route not named after a fish
was one of the most difficult and was called
Passage to Kham
because that mountain, in whose shadow
my brother would finally disappear,
caused us sleepless nights long
before we struck out for Tibet.

I clearly remember the night
when he woke me
because he needed help to tie down a corrugated-
iron sheet that was flapping in the gale.
The sheet had come loose from his observatory
(a dome-shaped extension built onto the eastern side
of the house) and was in danger of being swept away.

But the force of the wind tore the long strip
of metal from our hands,
sent it spinning like a thundering sail

over the edge of the field and down into the void,
and we turned, drenched
and cursing, back towards the house.

There, on the screen in his study,
Liam showed me a black-and-white photograph
from the previous century.
During a (storm-interrupted) expedition
into the Net that night
in search of details of the history
of surveying in the Transhimalaya region,
he had stumbled upon this photograph
and seemed obsessed by the sense
of having made a discovery.

The picture, over which the shadow
of an aeroplane wing lay like a roof,
showed walls of rock crisscrossed with hanging glaciers,
crevasses and avalanche corridors;
the southern precipices of a mountain,
whose height a Chinese bomber pilot
had estimated at 9,000 metres
—a peak higher than Mount Everest!

The pilot had firebombed
a fortified monastery near Dege
as Kham warriors offered hopeless resistance
to occupying forces under Peking's command
and on his way back a storm front
forced him to take a long detour.

This manoeuvre brought him close to the flanks
of a nameless mountain,
its eerie, towering peaks
eliciting heartfelt patriotic shrieks
that were relayed over the radio to his base: This mountain,
this colossus! was the highest pillar
of the revolutionary world!

Queries from the ground staff
went unanswered,
breaking up in the atmospheric crackle
of a snowstorm over Chamdo,
into which the bomber then
vanished without further report.

The wreckage would only be discovered
twenty years later by zoologists
on the trail of a snow leopard.
The pilot was never found.
No trace. No remains.

For someone like my brother Liam,
who was interested in atlases and maps
produced with surveying techniques
based on terrestrial satellites and laser technology;
for someone capable of writing
geodesic computer programs, like Liam,

who, with a few taps on his machine,
could make the
hatched contour lines

that were caged in by coordinates
rear up into three-dimensional uplands
and mountain ranges,
into virtual landscapes, over whose folds
skimmed the shadows of the passing day
or the seasons' changing colours;

a man like that obviously knew that the history
of surveying abounds in radio messages and rumours,
daydreams of supposedly undiscovered
secrets of the earth's crust,
inaccessible gorges deep in the Himalaya
or the Karakoram, gigantic mountains
or volcanoes buried under glaciers . . .

On his computers Liam simulated
the movements of the Earth's mantle
for digital atlases and globes,
sold his animations over the Net
to every corner of a world
calculated to within a fraction
of a second, and knew of course
that captions such as the one
to the glittering, icy photo
on his computer screen
had often proved to be errors,
surveying mistakes, hoaxes or downright lies.
Still, he shouted at his screen
on that stormy night, still,
a survey expedition carried out
the year after the bomber flight revealed

that the cliff face was part of a massif
which the nomads of eastern Tibet knew as *Cha-Ri*,
just one of the world's many six-thousanders,
and Cha-Ri, the caption concluded, meant *Bird Mountain*.
When I try to pinpoint what first
led us from the beaches of Horse Island
to Kham, to our ascent
from sea level in the Atlantic to the passes
of Sichuan and the highlands of Tibet,
from yak pastures veiled with clouds
and bounded by glaciers to the fires
and black tents of Nyema's clan,
and on to the avalanche corridors of the Flying Mountain,

I always find myself recalling
that night with my brother
in his study,
that picture shining in the half-darkness,
that wall of ice that appears to be pouring down from the
        zenith.

Though nearly two years were to pass
between that stormy night
and our calamity in Kham,
what launched us on our journey
was the mystery my brother uncovered back then—
a barely distinguishable detail in that photograph:

at its edge, almost entirely concealed
by the aeroplane wing and a foaming front of cloud,
one could make out

beyond a glacier-covered saddle
another ridge that seemed to sweep
forcefully and steeply up towards
a second peak, even higher than the battlements
of the visible wall of ice!

But whichever topographical grid
from atlases and maps
my brother superimposed on the picture
of the ice-wall, it revealed nothing but contours
under the seven thousand mark around Bird Mountain,
an uninhabited wilderness with no paths and no names.

There was certainly good reason
to doubt the accuracy of these maps,
and Liam knew many possible ways of settling
questions or contradictory height readings
by consulting geodesic sources or, occasionally,
army geographical institutes.

But he did not do so,
he chose not to this time
and instead, in the days following that stormy night,
began to dream of a journey
to eastern Tibet.

Perhaps it is an urge
that can never truly be satisfied
that drives us to search for the unknown,
for what remains unspoilt
by tracks and names,

even in minutely charted areas;
to seek that immaculate blank spot
on which to stamp
an image of our reveries.
After all, projections of the imagination
or sheer greed have launched
entire fleets upon the waves,
caravans and dog-sled teams,
armies of conquerors and explorers,
who, when in doubt, trusted
in the vanishing lines of a dream
rather than measurements as their guide.

Likewise, Liam's astronomical observations,
made through a computer-controlled telescope,
sometimes reminded me
that we use precision instruments
to keep watch for worlds
that may not exist anywhere
but inside our heads.

Hence the foot of the flying mountain surely lay
not in Tibet, the land of the Khampas,
but instead by the sea,
where three hundred and fifty million years ago
the black rock walls of Horse Island
arose out of the surge.

For Monkfish, Turbot, Hake and Cod
and all the other cliff routes
we had named after fish,

led out of the water
through a fog of spray, up crumbling belts of rock
and past seabirds' nests
not just to the edge of a field
but on, beyond life
and any earthly pasture,
to the icy pyramidal peak of Phur-Ri.

Still, with every step we took
away from the ocean's mirror and on to greater heights,
we simultaneously
plunged deeper into our own past.
For, like any vanishing line
that leads to the margins of life,
those climbing routes bound us
from our very first ascent
not only to that which was furthest away but equally
to that which was nearest and dearest—
to memories of our first walking trips,
the childhood treks to our father's
high peat fields and sheep pastures
and, in summer, to the lakes of Kerry and Cork,
along whose rocky shores
climbing had been a game.

Even our family pilgrimages
to a bubbling spring in the Caha Mountains,
accompanied by prayers and hymns to Mary,
surged up once more out of the depths:
at that wishing well, a ribbon had to be woven
into the branches of a rhododendron bush

and a sip of spring water
drunk from cupped hands
to bring a well-kept secret wish
closer to fulfilment.

Should anyone ever reveal
his secret wish,
we were warned on these pilgrimages,
he would be tormented to the end of his days
by insatiable yearnings.

During the first few weeks after Liam's death,
as I lay on my sickbed in one of Nyema's clan's black tents,
I dreamt
that it was neither a desire to see far-off places
nor a yearning for some virgin, untrodden spot
on the world map
that had led us to Kham in search
of a forgotten mountain;
but that that mountain had found *us*,
its victims—two tiny silhouettes
on the rock faces of Horse Island.

It had drifted ineluctably towards us—
first as a white fragment of digital data,
then as a burgeoning hallucination,
continually disappearing behind scudding clouds,
and finally draped in glaciers and everlasting snow,
awe-inspiring, overpowering, rushing towards us
and past us, with blazing plumes of snow—

and had sucked us in its wake
from the shelter of Horse Island
and our life there
into the rarefied desolation
of its highest heights,
under a dark sky adorned even in daylight
with starry constellations.

3.

Sleepless by the Yangtze Jiang.
Sleepless in the Cahas.

How small my brother's fist was.
Mouth half open, his breathing shallow,
he lay beside me in his down sleeping bag,
entangled in a dream
that made him clench one fist
while the other hand groped at thin air.
Was he trying to hoist himself
up an imaginary cliff?

It was Liam who had shown me
how to push an exploratory hand
into a crack in a vertical face,
wedging your fingers inside the rock
or curling them into a fist,
then pulling yourself up on this anchor
to the next pocket, the next hold.
Was he dreaming of our routes
on Horse Island?

He couldn't remember when he awoke.
Undisturbed by the occasional shouts
and laughter of the Khampas
outside in the night,
he slept in our olive-green dome tent,
which crouched kennel-like
among the five black yak-hair tents
of this nomadic riverside camp.

A skein of saliva
trickling from the corner of his mouth
glittered when one of the torches outside
flared up, its glow slanting
through the open tent door
into the darkness where we lay.
This weak, flickering gleam
seemed mysteriously related
to the dancing signal lights
bordering our camp—flaming reflections
in the waves of the Yangtze Jiang.

Coyly, as cautiously as a child,
Asia's mightiest and longest river slid
through this night out of the silhouetted mountains
towards our camp—a slender mountain river,
casting back the nomads' fires,
showing no signs as yet of the monster
that poured into the East China Sea
nearly 6,000 kilometres
from its headwaters
and a thousand metres below our campsite.

At a safe distance from the torches
and a long way before the first
of the nomads' tents strewn along its bank,
the river appeared, however, to lose all interest
in human settlements,
winding its way into a meander
bordered by sand banks
and vanishing, deep in gurgling soliloquy,
into the darkness.

Liam's fist and hand as small as a child's,
the Yangtze Jiang barely more
than a wide, leaping brook,
even the silhouettes of the mountains
mere paper cut-outs; yes, the entire Khampa
community of forty-two people
(most of them women and children)
gathered in five tents,
ninety-six yaks and eight mastiffs—
sheepdogs the size of Great Danes—
that were meant to ward off wolves and other attackers,

all this a toy box full of tiny tents,
miniature sheepdogs, snow-dusted papier-mâché hilltops
and fist-sized livestock,
tipped out into the rocky landscape.

Everything I could make out in the dark tent
or through the lighter triangle of the open door
during this night in the second month
of our trip to the foot of the Flying Mountain

struck me as oddly shrunken,
detached from any semblance of reality.
Even sounds changed their meaning
as their volume ebbed and flowed,
the canvas flapping in the wind,
the growl of a receding storm;

the rustling of the sleeping bag
(when Liam shifted in his dreams)
—boulders, trickling sand, harbingers of a rockfall.

And, finally, the murmur of the Yangtze
—a chorus of voices and verses.
As incessantly and soothingly as a prayer wheel,
the Yangtze gradually began to permeate
and transform the other noises of that night:

the bumpy truck journey with a trader
from Ya'an, which for days had carried us closer
to the high valleys of Kham and whose roar still
rang in my ears as I lay in my sleeping bag,
were lost in the sound of the water,
as was the wailing pop music
to which the trader listened
every evening on his shortwave radio
as he drank himself to sleep
on the camp bed
on his truck's covered platform.

The man from Ya'an was willing, for a price,
to ignore laws and regulations

and take two Europeans in his truck
(his storehouse and mobile market stall)
along avalanche-prone mountain roads and tracks
to the camping grounds of his customers—
the Khampas who waited for him beside the Yangtze.

There we would take leave of him
and travel on with the nomads.

Occasionally I thought I could make out words,
whole sentences, in that polyphonic water music,
with which the river gnawed at its edges,
streamed past boulders, ground down gravel and sand
    banks,
leapt over low stepping stones
or frolicked in spiralling eddies.

I heard counting rhymes and the refrains
of songs from the Caha Mountains,
flywheels from the engine rooms
of freighters long scrapped or sunk,
and finally even
my father's snores.

Nights in tents.
I always hated those nights in tents,
hated too those endless, sleepless hours
in stuffy darkness,
and the excruciating wait for dawn.

Whereas Liam . . .
back then in the Cahas, Liam,
who as a teenager was passionate about the outdoors
and thus firmly on our father's side,
not only put up with damp sleeping bags
and dew-soaked or dripping tent canvas
running with condensation in the grey light of morning
as the natural backdrop
to our hikes through the mountains
of Cork and Kerry,
but appeared even to enjoy
this toil, these ordeals.
As we trudged, weighed down with gear and food,
peat sods for the campfire even,
through the high valleys of the Cahas
or Macgillicuddy's Reeks,
pitched our tent long before darkness fell
on the shore of a mountain lake,
and then lay in the darkness
to the left and right of our father,
who always blocked the middle and thus the tent door,
the time till daybreak seemed to fly past for Liam,
whereas for me it stood still.

During those boyhood nights, Liam never tired
of whispering to me across our snoring father's body
new interpretations for the mysterious,
menacing noises outside in the dark;
he promised me—his fearful, unsleeping brother,
three years his junior—protection
from all ghosts, trolls and monsters,

but then woke our father
when a sheep came too close to our tent
or a gust of wind tugged at the awning.

Manoeuvres was my father's name
for these summer nuisances,
which Liam hungered for
whereas I always had to be coaxed,
or tempted with presents and promises.

Disregarding the now-appeasing,
now-furious objections of our mother,
who could not forget
how, as a Red Cross nurse in her home town of Belfast,
she had tended gaping shrapnel wounds,
bubbling with blood, and burns
after a bomb attack,
our father acted on these hikes
as if he had to train
his sons in the mountains
for future battles
over Irish unity—

against the British Army,
against the Ulster separatists
and against every damn Protestant in the North;
he praised Liam as his *true* son,
thereby reinforcing my hatred
of marches and tents,
of mist-shrouded mountains
and life under the open sky.

The only things our father extolled as *true* and *real*
were those that fully lived up to his ideas
about the world.
A windowless corridor became known as *the true Ireland*
when he papered its walls with hundreds of photos
and a grease-stained map of the world.

Whenever, after much packing,
we left the house carrying our rucksacks,
either for a brief grace period
in the Ford Galaxy on the drive
to the start of a manoeuvre, or
panting straight out through the back gate
and across a gorse-covered slope
towards the mountain tops,
we would stumble—as always on our way out—
through this true Ireland.

The photos on the walls
showed close and distant relatives, family friends and
        acquaintances
who had emigrated years or decades before
and were scattered across the continents,
showed them at their weddings, their birthday
and Christmas parties, at christenings and
St Patrick's Day parades, in front of memorials
and their new houses, new cars,
new swimming pools even.

Caught in an unchangingly blissful dream
that had apparently come true

in a far-flung corner of the world,
they stood laughing or with solemn, immortal expressions
in front of the trophies of prosperity,
elders resting their paws
on the shoulders of their descendants,
the descendants seemingly petrified by this burden,
and so they would remind our father, remind us:
This is how far we've made it!
Here we are! Remember us!

All of these photos, black and white
or in screaming, flash-lit technicolour, clustered
like butterflies impaled on pins
around one particular picture—the portrait
of the staunchly Catholic inventor Henry Ford,
whose ancestors had once fled from poverty
in Ballinascarthy,
our father's birthplace,
to find in America if not a new,
then a second homeland and
exotic happiness.

How strange the contrast
between the summer skies
on these family snaps and portraits—
the weekend skies, the skies over gardens,
weddings and the sea,
and all the other bright backgrounds
illuminated by candles or even bursts of fireworks
to these scenes of frozen cheer and celebration—
and the darkness of our windowless corridor,

which smelt of wet clothes and damp boots
even in midsummer;
a gloomy gallery of yearning,
lit by a single, naked light bulb.

My father spent many evenings in this bulb's dim glow
with a box full of photos,
beside him some scissors, a pin cushion
and threads of many colours.
For on the second wall, facing the photo mosaic,
was spread the metre-square map of the world,
on which he used pins and cotton

to mark all the interconnected places,
where not only these fortunate relatives,
friends and acquaintances were to be found
—their houses, gardens and garages—
but also every Irish community
of whose existence he'd learnt.

All these settlements, havens and ports of call,
both accidental and planned,
were closely connected by threads
whose different colours
specified the type of relationship,
the degree of relations and
networks by marriage, or origins
in a birthplace abandoned for ever.

It was this Ireland
that so many emigrants' dreams

or sheer poverty had spun into an endless web,
a cat's cradle spanning Australia and both Americas,
New Zealand and various South Pacific islands,
the shores of Indonesia and southern Africa,
that my father finally felt was grand enough,
big enough, to merit
the distinction of being called *true*.

All along, his own pinhead remained immovable
on this map of the world, motionless,
stuck between the letters O and U
in the words Caha Mountains,
a crotchet, a floating note
between two contour lines just above the sea.

For my father could only speak of farewells
and never of arriving;

as a boy he had waved to so many emigrants
from the piers of Cobh and Dun Laoghaire,
and scoured the stormy main around Fastnet lighthouse
with binoculars on clear days
for America-bound vessels;
for container ships and passenger ships
that shrank to dots far to the west
before sinking, tiny and silent,
below the watery horizon.

How often had he announced
at bars in Glengarriff and Bantry,
over Sunday lunch and even (almost inaudibly)

in his dreams
that he would one day follow
the vanished passengers of these ships: *I'll up and leave*!
And yet he had stayed
beneath an immovable sky
in an immovable place.

Throughout my childhood years
I took all these pins
on the world map—these frozen droplets,
tears in the dragnet
of longitude and latitude—
to be markings for tents: tents of red,
tents of black, blue and the other coloured
threads stretched across mountains, deserts and seas;
tents, because my father
always spoke of Irish camps
when referring to one of these points.

And so Ireland, the *true* Ireland,
long remained a swarm of pins to me,
a mysterious collection of tents,
scattered around the globe,
and I hated each and every one of them.

True and *real*:
I grew to hate these words,
and I would start to complain of sickness and headaches
the day before a manoeuvre,
yet my only escape from the mountains
was if I was truly suffering

from these or equivalent ailments.
(And that rarely occurred,
for oddly it was Liam
who struggled with nausea on our hairpin drives
into the mountains, and therefore always chose
to set out on foot,
preferring to leave directly from the corridor
through the garden into the mountains
rather than approaching them in the Ford Galaxy,
and he thereby extended many of our manoeuvres
by many exhausting miles.)

Decades later, after my return
from the seas to dry land,
after my move to Horse Island
and into my brother's world,
it took summer trips together
into the pleats of the European continent
(hikes and finally high-mountain treks
into the Mont Blanc massif, bivouacking, nights in tents,
to which Liam had not just to invite me
but also to persuade me)

for me to begin to regard the lightweight, flapping tent
    sides
of high-visibility canvas, woven from paper-thin
weather- and waterproof polyester,
under which we lay awake during storms,
once even in a late-August blizzard,
as a life-saving barrier between survival
and death.

The things I had hated for so long
became familiar. I even began to take pleasure
in spending nights outdoors,
nights without the protection of walls
and a fixed roof, pleasure
in the strange sense of security
inside a portable, foldable, rollable skin
that could be stretched over a few metres of stony ground.

How often I've reproached myself
for the futility of this reasoning, but Liam
might still be alive
if we'd struck the tent at our final high camp
on the way to the summit of Phur-Ri
and carried it with us, rather than leaving
the shelter behind under an overhanging ridge;

left it behind, trusting
that in one day we would be able
to scale the remaining few hundred metres
to the summit and climb back down
to the safety of the tent.

Maybe that tent's weight
in our summit backpacks would not have
represented merely wasted energy as we feared,
but also the reassuring certainty
that we could survive and sit out
even a sudden storm inside this protective skin.

Maybe that tent would have
preserved us from frenetic panic,
as, with horror, we climbed back from the summit
above the tower of cloud boiling up out of the abyss
after a sudden weather change,
and hurried down into the deep,
faster! onwards!
and then past the overhang
and the abandoned tent
along the wrong path, towards death.

Yet near the summit, of all places,
in the final desolate heights
that suddenly seemed to fall away
beneath our feet that day
and begin to curve back behind the mountain—
there of all places, high up, we would have found
hollows, dips and shallow, sheltered bowls,
in which a tent
could have withstood the storm,
as if cupped in a protective palm,
with us safely inside.

Up there, way up there! only up there,
I have told myself so many times,
only there was the shelter at hand
that was no longer to be found
on our way down into the depths,
back to the world of men.

Or did we merely dream those bowls?
Merely dream, in our exhaustion
and breathlessness, the dips and hollows
and the flat snowscape around the summit,
reminiscent of the rolling, fenced pastures
that so often awaited us at the end of our routes
up the cliffs of Horse Island?

For so long, an eternity,
during our last agonizing hours of ascent,
the peak of Phur-Ri had hidden
behind icy clouds and crystalline plumes;
yes, it seemed—when it finally
and scornfully revealed itself,
a blazing dome in the low afternoon sun—
to retreat before us,
farther each time
it flared for a few painful breaths
through the clouds
before immediately disappearing again,
retreating before our every step
into the deepening blue of the sky
and then into the brooding black of space
which began to descend on us
through shredding curtains of ice.

And when the whole sky was finally rent,
cleared and darkened only
by that monstrous towering cloud to the north-west,
we no longer knew if we were gazing up or down
at glittering, star-like dots of light,

exploded suns, because at the top, the very top,
height and depth were one
and indistinguishable.

And we stared at each other
and stared up and stared down
and fought for air, gasping and panting,
felt the floor of snow
subside beneath our feet
and then begin to fall away again,
gently, ever more steeply.

We had reached the summit.

From here, at last,
no more paths led upwards,
every path led only into the abyss,
and I stumbled into Liam's arms
because suddenly the Flying Mountain
offered no further resistance, no gradient,
no ground.
I stepped off the edge and after
Liam had saved me from falling
and immediately released me,
and the mountain bore me once more,
I began to write our names.

Our names,
with the shaft of my ice-axe
in the snow.

How placid it was on these heights,
from where all routes pointed into the deep.

And was this ugly, bestial noise
our breath? My breath?
An hour? Was it only minutes?

I don't know how long we stayed
at the top, the very top,
nor can I recall
when the towering cloud to the north-west
began to tip and fall, to collapse
and crash down upon us.

Arcades, cornices, buttresses, struts,
demons, praying saints, gargoyles
—all the colours of weathered stone
and all raining down on us.

I felt the vast pressure
of walls rupturing, bursting around us,
waves of icy air
that threatened to sweep and blow me away,
heard the thunder of an abruptly gaping vacuum
and, in the sudden ensuing silence,
the crackling of ionized empty space,
saw in that same instant
the flamelets of St Elmo's fire
on my ice-axe—a blazing,
immediately extinguished garland of fire—
and only then
the lightning smothered by snow flurries.

Now it was Liam clinging to me.
Throw away the metal! Throw away your ice-axe!
Away, let's run, down into the deep,
into cover, into a cave, a shelter.
Throw away anything metal, trekking poles, ice screws.
Throw them away, and climb down. Down and away
from inside this exploding cloud.
And another crash,
followed so closely by lightning
as though the glare
were thunder made visible.

Get down! Flat. In the snow.
And then move on!
Faster.
Down.

Yet the holes, furrows and ditches
that we, both victors and terrified fugitives,
kept trying to dig as we rushed downhill,
jumping up, then, barely back on our feet,
falling into cover again, lying,
panting, and here and there
and always along an escape route determined
purely by gravity, trying to beat a path
with our clotted, gloved claws,
revealed nothing but inviolable, shallow rock.
The peaks, the ridge and our path
were swept virtually clean: no shelter.
And without a tent there was no staying, even
in the snowy hollows; the storm scraped them from the
    rock

or levelled them out, filled them with needles and crystals
like sand fills the glass body
of a suddenly inverted timer.
Time, our time, was running out,

and we chased after it, after fleeing life,
bounded, ran, fell and bounded
for heaven's sake! back towards the col
where our tent had to be;
always down, farther and faster down,
until we lost each other,
one screaming to the other,
one inaudible to the other,
gagged by the force of the wind,
full of doubt about his own life
and his brother's life,
each alone in the thundering void.

The tent we had left,
the tracks of our ascent,
a safety rope we had screwed into the rock-hard snow,
the rock formations along the summit ridge;
all were gone,
engulfed by a chrome-like,
lightning-spitting wall. No tent.
No shelter anywhere.

Thus we strayed, each alone, past all of this
and were trapped, each alone,
in the ruins of a sky
from which no clemency came.

Heaven, heaven have mercy,
I heard myself
twice, thrice utter
our father's terrified groan.

I stammered words
that *he* sometimes murmured
in our nights under canvas
in the mountains of Kerry and Cork,
and had even shouted, *Heaven have mercy*
when he dreamt of battles for Ireland,
of comrades stumbling to their deaths,
the salvoes of executions
at Mountjoy prison in Dublin, of everything
he used to invoke in his tales of war:
Heaven have mercy!
And Liam and I, torn from our sleep
or dozing by his sighs,
would look at each other in shock
over the dreamer with his sour, sweaty odour
before breaking into a baffled giggle,
and our father would turn towards Liam or me,
moaning, eventually snoring,
never opening his eyes,
and would carry on sleeping: *Heaven have mercy*.

If the old man had drunk whiskey the previous evening
while telling his stories of Irish martyrs and heroes
by the campfire, a trickle of spit
would sometimes run from his mouth.

I recall that as I lay awake in the unquiet darkness
of our dome tent on the banks of the Yangtze Jiang
I thought I saw not Liam but my father,
caught in his dreams, again and again—
this father, who could tell such passionate,
rowdy tales of rebellion and civil war

but who on sheep-slaughtering days
would leave the killing to a neighbour,
had oddly small hands and small fists,
which seemed to belong to a different body,
to a different man.

Even when it came to the chickens,
it was our mother or later Liam
who would bind their claws and chop off
their heads on a wooden block in the shed;
Father couldn't do it.

My hands, he would say
whenever his wife protested at this slaughtering
or at the wage the neighbour
demanded for his efforts, *my hands
are too small for it*—and grinning
would hold up his arms like a soldier
offering to surrender.

What cold images
came to me out of the darkness
of our dome tent by the Yangtze Jiang:
the manoeuvres in the mountains of Kerry and Cork,

as present as if they were only just past,
and even the slaughtering days on our parents' farm
seemed so vivid that it was as if headless chickens
were fluttering among the yaks
grazing out in the darkness.

I lay sleepless beside Liam as if at the hub of a wheel,
equally far from everything
and equally close to everything; not only
that which lay far behind us, but also
that which the future still held hidden,
as close to the pathless expanses
of these mountains and glaciers
as to the cliffs of the Irish coast;
no farther from the yaks
of a nomadic clan than to the cows
that gawped at us in astonishment
when, after hours of climbing,
we ascended the overhanging walls of Horse Island
to the cloud-hugging edge of the void
and on beyond the rim of the sky
to the top, the very top,
where we stepped out onto grassland,
luscious grassland.

Close beside the looming ridges
of the land of Kham lay the Irish mountains,
whose bare summits were no more distant
than the final apex of our life together,
which for a few gusts of wind

was to bear our names, before vanishing again
behind curtains of darting ice crystals—

all so vivid in the darkness
of our olive-green dome tent, in which I
heard the Yangtze Jiang whispering the verses
of songs from the Caha Mountains
and even the snoring of our long-buried
father as he dreamt of war,
he who couldn't kill and couldn't fight
and could never leave Ireland.

During our days at Nyema's clan's tented camp
Liam and I, two shallow-breathing guests from the sea,
would get our first unclouded
view of a mountain that
the clan called *Cha-Ri*, Bird Mountain.

Cha-Ri, a flaming keep
rising from a curtain wall of mountains,
was the first of three ice-clad giants.
They kept watch over mountain valleys,
whose stepped bases led
up into the clouds like a stairway;
on each step new pastures greened
as the year crept ever higher.

If the weather had been clear that sleepless night,
I might perhaps have seen
Bird Mountain's cascading glaciers shimmering
in the moonlight through the tent's open door.

But the night was moonless, cold
and overcast, and as day broke
it began to snow.

4.

Arrival of the seamen. A feint.

Mountains in the blue-black watery depths, ridges
on which seaweed waved in the tidal currents,
ravines that led neither into the clouds nor to a valley
but down to the murky bed
or up into the light of the waves,
coral reefs, shallows, beaches,
the roar of the surf;

Liam had smiled with pity at my ravings,
interrupted one of my evocations of the sea
by the hearth of Tsering Dorje, Nyema's father,
and asked mockingly whether
there were submarine summit crosses
on the coral reefs in the sea off Horse Island . . .
But what else could I have reported,
what else could I have answered?

How could I answer a herder
who had never left his high valleys

and precipitous pastures, and never would,
who in summer weeks took his yak herds
to the lip of hanging glaciers,
and yet followed only the seasons and fresh grass
and found refuge, even in winter, in valleys
four to five thousand metres above the distant,
unimaginably distant surface of the sea?

How to answer a man from Nyema's clan
for whom even Lhasa seemed to be on a different planet,
the Potala Palace no more than a mirage,
the long-disappeared Dalai Lama
as remote as a god . . . ?

Which place names might be intelligible to a nomad,
a walker, a rider,
whose lifetime travels, set end to end,
amounted to less than the length
of our journey from Horse Island
to the southern flank of Phur-Ri?

The first question Liam, myself and our guide,
the trader from Ya'an, were asked
when we reached the tents by the Yangtze
was always, in translation, simply:
Where from? Where do you come from?
Where do they come from?

We were crouching on the load bed of the truck
of this Chinese man from Ya'an, to whom Liam's
web-based search for an ally had led us—

the fruit of an electronic correspondence
with business partners in Shanghai and Hong Kong.

The mud-encrusted vehicle
was escorted for hundreds of metres
along the boulder-strewn approach to the camp
by children who hopped barefoot through the slush,
before it was besieged by their mothers—
women adorned with coral and turquoises
(among them, as I later learnt,
laughing Nyema too)—and herders
wearing red ribbons and gleaming gold threads
in their long hair, woven into a dense, plaited turban.

We didn't dare to get down
as long as the tumult of our reception
included mastiffs barking, howling
and leaping against the sides
of the truck with bared fangs.
(During the weeks we travelled
with the nomads, we twice had
to dress bite wounds which these ferocious guard dogs
inflicted even on their masters.) We stood in wait
and waved to the throng
until the dogs were tamed
and chained to tent pegs.

Where did we come from?

The trader from Ya'an was familiar to the nomads,
a guest who appeared twice a year,

and seldom more, at their camps.
Yet in the high valleys from which Nyema
and her clan ventured as far as the switchbacks
of the landslide- and avalanche-prone pass road,
by which we had proceeded from the paddy fields
of Sichuan into the highlands of Kham,
most place names and the epithets
of seas, rivers and continents
carried no meaning.

Of course, Horse Island, an isle of horses,
might still chime with a livestock herder,
but the name of a valley, of a plateau
in a country somewhere in Europe?

If anyone from Nyema's clan
ever left his high pastures and these mountain meadows
spilling down out of the clouds and ice
it was only to undertake a pilgrimage to Lhasa
or to join a yak caravan
that would take him to the edge of his world—
to the great salt lakes to the north-west.

And yet the men and women who surrounded
our truck (when it finally came to a halt)
bedecked themselves
with fantasies of unattainable foreign parts,
treasures from the flipside of their world,
wearing on their belt buckles, bracelets and rings
turquoises whose hue had faded

under the Kham sun from deepest blue
to glowing green—ocean colours;

they even wore, as their most precious ornaments,
necklaces of shells and red corals
from the South China Sea and the Indian Ocean,
gems hauled from the depths of seas
on which even the pilgrims and salt-carriers among them
would never set eyes,
and yet everyone saw them again and again

in fireside tales, in dreams,
sometimes even in pictures in months-old newspapers
(mildew-spotted and used as wrapping paper)
and in reports by traders
such as our guarantor from Ya'an,
who transported these treasures
and other wares up into the thin air of their yak pastures
where he exchanged them for wool and leather, hides,
fetishes and medicinal herbs
and even for soot-smeared pieces of paper—
Chinese banknotes, magic paper!—
with which even the most secret wishes
might be realized.

Turquoises. Corals. The sea.
Forever separated from coasts, ports and beaches
by the world's highest peaks,
every member of Nyema's clan had
nonetheless seen towering waves—
watched, with dreamy eyes,

the incoming rollers, the deep-blue bottom,
from which shells and gemstones
and all manner of jewels, life itself,
had been salvaged and raised into the clouds.

One of the first laws Liam and I
learnt in the Khampas' settlements
was regarding water.
To the nomads all water was so sacred—
that of rivers as much as the still water of lakes
and, deepest and mightiest of all,
every undrinkable drop of the sea—
that humans were forbidden
to eat fish.

Water brought everything and carried everything away,
flushing and flooding, uncovering and burying
and washing away prayers
engraved on stones sunk in fords,
depositing them by the sea beneath the open sky,
and thus beneath the eyes of the gods.

Water liberated one valley of ice and scree
and blocked off another for ever with glaciers.
Whatever came, whatever existed
had crystallized from water
and returned to water,
like the salt in tears.
To kill a fish was to disrupt this flow—
no, to disrupt life itself—

and squander one's strength
on the dark side of the world.

Where from? Where do you come from?

We came from the sea, Liam and I.
This I said, I shouted, at the very moment
of our arrival, from the truck
of a trader from Ya'an, and later
at firesides and in darkened tents,
and even later, as I accepted roasted barley and salt
as a welcoming gift in snow-clad valleys,
I shouted or whispered it
over and over again: *From the sea. We come from the sea.*

In nearly two years of preparation
Liam had spun our trip to Kham
from so many yarns from the Net,
during many nights at his computer screens
(always with a view of the sea)
behind a camouflage web
of polite enquiries, requests
and his connections
to digital cartography offices,
party headquarters and marketplaces
dealing in adventure and expeditions.

Shielded by this cocoon,
our route to the Flying Mountain
gradually and irreversibly took shape,
like an insect inside its pupa.

Liam badgered trading partners in South East Asia and
     China
and agencies in Hong Kong and Shanghai
with travel plans dressed up as field trips,
and asked copyists with whom he was friendly
to intercede with the central authorities.

(These copyists in southern China—
Liam showed me an Internet video
of their exhausting work—supplied him with the raw mate-
     rial
for geodesic animations
by putting their apparently limitless graphic abilities,
gleaned from tracing Chinese characters,
to use by translating atlases
and encyclopaedic works
from the Latin alphabet
into binary code.
They reminded me of medieval monks
and their richly illustrated transcripts of the Bible—
and they also did their best for our trip.)
While the animals grazed
on the windy pastures of Horse Island
and the cliffs of our island gave up another secret
with every new route we named after a fish,
Liam wrote electronic (and even, though rarely,
     handwritten)
letters decorated with drawings
and photos of Horse Island
to Tibetan communities in exile
in Indian Dharamsala,

to party offices in Beijing and Chengdu,
seemed willingly to provide diplomatic delegations
and authorities on the other side of the world
with details of his island life, our origins and plans,

and in all his descriptions, embellishments
and illustrations he was careful to hide
the true reason for our journey to Kham—
the quest for a forgotten mountain.

For in those months and years,
Kham was once more regarded by every travel agency
as a practically inaccessible, even forbidden land.

Very few pictures and reports made it
through the news blackout on information
from the autonomous Chinese province of Xizang,
from Tibet, during our preparations.
That which did resembled coded messages,
rumours almost exclusively
related to a mysterious rebellion,
revolts in the great monasteries of Tsang
and also those in Kham,
attacks on occupying Chinese forces
by pilgrims in Lhasa.

On the Net flickered blurry pictures of monks
brandishing banners and placards
bearing the banned portrait of the Dalai Lama,
and even pictures of monks
armed with assault rifles and stones.

The insurrection, it was said,
was threatening to spread to the provinces
of Xinjiang Uygur and Qinghai and Sichuan.

Travel to eastern Tibet? To Kham?
Impossible was the final conclusion
of the replies Liam received.

A change in the Beijing oligarchy,
a scandal at the top of the world's most powerful party
had led to price slumps on the securities exchanges
and, in the remotest foothills of the Tibetan plateau,
to renewed outbreaks
of a supposedly extinguished blaze,

an age-old creeping fire
which, according to comments on the Net,
might swell into a storm of flames and sweep
through the deserts encircled by the Himalaya, Karakoram
and Kunlun Shan mountains and the bastions of a People's
    Army,
where many embers still smouldered
beneath the ashes.

Rebellion? Revolution? The beginning of a new era
which, after unshackling a voracious economy,
might finally do the same for minds and thoughts?
News, rumours and coded messages contradicted one
    another
as did the information in broadcasts and the print media.
Despite hundreds of orbiting eyes and ears,

camera lenses, emitters and satellites,
Tibet remained as silent and enigmatic
as back in the mists of time.

Unperturbed by events that pointed
not to the future but to the past,
Liam kept on spinning his cocoon
and gradually persuaded me,
as he had previously with the path from water to dry land,
to take the path into the heights, into the mountains,
winning me over for a daring, impossible journey,
finally presenting me
with plans for a metamorphosis:

Disguised as harmless lovers of peasant culture,
tourists interested in grazing methods
and cultivation techniques and, more generally,
in the history of the transition
from nomadism to sedentary life,
we would become trailblazers, nay explorers
and land-namers. Adventurers!
And all of this under the eyes
of suspicious, ubiquitous authorities,
under the eyes of escorting officers
and helpers assigned to monitor and report on us.

If my brother Liam had a second uncontrollable passion
other than for vertical ascents,
it was for tricking and circumventing
all forms of authority, making a mockery
of actual or supposed power.

Barely fourteen (and disguised
as a legal driver in hat and coat),
he had parked our father's Ford Galaxy,
which now lies rusting under thistles and briars,
in the very month the vehicle was purchased
so close to the church doors
that neither could be opened,
and those attending Pentecostal Mass
had to leave God's house through the sacristy window.

This prank was Liam's retaliation
for our father's angry *No*
when my brother had asked to demonstrate,
at the wheel of the new Ford, the driving talents
he had recently and secretly acquired
steering tractors on a farm in the Bantry hills.

Liam refused on principle to obey any rules
whose necessity he did not accept;
he did what he considered himself capable of
and remained unfazed by masquerades of authority,
comparing cassocks and uniforms with servants' outfits
and processions, marches and even parades
with a fools' ballet.

That he had swapped promising positions in programming
for the ruins and pastures of Horse Island
might perhaps be attributed to the simple fact
that most borders appalled him—
unless they were shores.

Only in his virtual animations
did my brother enjoy untrammelled domination—
for instance, when he ordered contour lines
and swarms of summit survey points
to rise up out of their two dimensions
into shadow-casting mountains
or wave-battered continental shelves;
when he drained oceans from their deepest basins
to highlight the dried-out trenches
and strata of their beds in the shades
of prehistoric fault lines.

He could even depict the future of the highest mountain
        ranges
as waves rolling through the ages and flattening out
under the impact of erosion and tectonics
as they were transformed within the parameters
of a program into deserts or fertile plains
from which reared nothing but towers, mosques,
cathedrals (or palaces of government as bombastic
as the cloud-wreathed tower of Babel).
But what then happened, or rather,
what Liam made happen:
he always decorated his cartographic works
(like a monk copying out the Holy Scriptures)
with something like illuminations, background pictures,
and in so doing expressed the imperceptible processes
        of change
and their disastrous tremors
as micro-modular definitions—
verses, columns and outpourings of binary code—

letting lava flows ossify into reefs
in the background of a relief map, then a hundred
        millennia later
scatter as sandstorms once more.
Continents flared up one last time
before sinking, like an after-image,
into the pitch-black vacuum; seas evaporated
into ancient rock springs and volcanic vents.

Only across the pattern-like surface
of these electronic mosaics did roads,
provincial borders, shipping and railway lines
and all the cartographic signs of civilization run
like irrelevant, fluid ornamentations
over the inexorable geological drama,
forming reliable scale maps ready to print.

Combining his persistence with the resourcefulness
and playfulness of an inventor,
my brother not only managed
to obtain entry visas for us to Lhasa
but also permits to travel
through the smouldering east of Tibet—
two seats in a convoy of four off-road vehicles
that would crawl over passes of almost 6,000 metres
from Lhasa to Chengdu in Sichuan
and, in passing, demonstrate
to travellers (and probably to the public as well)
that peace prevailed across the country.

A delegation of trustworthy
surveyors, agricultural engineers and botanists
from Nepal and India, Bhutan, Sichuan,
North Korea and, as a curious
and enviable exception, two island-dwellers,
representatives of Horse Island!—in any case, experts
in agriculture and forestry;
a party of travellers loyal to outdated revolutions
and dogmas, mandated by Beijing to find answers
to technical and scientific questions
about cultivation, fertilizers and yields,
should by the same opportunity conclude
that nothing was ablaze here—
not in the valleys
and not on the mountains
(on whose steep slopes we saw
vast fields of prayer flags fluttering,
rows of flagpoles hundreds of metres long,
as countless as the stalks of monoculture crops
rustling and undulating in the wind).

We were to find everything calm,
everything under control,
and the alleged noise of unrest
nothing but the clatter of progress,
and yet it had become necessary
to erect some dykes
against the gluttony
of mass tourism
endangering peace in Tibet—
measures taken for the good of the country.

Our convoy—we read this or something similar
between the lines of this correspondence
(in which I was never a participant)—
was to be part of a group of observers—
no, invited witnesses—who were to hear and see and
    confirm
along a 1,600-kilometre route
whatever was deemed worth hearing and seeing
in the opinion of China's great party
and its army recruited
from the people (and only the people).

After a night of leave-taking on Horse Island,
during which everyone who was to look after
Liam's farm, the pastures and the cattle
for the three (at most four) months of our mountain tour
—that is, our friends Eamon, Marian, Declan . . . —
drank until daybreak
and even ended up singing (but not dancing—
Liam didn't like dancing), and saw at sunrise,
like a message from our destination, ragged fields of snow
on the distant slopes of the Caha Mountains
(it hadn't snowed there for years)—
snow! which melted away in the morning sun—
we bumped across the heavy swell
in our cutter to the mainland
and, after a weary chorus
of last farewells in Eamon's Bar,
travelled from Dunlough to Cork, and from there
to Dublin and London and Beijing and Lhasa.

Yet even at cruising altitude
mountain peaks pierced the pack ice of the clouds
and drifted away like islands,
and we were buffeted by the spray, buffeted by the waves,
breakers, jet streams, seasonal turbulence,
as if the Irish Sea were surging after Liam and me
(as every other emigrant) into the highlands
of Tibet. Spring must
be well advanced there.

Barely fifty hours after casting off
from the pier on Horse Island
I was gasping for air in Lhasa,
ashamed by my sudden breathlessness.
How many times before
had I been at such altitudes?
Thrice? More? In any case, always and only by Liam's side
in the Italian or French Alps;
this time, though, we had come straight from the sea.

Breathing trouble. Already? Here on the steps
and in the courtyards of the Potala Palace,
which no god-king was ever to enter again.
Here, in the Jewel Park and at other stages
of a whirlwind tour
under the supervision of a translator
who took us, like prisoners,
from the airfield to cold lodgings.

(The slopes here were indeed as thinly powdered
with snow as the mountains to the west of Cork

on the morning of our departure,
only two days earlier and yet already so remote.)

How tired we were.
And still the next morning we tossed
our luggage containing the recommended gear
(sleeping bags, boots, mats, a tent,
but not yet the picks, crampons, carabiners
and ice screws secretly awaiting us in Chengdu)
into the second of the four off-road vehicles of our convoy
and made acquaintance with our academic travelling
        companions
and three tight-lipped escort officers.

Only three spies? It was hard to say, thought Liam
(who, from his years in Hong Kong,
spoke faltering Cantonese
that elicited surprise as well as mirth),
which master the other members
of this twelve-strong delegation served.
Caution was therefore advised,
even when talking about trees, high pastures or mountains.

Liam was satisfied with all these constraints
and did not take offence at a single ban
during those mistrustful days.
For him we were still engaged only
in a minor, preparatory
feint that would bring us,
disguised as surveyors
on an officially endorsed trip,

closer to our true goal without arousing suspicion.

(And wasn't this plan, Liam whispered to me with a grin
during an escort officer's welcoming speech,
reminiscent of the old days when, as dream fighters and
    scouts
in our father's war games, we would
roam the mountains between Kerry and Cork?)

From now on, like spotters, we should
keep watch for hidden tracks, clues
and rumours about valleys above which
rose a mountain named *Cha-Ri*, Bird Mountain,
in whose vicinity, shadow or rain shadow
we must seek our hidden goal—
the blank spot, the base of a peak
that flew: *Phur-Ri*.

(Yet this name was never mentioned
during the weeks of our official trip to Chengdu.
I first heard it when we arrived
at the large camp on the upper reaches of the Yangtze.)

Our travel papers included official recommendations,
copied, laminated in transparent film
and adorned with the stamps
of two universities and one Red Army.

As beneficiaries of protection that was reliable
because related to business and profits,
our hosts and our guards viewed us as

if not dependable, then at least harmless.
What need they fear
from two European islanders, two seamen,
among the world's highest mountains?

But *our* journey to Kham
(so Liam had decided, and so it came to pass)
was to begin, like the start of our climbing routes
on Horse Island, as a descent to the sea—
from the high pastures to the sea.
For did not every road from Lhasa to Chengdu
eventually lead downhill
to the rice fields of Sichuan?

As members of the delegation, we were
to grow accustomed to the thin air
along these treacherous tracks and pass roads,
these Red Army supply lines, and become familiar
with the hardships and the towering scenery
that lay both before and behind us on the understanding
that, having concluded our official trip to Chengdu,
we would make our way back, unsupervised but with the
        aid
of the waiting trader from Ya'an,
from the mirroring rice fields of Sichuan
into the clouds of Kham.

For hadn't all our journeys
from the very start been *return* journeys?
A return from the breakers to land;
from the whirl of messages and the hum

of the programming industry to the wind of Horse Island;
and, on climbing routes such as Hake and Turbot and Cod,
from the line of breakers back to the familiar world,
to the pastures high above.
When else, if not after a return journey,
could we decide whether our departure
had led us to life and bliss
or into oblivion and death?
Only when we had returned to the place
from where we had once departed
could we state something as puerile,
as consistently provisional and uncertain,
as: *We've made it.*
(Made it? Made what? And to escape what?
The world? Reason? Our greed?)

At the end of our official trip, in Chengdu
(so Liam had decided, and so it came to pass)
amid general relief
at our successful journey across eastern Tibet
along pass roads and supply lines,
with waning attention
and even perhaps in the mellow mood
or cheeriness of farewell,
we would have to become invisible,
Liam and I. Invisible.
For after arriving in the plains
and being released from official supervision
we would prolong our authorized, documented trip
with an innocent excursion
far from any smouldering fires—

into the bamboo forests at the foot of Mount Minya Gongga
(a 7,600-metre colossus),
prolong it with an outing into the subtropical wilderness
where pandas had their territories—
a regional tourist attraction,
(and also a plausible, obvious destination
for discharged members of a delegation).

It was only during this sightseeing tour
that we were to meet our guarantor,
the trader from Ya'an, and slip away,
driving back with him along the same routes into the heights
whence we had just come,
but then switching to other tracks into forbidden country.

When all supply lines and roads petered out
(so Liam had decided, and so it came to pass)
we would continue at our own pace,
on foot, ever onwards, with yak herders
until we reached a valley above which must tower that peak
whose clouded, ice-bannered ridges
my brother had so often conjured onto his screens,
and onwards into the very heart of that mystery
that he was bent on solving
(and which would turn out
to be his own death).

How carefully Liam had planned our trip
and all its attendant diversionary tactics!
And by and large it played out as he had foreseen
Liam found everything easy to grasp

(it was indeed very simple):
every one of our steps served the sole purpose
of eliminating a blank spot from his maps.

For me, though, as the brother he had torn
from an unstable life, from the sea to the coast
and to an island in sight of our childhood, for me,
the ship's machinist converted to cliffs and mountains,
everything, on this journey too,
as before in Beijing and Lhasa, everything
was different from the very start.

I was resentful, angry at my brother
and at my decision to accompany him.
Was I travelling and living in his shadow?
Was I his shadow? Was my goal
a fragment from the Net? A blank spot on the map?
Or might it perhaps be *he* who understood none
of what *I* wanted to see and understand?

In a dim hall smelling of the cold smoke
of extinguished butter lamps in the Potala Palace
in Lhasa, the residence of an exiled god,
I had seen a gasping guard.
He stood before rows of shelves that were in danger
of collapsing under the weight of Tantric books—
there must have been thousands of wood-bound
       manuscripts
lying there, illegible and dusty.

The subjects
of the last Dalai Lama had believed
(no: *still* believed,
even if his reincarnation was no more
than a rumour denied by the occupiers)
that even if they were unable to read and write,
pilgrims had to crawl under these shelves—merely crawl—

,

brush off, with the dust, a scrap
of the ancient teachings stored here,
and they would become wiser and gentler,
more closely connected to the sky.

The gasping guard in the green army uniform
did not, however, fall to his knees
to brush against some teachings as he crawled,
but stood ramrod straight and,
clutching in his arms one of the biggest tomes,
which had the shape and presumably
the weight of a trunk,
began to hoist the book into the air,
lifting it over and over,
again and again, as a bodybuilding exercise.

When the dusty dumbbell weighed on him too much
he grunted, groaned and struggled with his waning powers,
suffering under the weight until one saw
trickles of sweat glisten on his face in the twilight
and drip onto the breast pockets of his uniform.

Suddenly, he heaved all the prayers, invocations,
teachings and advice for the path out of time
back onto one of the shelves
with a cry of relief and, with a grin,
waved to Liam for a cigarette.
But Liam ignored him. Unmoved, Liam followed
the already-disappearing members of the delegation.

Late in the afternoon of our first
and last day in Lhasa, I saw hundreds of pilgrims
in the square outside the Jokhang,
ancient Tibet's holiest temple,
against whose columns
a sea of light still broke—
the flames of thousands of butter lamps.
But none of the pilgrims, of whom
some had measured the arduous route,
which sometimes took years, in body lengths:
walking, pausing after three or four paces, kneeling down,
then lying on the ground with outstretched arms,
standing up again to walk three or four paces
and repeat the exercise all over again;

none of the pilgrims, not one of those waiting,
was allowed into the holy of holies,
but we members of the delegation were led,
along with other indifferent paying guests,
sightseers, and temple and museum visitors,
past the excluded worshippers mumbling their mantras
and into the sanctuary
where we strode past shimmering rows

of stone, wood and bronze buddhas and bodhisattvas,
like a parade of dethroned gods, disempowered demons,
spirits, incarnations and reincarnations
lined up solely to greet us,
about whose lost empires
we were informed by leaflets
containing information in three languages,
which we took from readied cardboard boxes
before entering the chapels and shrines;

yet even these aids merely demonstrated
how ignorant we were, light years
from the paradise invoked
by those locked out in the bright daylight.

In passing we spun prayer wheels
that should have revolved under the hands
of believers until the end of time.
Behind us they stood still.
And then (it was just before darkness fell)
I had—we had—seen men condemned to death,
crouching on an open truck,
prisoners with signs around their necks.
Accusations? Lists of their crimes? High treason?
Rebellion? Resistance to progress?

Our translator told us only that the condemned men
were thieves, and that an individual
who misappropriated the property of the people
had committed a crime that merited death.

Bound to each other with rope, exhausted,
shoulder to shoulder with their executioners,
five men, none of them older than Liam and me,
crouched on the loading bed,
blindfolded and on their way to a place
(the translator gave an untranslatable name)
where a bullet in the neck
would shatter their vertebra.

Liam remained unmoved.
Liam observed what he saw in silence,
as if on a screen—soldiers, pilgrims, condemned men.
He bathed in the glow of this sight and everything else
we encountered on this and our other days of travel,
and observed the changing images
with the same immobility with which he followed
what appeared on screens and then vanished again;
alert, prepared for anything,
but without anger or indignation.

My brother Liam seemed to judge everything
he heard and saw purely according
to whether it obstructed or abetted his plans.
And, like writing in the elementary language
of programmers, there was for him
no question in Kham that could not
be answered by *Yes* or *No*.

He even converted our passing days
into binary columns, rows of numbers
that had to rise up and coalesce

into ideals and illusions:
into the shadow of an unscaled mountain
or a pattern of contours,
places so dazzlingly white
that everything real, tangible
and undeniable began
to fade in their glare.

Liam didn't want to see anything.
Liam didn't want to hear anything.
Liam imagined. Liam dreamt.

5

Master Coldheart. Billiards in the snow.

All right, Master Coldheart,
I whispered to my snoring brother
(what adventures did Liam have to endure
every night, as he stammered entreaties—or curses?—
in his dreams and struck out in the darkness,
as if his sleeping bag were a trap, a net,
and he the beast, the prisoner, caught in it);

all right, Master Coldheart, I repeated
the next morning and the next night
and so many other nights
and through so many hours of walking
in his footsteps:
All right, create the world,
attach it to your modules, Master,
pin it to your screens,
make it appear on cliffs,
yes! project it, for all I care, onto the wall!
But count me out!

I screamed into the engine's wail, as our convoy
manoeuvred through the snow and mud, and I screamed
up the polished rock sides of a chimney,
which Liam had fitted with rope and ice screws
so that I too could climb it,
and once I even screamed
at a bouquet of prayer flags
(snapping in the wind on top of a pass):
Count me out!

I sometimes managed to remain completely calm.
Listen, I mumbled, as if to myself
and full of the best intentions,
(I wanted him to understand my concerns):
Listen, Liam, this is how far we've come.
Are you not surprised that the snow,
the wall of ice, every metre of altitude gained
on this damned route refuses to bow to your schedule?
That nothing is going to plan?
Do you still know—did you ever know—where *we* are?
You don't know. How could you—
you're blind. Blind and deaf.

Blind, deaf, poor Liam,
I would sometimes say in pity . . .
but the next instant anger once more overcame me:
Should I whisper to you, Coldheart,
should I whisper to you where we've ended up?
Liam, my Liam, my brother:
Did I not whisper to you as you snored
and shout at you?

Did I ever say
that I would no longer continue
to live and stumble on in your tracks,
tied to your rope, on your island,
in your projects—damn it, Liam!

I didn't.
I failed to do it.
I was furious, I was often furious,
but I was silent.
Silent, as I'd always been silent
in the old days in bivouacs at our father's side
and in our radio conversations
and across the oceans
and even after my return to Horse Island
and always. I mean . . .
once, yes yes, once only I called
Liam, loudly and unmistakably, Coldheart (he laughed).
But otherwise . . .

How many times I addressed my brother
wordlessly, dumbstruck, and yet every time
only addressed myself;
and when finally—it was a late afternoon in May
when it was so silent that the crackling
of ice crystals was audible in the glassy air,
as the sunlight cast them back into the sky
as microscopic flashes and they burst—

when finally I began to speak
and for the first time uttered what I'd wanted

to say all that time, my whole life,
I was suddenly alone;
I had been alone for hours.

I admit, I profess: I failed
to speak, to whisper, to shout;
I failed to confess my anger to Liam
or maybe simply to ask him:
What am I doing here?
And on Horse Island?
In your house?
In your life?
How easy I found it to ask
and at last to confess,
on that cone of scree under which he lay buried;
the phrases and words came flying to me,
and I let them all out.

I said, Liam, I can't go on,
I don't want to go on,
I want to go back to my own life,
not to your island
and certainly not back to your house
but back to my ships, to the sea.
I don't want crystal screens flickering around me
and computers humming me to sleep;
I want only to be rocked to sleep by
ships. My ship. The sea.

This, or something similar, I said
and screamed and finally mumbled

in exhaustion, pouring it all out to Liam now,
but even with the best will in the world
(which he had so rarely shown to me)
he could no longer hear me,
not any more,
for he lay buried under ice and scree
and splintered trees and snow,
secure, inaccessible as always
under his avalanche,

on whose settled, petrified cone
I crawled around for hours,
deep into the night;
I crawled up and down, digging in the debris
and scratching at the ice until I lost my fingernails.

Now, at long last, I wrote, I really wrote
not just our names, as on the summit,
and not with the shaft of my ice axe,
but, with frantic fingertips,
illegible, pale-red signs in the snow.

It was these scribblings, these red engravings,
I remembered most as, months later,
—saved, a survivor—
I walked through Liam's house on Horse Island again,
and I had never known that house warmer
or more alive than at the moment
when it had finally been emptied—empty!—
and my inheritance shipped to the Irish mainland,
to Dunlough and into the shed behind Eamon's Bar.

The echoing rooms flooded with sunlight,
in the bolted sliding glass doors
and every window: the sea.
And the salt flowers on the glass like crusts of ice and snow.

That day too stayed so clear that the Caha Mountains
were visible in the distance,
the slopes in whose shadow the pastures, cattle sheds
and our parents' farm lay, reverting
over the years into wilderness,
vanishing under gorse and brambles,
just as, long before, *Ireland*,
the *true* Ireland of our father, had vanished,
peeled from the cold, windowless wall of a corridor,
plucked by the draught from a mosaic
of unrealizable wishes, and the last
remaining colour photographs on the wall,
blurred and mottled with damp stains and mould.

Although Liam never talked
about restoring our parents' farm, *these* ruins,
instead of the collapsed stone buildings on Horse Island,
to their previous condition
and in so doing salvage them from the past,
it was surely in fact

our parents' house, pastures and fences,
the backdrop to our childhood, that he had rebuilt
on Horse Island (long before I arrived);
a reconstruction that eventually
only lacked actors,

its vanished inhabitants,
me.

I alone, though missing on ships and in engine rooms
somewhere on the seas of a world
that had seemed to our father during his lifetime
to represent the *true Ireland*,
which Liam had left years before I did
(in favour of a rock in the Atlantic
off Dunlough, overloaded with derelict houses
and memories)—I alone could be reached.
Our mother, whom Father ambiguously called Mummy,
whereas Liam and I only said Shona—
we called her by her first name, Shona.
Shona could no longer stand
Father's ramblings, his manoeuvres,
his endless wish lists and fulminations,
his invoking of the civil war
and all the battles over Irish unity,
and she went back to Belfast.

Deserted to the North! as our father complained,
but she hadn't left him;
no, she hadn't *divorced* him,
for only death could separate what God himself
(these too were Father's words) had joined together.
Shona, Mummy,
had done something worse than dying:
she had betrayed her husband and with him, Ireland;

she had up and left,
with a *souper* of all people,
a man whose ancestors had, in the years of famine, sold
their rightful Catholic faith
for a bowl of soup
and their soul to the devil—
Protestant missionaries;
in our father's eyes
a disgrace that still would not be forgotten
three hundred, five hundred years from now.

Shona had run away with a man named Duffy,
an electrician from Bearhaven,
whom Liam and I proclaimed a magician,
for he had brought the first screen
in our childhood home to flickering life,
a television set that would sometimes
(even during weather favourable to reception)
produce only a steady roar and almost inaudible
crackling voices, ghost songs,
presenting us with electronic flurries
and snowstorms.

I believe that in the end it was
neither his corroded lungs nor Father's grief
at the loss of his wife,
but his anger at her treachery
that a mere three years after her escape to the North
took him to his final immovable place
under an immovable sky,
six or seven feet under a stone
in Glengarriff graveyard.

The gravestone bore his name
and beneath it one could read *A Gentleman*
but no birth or death year,
and it sank so quickly into the earth
that it seemed empty again by the time
I first saw it after my return to the mainland,

as though the name had followed its bearer
into an overgrown grave in the shadow of the church
in Glengarriff, where the A71 main road forks:
the left spur leads
further along the coast
(to Adrigole and Bearhaven),
the right one up to the pass
and the county border with Kerry.

The old man's head, Liam told me over the radio,
pointed now and as always towards the mountains.
So his feet, I replied, pointed
out to sea.

I learnt of Father's death and burial
over the ship's radio and also heard
that even this occasion had not brought
Shona back from Belfast.

For one day and one night the old man
had been laid out in an open coffin—
on a counter in Glengarriff, in fact, shrouded
in an Irish tricolour by way of a catafalque.

Dressed in an Irish Republican Army uniform
redolent of mothballs,
he at last resembled Michael Collins, the IRA hero,
his Collins (one of Father's two saints
alongside the inventor Henry Ford)—Collins,
who, after being shot in an ambush
in the hills of Bealnablagh near Macroom,
had been laid out in Dublin city hall—
and now awaited eternal rest and undying fame
in the same uniform.

Father—a freedom fighter, a warrior, a hero at last.
The wake in the Sandboat, his local in Glengarriff,
was among his final wishes
(one of the realizable ones), but it was Liam
who had to pay for the pints for the mourners
raising toasts at the bar,
the dead man's cash reserves being insufficient
for this kind of send-off.
(I even heard about the size of the tab via radio.
I heard about everything—I alone could be reached.
Liam made sure I knew every detail.
Liam wrote to me. Again and again.
Begging me, finally calling me back.
And I came.)

But had I ever been, on Horse Island,
and before that in our parents' house
or in the tent by our father's side,
anything other than a poor substitute?
I was not—definitely not—that forbidden friend

and never the lover whom Liam presumably sought
in vain during his wandering years
in London and South East Asia.

The taboo of the love Liam meant
whenever he spoke of love
could be broken, like other bans and rules:
in Dublin and London and with rent boys elsewhere.
Insurmountable and unbreakable,
however, was the impossibility of showing
this love where he, where we, came from
(not without disturbing our own peace
and our neighbours' peace, anyway).

So, like our father, Liam had surely begun at an early age
to make lists of unrealizable wishes,
one of which must have been for a life
with a partner or lover,
not in secret
but on that coast ruled by westerly winds,
to which he longed to return
(*that* too figured in his archives)
during all his years elsewhere.
And you? he asked me in a letter
written on the pages of the logbook
of Dunlough lighthouse: Were you never homesick?
Before I exercised the first power of my inheritance
to reformat the memory of Liam's computers
and wipe them for ever
(after all, even *I* could do that with his machines)
I found in his digital archives

copies of adverts, appeals, cries for help
on the Net, in which he extolled himself
and his island, even advertised the idea,
in return for money and as a disguise,
of fetching a wife to Horse Island, to be followed
by a lover whose heart was set on the country life
in the role of an irreproachable farmhand (whose work
on fences and pastures I then assumed).

My life on Horse Island had never been more
than a form of temporary and stopgap solution
in the years when Liam still had to pursue his dreams,
and was supposed to end
when the person he truly sought at last turned up.

Without ever telling me,
Liam used coded online adverts
to arrange discreet meetings with several interested parties
in Dublin and Cork. With no success.
For such secret discussions of his plans,
along with the odd fleeting adventure
(his archives proved as much before I deleted them)
did indeed occasionally take place, but nothing more.

No, Liam certainly dreamt of a different companion
than the brother he had lost to the sea.
I was merely temporarily to fill the space
that he had created for a fantasy,
a figure in one of his programs.

Even our weeks in the convoy sometimes struck me
as just another example of our time together
on his island or from decades past,
as just a continuation of a play in which I
had been, if anything, only a silent character, an extra,
at best a listener or a prompt.

For even in the convoy to Chengdu my brother
never lost sight of his goal, his true goal,
the taboo, the blank spot somewhere in the distance,
but remained always utterly calm and unmoved,
focusing his attention entirely on illusions
and showing no particular interest
in the circumstances, voices
and real people around us
or those we met in villages and camps.

But I was confused and often enthused by it all
and sometimes so overwhelmed
by what I heard and saw
that I either grew indifferent to
or simply forgot
what my brother regarded as the truth,
the essential part. (I had seen more than enough
of this kind of truth in the corridor
of our parents' home, to be honest.

There too, the guide to fulfilling
one's dreams was no more than a wall
stuck and pinned with memories,
postcards and fading snapshots.)

The Chinese drivers of our convoy's four-by-fours
wore white cotton gloves,
which they changed every day
(so quickly did they turn grey,
then blackish with the grime of our journey).
And these gloves struck me
as one of many gestures designed to show us
that Kham, the occupied land, our goal,
was not to be grasped with bare hands.

It's a barbaric country, our drivers said,
a barbaric country inhabited by superstitious savages,
tribes obsessed by their belief
in demons and rebirth,
incorrigible people, of whom a traveller
had better beware.

The Khampas wore decorative cords in their hair
and chains of shells and turquoises around their necks,
sharp, finely wrought swords at their belts
and the occasional rifle
in saddlebags or on shoulder straps.
(I had even seen hand grenades dangling
from the saddle of one rider crossing the pass road . . .
But before our uniformed protectors
could raise the alarm, the rider
had vanished among the rocks again—a spook.)

These intransigent men, these rebels,
said one of the lookouts, an officer from Nanchong
(who also wore gloves) might be dominated,

described and studied
as hunters using stone-age weapons,
as shepherds, self-sufficient nomads,
yet even in captivity they remained
unresponsive, unwilling to convert and incapable
of grasping the benefits of progress
without the aid of an army.
The army! reiterated the man from Nanchong
in a solemn farewell speech
to the delegation in a cold hall in Chengdu;
the army alone had brought a new age
from Beijing to Lhasa
and with it countless everyday comforts:
peace through equality, the right to a future . . .
And Liam, Liam!
of one mind with our guards because he cared
only for the smooth fulfilment
of his own plans or for other strategic reasons,
agreed in a toast that evening
(as he had a few times already on our trip)
with our uniformed or chauffeuring,
denouncing glove-wearers;
he agreed with them!

I was familiar with his behaviour and his calculations,
and in the convoy they had led to the occasional quarrel
between us, but I began to find them unbearable
when Nyema eventually came into our lives—
no, into my life.

Through the windows of our convoy and from the safety
of our guarded encampments we saw many things

that our drivers and guides regarded
as unfit for our eyes.
The vehicles would then sometimes be ordered
to pick up speed with no explanation
(and no regard for the state of the road).

So we rattled past metre-high pyramids
of yak skulls and bones,
the decaying remains of herds
that had starved the previous winter,
victims of a season whose deep snows
and temperatures also laid bare the weaknesses
of an occupying army sure of its power.
Armoured vehicles, trucks and even personnel carriers
had simply disappeared under the snow.
On the verges we even saw some burnt-out wrecks
(in skirmishes or merely in unguarded night-time corrals?)
from this army's fleet of vehicles.
And we saw, on our authorized travels
beyond the blood-red walls of monasteries,
whose reconstruction had been approved
in the years before the uprising as a sign
of Beijing's goodwill, the incomparably greater ruins
of entire monastic towns—fields of rubble and scorched
      remains
whose scale gave an indication of the fury
with which revolutionary reason
had countered such obstinacy.

And along the wide meanders of high valleys,
into which our route from Lhasa to Chengdu

finally flowed, we saw columns of trucks
crawling along, piled dizzyingly high
with the trunks of Himalayan cedars,
Chinese hemlocks and blue pines—
raw materials for China's future mined
from the virgin forests of Kham; in their place
bare hills, studded with millions of tree stumps,
rolled off in every direction
to the horizon,

clear-cuts from which wildlife, birds
and humans had fled, abandoning them
to the insects, ants, bark beetles
and other related species—
a shadeless, wasted land.
And Liam, Master Coldheart, merely nodded absently,
when one of our guides, our guards and keepers,
talked of progress, development programmes
and the reasons and need
for radical forestry measures.
Liam was interested in an empty space, a blank spot,
not in woods.
But I recall that we were sometimes united again
in cheerful camaraderie, as we had once been
as we laughed at our snoring father
in his warrior costume
during those mountain nights in tents,
an intimacy that suggested that our childhood
was far from over.

It was that night in the nomads' camp by the Yangtze,
barely a week after the delegation
had broken up in Chengdu and a day
before the trader from Ya'an left us,
and Liam and I were alone with Nyema's clan
at last and were to continue on foot—
a night of clear skies and no wind, at whose end
it began to snow again.

The sudden rise in temperature had thawed
the rock-hard mud and the glassy puddles,
and the night had such a mild spring-like feel
compared to the cold of previous days,
that Liam and I were crouching
by a cooking fire under the stars
while our hosts
(they too outdoors)
were engaged in their favourite game
and the trader from Ya'an was asleep in his truck.

Unperturbed by the laughter
or the approving and sympathetic cries
of a knowledgeable crowd,
four Khampa warriors were playing pool on a table
that stood in the quagmire between yak-hair tents
and were doing so according to the same rules
that we had used only a few weeks before,
an eternity, in a backroom at Eamon's Bar,
and by the light of pitch torches as tall as a man
they continued to play
long after our fire had burnt down,

the crowd had grown sleepy and left,
and, as day broke, it began to snow.

Liam and I crouched outside our dome tent
and talked about our nights in the Cahas,
looking up in amusement whenever a cry
of enthusiasm or disappointment rang out
from the pool table among the torches,
and even went over to the table two or three times
to watch a particularly difficult,
game-defining shot.

The trader from Ya'an carried two of these greasy
pool tables around on his truck,
hiring them out to customers in the nomad camps
of Kham, at markets in Chinese garrison towns
or on squares outside rebuilt monasteries;
there one might see holy men, ascetics
and red-robed monks
triumphantly wielding their cues.

Even Kham's holy men played pool,
showing the same intensity as our hosts,
who were bidding farewell to their pastime that night,
for tomorrow the trader would have moved on
and would not return for months.

As if they required one final justification
for doing business with the man from Ya'an,
the warriors played for the money that he
had given them for leather, herbs, wool and skins

and carvings on bone and stone.
The loser paid for a night's table hire.
The torches cast long, flickering shadows
over the Khampas wrapped in their fur coats
and they didn't only light the table,
but were also arrayed in a magic circle
to keep the ghosts of the icy regions
from attacking the sleepers in the black tents
or the stock grazing in the darkness.

Still, none of the warriors had put down his sword
(even if its silver scabbard sometimes
beat against the folds of the fur coat
and hampered a shot).
The brightly threaded ribbons
in the players' hair that hung down to their belts
glittered sumptuously when one of them
leant far over the table and yelled
after sinking a difficult ball
into one of the corner pockets.

The players barely looked up
if the mastiffs barked furiously,
alarmed by these cries, a shadow
or an animal peering out of the night.
The click of the ivory balls hushed any alarm
and any noises back into silence,
into a quietness in which only the Yangtze
chattered ceaselessly to itself with no respect
for the seriousness of the game.

Completely absorbed, the warriors
seemed indifferent to all dangers
from the menacing mountains, those lightless walls
that surrounded the bed of the infant river,
the pastures and camp to such a height
that the tops of those walls touched the stars.

Everything beyond the game was forgotten,
even the snow leopard and the fiercer demons
who bear so many names and can assume
as many shapes as a tree produces needles
or fruits or leaves.
All forgotten.

The peace that reigned over the Yangtze in those hours
transported Liam and me back to a time
when fear had been passing, fleeting,
and security the norm.
We saw the silhouettes of the Transhimalaya
as outlines of familiar mountain ranges,
recalled our camouflage-garbed father
and giggled about him,
as we had as boys in those nights under canvas,
a sleeper's soldiers, invincible, immortal.

As Liam grew tired and increasingly quiet, then,
without drawing the tent flaps closed behind him,
crawled into his sleeping bag and, shortly afterwards,
started snoring as Father once had,
I laughed and continued giggling alone
(the rice liquor in our luggage might also

have taken effect) and our peace held
and became as joyous as in times past
when I woke Liam because it had begun to snow.

The snow tumbled down onto the torches, the players
and the table, falling in heavy flakes
onto the greasy felt, and the ivory balls
momentarily uninvolved and untouched by the game
received crystal caps—billiards in the snow.

Liam, I said, Liam, and he
sat up from his dreams without protest
and understood my wake-up call the very instant
it reached his ears, understood
why I wanted him to see what I saw:

Framed by the open door of our tent
were the ring of torches, the table, on it
white-helmeted ivory balls and, in the foreground,
richly adorned, long-haired warriors in fur coats—
a game being played in a storm of snowflakes.

Liam said nothing, asked no questions,
just nodded at me with a smile,
and me, I crouched beside him,
laid my arm around his shoulders
and rocked him back to sleep.

6.

She says her name. Place without dreams.

It was enough for me to stay quiet and keep still,
holding my breath for a few seconds, simply listening,
tilting my head towards the west
where he had disappeared, simply listening
and holding still, to hear sounds
of the man from Ya'an, on and on, the next morning,

on and on and long after
the roar of his truck's engine
deepened in pitch in accordance
with wave theory as it drove away,
until it finally reached me as intermittent rumble,
echoing from the stone resonance chambers
of the Yangtze gorges, then died away.
It was the sound of a missed opportunity
not to take a single step more in Liam's shadow,
not a single step deeper into his programs,
but to find my own path out of the wilds of Kham
and back to my life—
even if that meant travelling with the trader from Ya'an.

(A route of your own? Don't make me laugh!
I heard my brother say,
I imagined my brother say.
A route of my own!
Like that time when a piton-less,
rope-less cliffhanger on the rocks of Horse Island
began to wail with terror,
scared by a summer storm
and the impending fall?)

As I held still and silent and listened
I felt something start to tug at me,
to tear at me and I asked myself,
Why did you stay, you idiot?
Why are you still here?
He'd have taken you along,
by now you could be as far away as that noise . . .

The man from Ya'an would certainly have taken me along,
I had asked him in passing, *if, for some reason . . .*
But then what?

I would have wound my way towards Lhasa
for another two weeks or a few more days,
would have visited markets, camps, monasteries,
hidden from military checks with his help
and would then have returned with him
a second time to Chengdu—
but then what?
Where's your brother? the army would
have asked me at the airport (at the latest).
Where have you been? Where's your brother?

Am I my brother's keeper:
would I have dared to ask
the Red Army that question?

No, I had become so lost inside one of Liam's
programs that I could only find my way
back out of it with his help.
(Or was it fear that held me back,
fear of heading back without him,
in this land of Kham,
in Liam's land, his land?)

Fear? Had I not reconciled myself
to Liam's aims, to this journey
in our giggling agreement
at the sight of a group of long-haired,
pool-playing warriors obscured by the snow?
Or had the mollifying effect
of night-time melted away again
in the morning sun with the fallen snow?

We were brothers, after all. We were the sons
of a warrior who was now peacefully
buried under an empty, sinking stone
in Glengarriff cemetery.
And we were doing this hero,
awarded the title of gentleman
only on his gravestone, proud.
We, his giggling sons, were in the process
of conquering a blank spot, an empty space on the map.

The morning of our departure was as mild and windless
as the night before; apart from a few patches,
all the fresh snow had vanished by noon,
and the clansmen were just starting
to take down the tents (our green dome
had long been struck, rolled up and fastened
beside our rucksacks to a yak's saddle)
when at last this tearing and tugging within me
subsided, this secret self-abuse,
when the questioning and doubts fell silent,
giving way to a curious satisfaction

that I had passed up my last chance to run away,
and all that remained was the path into the mountains,
the path alongside yak nomads
who that morning were preparing
to depart for higher meadows—
their herds' spring and summer pastures
and that short, snow-free season
in which the highest peaks and fortress of the gods
moved closer to the tents of men
than at any other time of the year.

My satisfaction at being where I was and only there
owed little to Liam and much to the fact
that as we were setting out I learnt
the name of the woman,
to whom the trader from Ya'an had simply pointed
(without introducing her or speaking to her) and said,
That woman, yes, that one over there;
like everyone else in the clan she could

neither read nor write, but she understood and spoke
our language perhaps even better than he did.
What's more, she was the only one of these savages
who had once been to Lhasa, to civilization.

I have never been much interested
in descriptions of faces and physical attributes;
when some chronicler or bookkeeper
took pains over such details
like a forensic specialist,
I would generally skim-read and forget them
because I liked to put my own faces
to every story, and more important to me
than the curve of someone's nose, the colour of their eyes
or the size of their ears and mouth

was the question of *what* those eyes had seen
or wept for, what those ears had heard,
this mouth said and swallowed
and *what* of the wide world they had experienced,
endured or enjoyed—and yet I was amazed
to find, as I looked through my notes
about the day we struck the tents by the Yangtze,
that my first sentence about Nyema read:
She is taller than me—not much, but still taller.

As she stood before me that morning
and looked at me, I had to raise my eyes and
(though barely noticeably) my head.
Her long hair, woven into braids as fine as threads,
was as black as any other clan member's;

even her eyes, their irises dark,
almost as black as the pupils,
her face narrower than other women's faces here
and a uniform bronze colour, but her cheeks
were not coloured deep red like the others'
from the frostbite with which the icy wind
marked her people as if they'd been branded.

Only at second glance
was it clear that this woman's gently curving nose
must have been broken once.
A woman of the Khampa people.
Was she beautiful?
I recall that I was overcome
with a sudden, puzzling desire
the first time I saw her,
and almost as an excuse for this
the word *beautiful* came to my mind, *how beautiful she is*.
She's beautiful.

It was the day we reached the camp from Chengdu,
after the commotion of the first greetings,
after the pool table had been awkwardly unloaded
and amid the jostling din to see the trader's wares.
She was kneeling outside one of the black tents,
beating and stirring yak's milk butter
in a container circled by silver hoops,
half-cooker, half-churn.

I recall that I involuntarily tried
to picture her figure, her breasts,

her naked body, of which barely any outline
could be seen under her embroidered clothing: I ogled her
until she suddenly lifted her head and wrestled
my gaze to the ground. I think I even blushed—
one of the first Europeans to reach this camp
by the Yangtze, freshly arrived
and yet already caught gawping.

When, days later,
on the morning the trader drove away,
she looked at me for the second time, I was ready
for her gaze and was surprised once more
by the mistrust I discovered there
—as if she didn't believe in *that man's* innocent interest
when I asked her (the truck was still audible from afar)
how long before we all departed.

It was only now that I noticed the midnight-blue of her eyes;
she gave an answer that I didn't understand at first,
but which turned out to mean *two or three hours.*
In response to my next question she told me her name,
this too a series of such quick, darting sounds
that I had to ask again and then a third time
until she eventually repeated it very slowly,
as though spelling it out for an idiot.

Nyema, she said, and again, then with a laugh,
Ny-e-ma Dol-ma, beating the rhythm
to every syllable with large, slender and
(as I later found out) extremely soft hands.

Nyema was the only one in the clan who understood our
     language.
Tashi Gyeltso, the father of her barely two-year-old son,
had passed on all the words he had picked up
as a porter on nine different expeditions into the clouds
and to the empty dwelling sites of the gods.

Although his language teachers—snow walkers, mountain
     men,
climbers from lands of immeasurable riches—
even had their own word for the goddess *Chomolungma*
—for *Chomolungma*! whose name meant
Holy Mother of the Valleys they had invented
their own word and had called her ever since
simply *Mount Everest*—Tashi Gyeltso
not once let these sacrilegious words pass his lips
and he advised his wife Nyema to follow his lead.
Names were holy, and a single one of their syllables
mightier than any word.

Five times the path of Tashi Gyeltso's life
had taken him over Chomolungma's highest peaks,
five times to a place his language teachers
called *summit, summit* . . . a word
that seemed as much part of their equipment
as ropes, helmets, down jackets, lamps, sleeping bags,
blankets, ladders, ice axes, pitons and screws,
metal bottles full of compressed *English* air
and countless other burdens full of delicacies,
gleaming instruments, tools, plates . . .

And with all this extravagance his teachers
were heading nowhere—nowhere!—
just higher and higher, ever higher,
so that at the top—finally at the top!—
they might turn their backs on their goal
within an hour of their arrival
or after a breathless, exhausted rest—
an empty spot, clad in snow as hard as stone,
8,850 metres above the sea and deep
in the blackness of a sky
that finally proved merciless to Tashi.

Many people in the clan claimed
in their conversations with Liam and me, accompanied
and translated into lilting English by Nyema,
that it had been the wrath of the heavens
at the desecration of Chomolungma
that had ultimately killed Tashi Gyeltso and not
a Chinese soldier's machine pistol
at Nangpa La, the pass
where his murderers rather than burning his body
had buried him under stones
like a plague victim or a criminal.

And yet Nangpa La, on the border with Nepal,
should have been a gateway to happiness
for Tashi Gyeltso and his Nyema,
as for so many refugees before them,
to a new life in the Kingdom of Nepal,
perhaps even to a life on the monsoon-watered
slopes of Indian Dharamsala

(where the fourteenth and last Dalai Lama
had found peace and refuge from the Chinese army).
But whatever awaited them on the far side of Nangpa La
would be better, far better, than anything that existed.

His wife's pregnancy had induced Tashi
not to return from his final Chomolungma pilgrimage
to the high pastures of Kham,
but instead to flee their snowy country
with Nyema and twenty other Tibetans
from Dhatse Dor, Tawiu and even Lhasa,

if not to paradise and the sea,
then at least from the eyes of an army,
which scoured even nomad's tents for weapons
and forbidden pictures of the Dalai Lama,
destroying anything they found
and often punishing their owners with death.

Seven months were to pass before Nyema
was allowed to return from the barred cellars
of the army to the tents of her clan,
months during which the snow lay deeper
than it had for years;
snow into which she then had to give birth
to her firstborn—
that was on the track leading to Dhatse Dor.

She named the premature baby after the lost *Tashi*;
Tashi, so that the fortune contained in this name
would not remain buried at Nangpa La

but would instead rise up from the scree
and frozen earth into the light.

Nangpa La?
The grave of a murdered refugee?
A Khampa, a yak herder, who had not only scaled
the summit of Everest more times
than most of the western world's extreme mountaineers,
but had sought, and hewn from the ice, routes
to lead his language teachers and wards into the highest
        heights,
had secured them with ropes and ladders,
and preceded or followed them
with food and fuel, even in disasters,
and had stayed with them through and through,
pulling, dragging and sometimes even carrying them,
in constant peril of his own life, higher and higher—
and then back down into the safety of the lowlands . . . ?

Oh, Liam was acquainted with the lives
of high-mountain porters
and no longer particularly interested
in tales of expeditions,
which stormed peaks in the Himalaya and the Karakoram
year after year as if they were enemy strongholds,
with tonnes upon tonnes, whole wagonloads of material
and hosts of infantry willing, for a porter's wage,
to leave farms and fields, herds and tents
in the custody of women,
leave everything behind.
Sometimes for ever.

Liam knew these tales well—
they were still passed on by cartographers
and surveyors, and on the Net, of course.

No, here and now, on this trip of ours,
of far greater importance to him
than the life and death of a man from Nyema's clan
was the certainty that he was on the right path,
his path, as we joined the people
from the camp by the Yangtze
and followed them up to their summer pastures.
For on the very day of our arrival they had
confirmed a name: *Cha-Ri*, Bird Mountain.

So there really was such a mountain!
It overshadowed the high valleys to which the Khampas
were proceeding with their yaks,
and alongside this Bird Mountain—this too
the man from Ya'an was told after questioning from Liam—
towered two other mountains,
whose names existed only in the clan's memory,
in stories and songs,
but on none of Liam's maps:
Te-Ri, Cloud Mountain,
and *Phur-Ri*, a mountain that flew.

How high were these mountains?
Height? What was *height*?
Mountains had mighty names,
names that contained teachings about the sky,
about life, about death.

Seven thousand, eight thousand metres above the sea
and higher! Twenty-nine thousand feet . . .
The clansmen had naturally heard
of such measurements:
they meant nothing to them.

What was indisputable, though, was that anyone
who set foot in the snow gardens of the gods ran the risk
of crushing his own life,
for the frenzied rush up and up
and over these dazzling, forbidden heights
led anyone who was not himself a god
only into darkness and emptiness
and out into the night.
Everest. On this one question at least Liam
could agree with Tashi Gyeltso the porter:
it was a lousy name.
Liam had long given up pronouncing it,
didn't write it and never once
permitted it to shine forth from his digital atlases.

Not because he felt that to use it
would be sacrilegious, but purely
because it was the name of the British surveyor
George Everest.

While Ireland, under its English masters, was sliding
into the most disastrous famine in its history,
Sir Everest and his fellows were sizing up
even choicer pickings for an insatiable Majesty
in London: Indian colonies! Tea plantations

against a picturesque backdrop of mountain chains,
whose triangulation from a safe distance
produced unheard-of summit heights:
twenty, twenty-five, twenty-nine thousand feet!
Approximately, at least.

The British surveyors hadn't spent long
asking after names, instead hurling
the inventory number *Peak XV*, for instance,
at a gleaming, supernatural thing among the clouds;
but George Everest alone was honoured for his temerity
the year before he died when this apparition
was renamed *Mount Everest*—
and yet even this did not make him immortal.

No—and with this Liam gave voice
not only to the convictions of a porter
who had been hastily interred at Nangpa La,
but above all to our father's belief,
that of a gentleman who had so often longed
to leave his homeland for a paradise
and now lay buried under the stones of Glengarriff:
Everest was not a good name,
neither for a living nor a dead man,
and most definitely not for the highest mountain
in the measured world.

Even Liam didn't call this monster, whose summit
had become just one of countless survey points
on the boundary line between occupied Tibet
and the Kingdom of Nepal,

Chomolungma,
preferring a title
that had currency in Nepal, on the mountain's
southern slopes and precipices—

Sagarmatha—as it could
also mean (translated from the Sanskrit)
Mother of the Ocean, Mother of the Seas.
(And that was more to Liam's and, I confess,
to his seafaring brother's liking,
whichever interpretation we chose.)

For us Everest was just a word in a children's game
that had regularly led to arguments between us
on our manoeuvres in the Cahas—a game
that we had christened *Air Battle* and played
to make Father's wars in Kerry and Cork
pass more quickly (above all
the hours of resting while the captain
snored on cushions of moss or heather).

We would point to a hulking cloud drifting
in from the sea, a veil of fog or just the fast-moving,
wind-torn tatters of an Atlantic front
and guess their cruising height
above an agreed point far out at sea
or at least before they reached the coast
(above the Fastnet lighthouse, for example,
above Hog's Head or Crow Head or Perch Rock),
depending on where our manoeuvre was and only
when the wind blew from the south or southwest.

At the latest when these clouds,
which were to our eyes enemy airships,
English barrage balloons or flying Protestant fortresses,
collided with our mountains
we could verify their estimated altitude,
for our father had not for nothing
forced his freedom fighters
to learn the height of the summit
of every mountain in the Cahas, the Sheehys
and Macgillicuddy's Reeks by heart.
If a cloud met Hungry Hill roughly at the rocky terrace
where our summer bathing lake lay,
its cruising altitude was 2,000 feet;
should it scrape over the summit,
whichever of us had guessed 260 feet higher
scored one point (for the imaginary kill);
if the cloud hit the Sugarloaf
or even Carrauntoohil, the one who wished to emerge
victorious from the air battle
had to raise his guess to heights
of up to 3,400 feet.

The first to have five of his predictions
confirmed to within a hundred feet
or less was the war hero
and the winner;
if one of us was wrong by the same amount,
he was demoted.
Sometimes we were both wrong;
but there could only ever be one winner,
and his name was usually Liam.

Yet our father, the captain, was not satisfied
for his recruits to be able to reel off the heights
of their area of operations as indicated on the map;
one of their duties was also to know
their Gaelic—no, Irish!—names.
After all, an Irishman only used the language
of his English foe for strategic reasons
and favoured—at least as far as the place names
of his homeland were concerned—
the vocabulary of his ancestors;

an Irishman spoke neither English nor Gaelic
but Irish!
Was that so hard to grasp?
And for that reason it was not
Hungry Hill, damn it! but *Cnoc Daod*,
not Sugarloaf but *Gabhal Mhór*,
not Baurearagh Mountain, you moron!
but *Sliab Bharr Iarthach*,
and, naturally, an Irish fighter
would never say Carrauntoohil,
for his country's highest mountain was called
Corrán Tuathail!

Anyone who wanted to ready himself
for the fight against England and
against Protestantism
in the mountains of Cork and Kerry
must know the peaks' true names
in his sleep, and all the more so
when he raised his eyes to appeal

to the triune God for victory and benediction.
A recruit unable to pass these simplest tests
was allowed to sing along to Irish ballads
by the campfire on the night after a manoeuvre,
but got only tea and dry bread for supper.

Sometimes, however, bands of strato- and altocumulus,
drifting far out of range above the attacking
cloud squadrons, neared the battle zone
above our native hills,
then soared over them and away, unscathed,
in a northerly and north-easterly direction and perhaps on
towards British headquarters!

We always counted these invincibles
among our own forces. They belonged to us!
They unleashed a silent hail of bombs
on our lower-flying enemies,
triggering panic in their formations
and headlong flight: *Broken Arrow*!
Battle over, honours even.

To these and only these high-flying,
invincible cloud-ships
we gave the honorary title of *Everest*,
christened them *Everest* clouds, *Everest* cruisers,
Everest bombers—until one day,
that is, our captain awoke
unnoticed from his midday nap
on the moss outside the tent,
listened in on our transmissions and then
held a sermon on the indignity of this name.

Yet he never told us
what else an invincible cloud-ship
might be called,
and he knew no other of the many names
for that Peak XV, which even the British
at the height of their dominance
had not conquered but only measured from afar.
Oh no, our captain . . . our captain
insisted, obstinately and unwaveringly,
that on his battlefields and in his army
nothing invincible and no summit
should be named after a British land-grabber . . .

The day Nyema told me her name
and, hours after the trader's departure,
we struck out with a heavily laden yak caravan
into the mountains, a blizzard set in
around noon and soon rendered even the marks
of hundreds of hooves invisible.
By early afternoon we gazed back down an
endless steep slope. The countless hairpins
of our ascent were lost in the pristine whiteness,
amid clouds and drifting banks of fog
that were unable to follow us up to the saddle
I had been longing for hours to reach.

Up there! We would surely have a rest up there.
Though the yaks were carrying our luggage, I was still
        exhausted
when we finally reached the top.
For the first time on this trip I was wearing the altimeter
on my wrist: 5,400 metres above sea level.

Far below us lay a valley in the afternoon sun,
so wide that it could have harboured cities, and so long
that its end was lost in a bluish haze.
On the valley bottom, whose lowest point
was nonetheless 4,620 metres high
(as I was to measure the next day),
a river meandered away into the distance.
No trace of roads, houses, tents or tracks,
even through binoculars—
a valley without humans, a land without us.

After the descent to the river
and two days' march along its banks, said Nyema,
a monastery awaited us, another ascent,
another pass and, beyond that,
that year's first lush meadows.

No rest in the saddle.
As slowly as during the ascent,
the yaks crossed over the eagerly awaited goal
and the herders gradually broke off from the procession
to mumble some prayers and bow low
in front of a spray of prayer flags on the pass
before hurrying to catch up with the train
as it headed downhill.
No rest, no fire, no pause for breath.

As dusk began to rise up from the valley
to our height like the slowly rising tide,
the river meanders continued to glitter
far down below,

but a bare terrace on our descent
offered enough room for even a caravan to camp.

Tents? For one night no tents were pitched,
for one night no hearths and clay ovens
were built, no sleeping places were
consecrated, the inner living space not divided,
no guardian spirits commended; for one night
travel offerings and walking prayers
sufficed, some lengths
of wool pulled over poles sufficed,
skins, blankets and open fires sufficed.
Only Liam and I—two sea-dwellers
in the trader from Ya'an's retinue,
left behind by the man from Ya'an—
pitched their green dome
and crawled into this burrow,
whose synthetic layers were repeatedly
buckled
by the nostrils of jostling yaks.

The yaks' breath, their grunting
so close to our down sleeping bags,
the wind that rose around midnight
and began to wail through the needles of rock
pointing up to the stars
and the barking of the mastiffs
kept Liam and me from sleeping.
Yet we heard no sound from the hearths
of our hosts and protectors,
no commands to the dogs, no talking, no laughter.

Nyema said the following morning
that the rock terrace we had camped on that night
bore in her clan's tales
and in all its memories a name
denoting a strange curse:
Place without Dreams.

7.

The Flying Mountain: Nyema's story

It is still Nyema's story, of course,
for it was above all Nyema
who told me of an age when the mountains
broke away from the sparkling swarm of stars
and sailed like bright rafts across the night sky
until they eventually floated down
onto the world's plains, which were flat
and composed only of marshes, stony and snowy deserts,
pastures, meadows and savannahs.

However huge and immovable
these mountains might appear now, Nyema had said,
none of them would remain
in the human world for ever; one after the other,
they would lift off again one day
and disappear whence they had come,

they would fly upwards and, with a roaring and a
    thundering

of torrents of meltwater and stones, rise higher
and higher and float away amid swirling plumes
of snow, homeward bound, back to the stars,
slowly, inexorably and blazing white,
like cumulus clouds on a peaceful afternoon.

Nyema talked so naturally of the circumstances
under which the greatest weights on earth
would suddenly grow light, light as a feather, and fly away,
as if describing natural laws that turned water
into rock-hard ice or rocks into flowing lava.
But she told this tale of flying mountains
not on a single day, one evening,
beside a single fire, but divided it
into passages and fragments spread over our weeks
in the mountains of Kham, as if to check
before every instalment or extension of her story
whether her listeners could cope with her words
and were capable
of recognizing the naturalness of it all.

I cannot exactly recall
when she began her story, for Nyema
did not simply *begin* and then continue
on and on to the end . . .
One could sometimes only tell
once she had long since fallen silent
if one of her references was part
of the story of flying mountains or simply an explanation
of some apparition in the towering landscape.
The links often only became clear

in my memories, in which words,
sentences and fragments coalesced into a whole,
and it is therefore probably true
to say that I gradually transformed
Nyema's story into my own.

If, for example, she spoke of *nails*
when describing the shafts of prayer flags—
the wood used, the prayers and mantras that fluttered
from it—she was in fact
absorbed in her telling of a mountain that flew . . .
Yet I thought at the time that these *nails* were simple
euphemisms, approximations of a word
she didn't know or that wouldn't come to mind
and I believed I understood and asked no more.
So where did her tale begin? And when?

Its beginning reaches back to the days when we
were descending with the yak caravans
from the cold campsite at the Place without Dreams
to the meandering river and then kept to the banks
as we headed towards the cloud-veiled valley end—
the yaks light on their curiously delicate hooves,
making their bulky bodies, fluttering with wool, seem all
    the heavier;
me, with sore feet that repeatedly broke out
into blisters as I trekked across
the wet ground and scree.

The clouds filled the valley like a trough,
occasionally rolling up the slopes in the thermal updraught

and vanishing like smoke over the ridges
into a dark-blue sky,
plunging the river, the mountain chains, the valley
each time into a different hue,
as if they brought not just rain, snow or hail,
but colour too,
alternately tingeing the highlands
with every wavelength on the spectrum of white light.

The clan occasionally broke its progress to the mountain
        pastures
for a few hours to allow the animals to graze.
Liam and I would then collect firewood,
bounce flat pebbles across the river
or attribute familiar shapes, forms and names
to the clouds;
we played.

However, on one of those spring days
the air was so clear
that one face of Bird Mountain appeared,
its terrifying scale visible
above the distant head of the valley;
at its foot not the promised monastery
(the distance was still too great for that),
but a delicate pillar of smoke, rising towards
a crevasse-riven glacier snout . . .
Most notably, though, patches of colour, triangles
suddenly appeared in the crystal air!
They must have been of enormous size
for us to distinguish them from this distance.

144

The triangles reminded me of the potato fields
ablaze with yellow-flowering gorse and purple
heather on the slopes of the Cahas,
of abandoned, overgrown farmland
that had lain fallow since the time of the great famine
and its tenants' death, displacement or emigration,
though its old boundaries remained clearly visible
more than one hundred and fifty years later.
The sight of those fields that had gone to seed
under British dominion never failed to stir an ancient anger
in our father on our manoeuvre days,
and what I felt at the sight of these colourful signs
at the head of the valley . . .
was it an echo of that anger?

The military! Flight beacons! Those bloody occupiers!
They must be the Chinese airforce's signal colours,
markers of conquest and settlement;
those arseholes painted
and labelled even the wilderness and the mountains
with directions for their bombers
so that they could add new scorch marks whenever they
        wanted.
Our land! Our booty!

But . . . I also felt, as I had back then,
staring at the fields glowing gorse-yellow
and heather-violet, that these marks on the slopes,
when separated from their meaning, looked
like a message to a . . . a divine power?
In any case, a power high up in the clouds

that was to be honoured, warned,
educated or appeased by this interplay of red and blue.

And as the signals at the valley head
grew more distinct with every step of the yak's hooves
and could then be seen moving like billowing fields of corn,
I pushed my way through the herd as it trotted
in an endless line and attempted
to catch up with Nyema.

It was the second time
I had tried to address a considered question
to the woman, not because I particularly cared
about what I saw in the distance,
but because I wanted to hear her voice;

I wanted her to look at me, and I didn't want
either her or my brother to notice
my longing,
for I still could not admit to myself,
with the excitable shyness of a man
who fears being rebuffed, and thus continually
searches for new excuses,
for a look, a word, a question, I . . . ran after Nyema.
I ran after her.

I didn't need to look for her,
for I always knew where she was—way ahead in the caravan
beside a yak cow from her herd that was entirely white
save for a few dark blazes, as if
camouflaged for an everlasting winter.

The sandy track running between large boulders
and a steep 3- or 4-metre-high embankment
was so narrow that the yaks
could only trot along in single file
and I was forced up against stone blocks
or the edge of the embankment
by every animal I pushed past.

And then, before I reached Nyema,
I heard her murmuring, a singsong,
prayers, nursery rhymes . . . I didn't know
whether she was talking insistently to her gods,
to the cow by her side or to her son Tashi,
whom she carried in a cloth on her back.
She murmured, sang to herself and spun yak's wool
with a hand spindle as she walked, and yet
the thin air made it hard for me to speak
and keep up with her at the same time:
Nyema, I panted, Nyema.

But it was Tashi, the child on her back,
who suddenly opened his eyes
and stared at me.
I was bewitched by that gaze—
and stumbled and staggered, in danger
of toppling into the river.

Only now, as if the opening of her son's eyes
and not my calling
had woken her from her absorption,
Nyema turned round and saw me fall,

dropped her spindle, stretched out her arm towards me,
pulled me lightly, almost playfully
back up onto the path by my hand
as it grasped for a hold,
and saved me from the imminent fall
simply by redirecting
the momentum of my slip

up to her, back onto the path—
she made me fall *upwards*!
and, still helping me up
and releasing my hand,
bent down for the lost spindle,
scooped it up and shifted like a dancer
into the next step;

all in one movement, all so smoothly
that I barely had time to feel scared,
and could think only
of the eyes the child had turned on me:
They are as dark as his mother's.
Nyema said something that sounded reassuring,
presumably to the startled cow beside her,
but did not resume her praying, singing, mumbling,
and merely drew her carrying cloth tighter
with a quick tug of her free hand.

I pointed to the yellow, blue and red triangles
in the distance and suddenly had no idea
what I had meant to ask—it was as if her hand had pulled
me out of an icy shadow into the warmth of the sun;

it was also impossible to say now
whether the child had really noticed me
or just opened his eyes in his sleep.
Tashi's eyes were closed. He was sleeping.

As I lowered my arm
I touched Nyema on the shoulder,
an innocuous, fleeting gesture of gratitude,
and thought I could feel her body's warmth
even through the coarse weave of the cloth; I thought

that she slowed her pace,
almost imperceptibly, maybe, but slow enough
to allow my hand to rest
for a second on her shoulder,
let me rest on her shoulder.

I might be wrong, but I think
it was around the time of this first touch
that Nyema spoke of the *nails* of the prayer flags
and explained that the far-off coloured signs were fields—
huge fields of hundreds and thousands
of blue and red prayer flags,
which had been planted
on the flanks of Bird Mountain
by the residents of the monastery
(a blood-red, fortified building which gradually
emerged from a dip in the valley before us).

The prayers, mantras and invocations
written or printed with wooden stamps

on these flags were to beat in the air,
and their ceaseless movement in the wind, their praying,
would be borne away until the end of time,
just as the scrolls secreted
in the prayer wheels were to be turned
and turned
so that these words would be repeated unceasingly
even by those who could not read,
so no breath, no syllable of truth
would ever fall back into the speechless,
soundless, godless silence.

Even then, right at the start of her tale,
before I had grasped that it was the start
of her tale of flying mountains,
Nyema fell silent when Liam approached,
as if what she said was a secret
intended for my ears alone.

But at that moment Liam did not wish
to hear anything, but only to assure me enthusiastically
that the thing that now loomed so sky-high and sparkling
with snowfields and glaciers above the head of the valley
really was *Cha-Ri*,
the Bird Mountain of his maps.
Tashi woke and started to cry.
Liam said what he had to say and walked on.
Nyema fell silent and did not continue her tale

and so I learnt only later, days, weeks later,
that the shafts of these prayer flags really

were *nails*—nails with which humans
had to tack the skirt of the mountains to the world,
nailing it down so that the mountains stayed with them
and did not lift off, fly away
and dissolve into air during storms,
such gigantic storms that even stones
were hurled around like snowflakes.

Yes! it took these nails, but above all
the hands of the humans who drove them in,
to ensure that the mountains would stay
as their bulwark and wall and protect them,
for even the greatest and highest mountains in the world
had not always loomed over human lives,
but had flown to their aid,

flown to them at a time
when humans began to raise themselves
from the animal kingdom in which they had
hitherto been trapped, and could at last
throw back their heads
and look up at the sky,
at the passing clouds.

It was then, and no earlier, that the mountains
settled on plains, deserts, meadows and savannahs
so that this feeble race, so exposed
to the snow and all kinds of storms,
might have leeward slopes on which grass
for its livestock and herbs would flourish, offering spots
for fires and tents, shelter and room to live.

For, robbed of one pair of feet
which had now grown into arms,
teetering on their two remaining legs,
the gusts and lashes of snow
and hail storms flung these humans
to the ground more readily
than when they had crawled, non-sentient, upon the earth.

But, one by one, mountains descended
upon the world, primarily so that gods and guardian spirits
might find homes in the eternal snows
of the peaks, airy pavilions
from which they might watch their creatures' progress
and see in which direction this upright,
often staggering being would tread.
Barely risen from the animal kingdom,
would humans now turn back to bestiality, towards
        perdition?

The staircase up which some of these bipeds
strode and down which others
slid back into a bottomless pit
could only be discerned from the mountaintops
as a series of valley bottoms reaching up to the heavens,
beginning at sea level
and rising higher, ever higher,
far above the clouds and stars . . .

The fact that whenever Nyema told her story
she only ever spoke to me and excluded
my brother Liam from the very start

had little to do with any preference
for me, let alone love,
but was merely the expression of her clan's belief
that the story of flying mountains
might only be told by *one* mouth to *one* ear,
told only by someone
who had an answer to him who asked.
And I had asked.

But a flying mountain
could not be the subject of a fireside tale,
never a story for a circle of friends,
family or any other audience,
only ever a question between two people,
one of whom listened while the other spoke.
For unlike the universal rule
that the dogs must be released from their chains
and leashes to vent their fury on wolves
and other demonic night-time aggressors,
or the rule stating that a tent's hearth
might be placed only in a location recommended
by the guardian spirits,

stories such as that of a flying mountain were to be
transformed inside each mind into something new and
        unique.
Each person was to spin his own tale,
his own story, and thereby make it
something distinctive and exceptional,
something he could believe in for ever like himself.

The course of such a story, said Nyema,
carried both teller and audience away
from all that was familiar, sometimes into the depths
of the night, but always ended up back
where it had all started,
back and ever onwards,
like the orbit of a comet which appears,
vanishes and, after eons,
reappears from the opposite direction,
or like the light that goes out in the west
and rises again from the east.

In Nyema's view, it was therefore only natural
and self-evident that her story
should also lead me ever farther from the sea
and my memories and my brother Liam,
away and at the same time home
to a world in which I was alone with myself.

Nyema's and her clan's calendar
grew so familiar to me on that journey
that I stopped subordinating my years
to the habitual count,
no longer gave them their traditional numbers,
but, like Nyema and her family, called
the present—the year of our journey from Horse Island
to Kham—the *Year of the Horse*, a year
followed by that of the Snake and succeeded
by a year of the Goat,
all stretching out into a future

which, after cyclical changes in character
from Monkey via Rooster, Dog and Pig
and Rat and Buffalo and Tiger and Hare
and Dragon kept returning, in long loops,
to the name of the Horse
until at last all time stood becalmed
and, like the water of a lake,
became merely a mirror of the sky:
it stood still.

In these new times I allowed only
my months to keep their old names,
and to this day I say:
It was the 20th of March in the Year of the Horse
when our yak caravan reached the monastery
at the head of the valley, at the foot of Bird Mountain,
and the fields of prayer flags there, with sides
200 or 300 metres long—waving
fields that rustled in the wind, fields of nails
that were designed to prevent
a 6,000-metre mountain
from taking off and flying away.
What did rise up with a commotion
from one of the red towers in the field of scree
outside the monastery walls as we arrived was not a
        mountain
(although its shadow was gigantic),
but a flock of enormous bearded vultures, startled
by an exploding firework
that a laughing monk, a shaven-headed boy,
a child, had fired into the sky
to mark our arrival.

I had heard and read about
these towers and these flocks of vultures,
even seen photos of such flocks
on the Net on Liam's screens,
but now, in real life, I was spooked,
and even the yaks, which could calmly cross
the steepest slopes and trot along precipices,
became nervous, anxious, as this flock
darkened the cloudless evening
and cast its shadow over our caravan.

The vultures, which had given
its name to *Cha-Ri*, a massif
that obscured most of the sky before us,
had taken off from a tower platform
where they had been devouring the scraps of meat
and shattered bones laid out for them,
had taken off from corpses,
spent, empty shells of transmigrating souls,
which were to be ripped apart by beaks and talons
and scattered to the four winds
—a Tibetan *sky burial* or *bird-scattering*.

The photo captions on Liam's liquid-crystal screens
were fresh in my memory, but it was Nyema
who first told me, on the evening we arrived,
of those consolers,
who, at the end of such ceremonies, awaited mourners
beside the towers dark with flapping and squawking;
ascetics, whose single task was to succour
the weeping, the horrified, often the screaming,

listen to them in silence, speak to them
of the labyrinthine wanderings of the soul,
or simply take them in their arms
and stay with them—until they smiled.

For could the abandoned feel anything but horror,
anything other than distress and despair,
and what else could they do
but weep and scream when they
had to watch, on a platform or
some other place devoted to sky burials,
a tower guardian dissecting and readying
a person they loved—a dead wife, father,
child, friend or brother—
for squabbling vultures to devour,

had to watch the beloved's head
being smashed with a hammer, the arms, shoulders,
the whole, now cold, so-often-caressed body
being hacked apart with knives and axes,
then disappearing among the wings
of vultures fighting over their prey.

And how steadfast must one be
not only to console these witnesses
but also to make them smile?

The child, the little red-robed monk,
who had played with fire to fete our arrival
and scared the vultures from their carrion,
might grow up to be one of these consolers,

mumbling mantras and prayers,
spinning prayer wheels and beating his drums
until he himself was carried to one of the platforms;

but that evening
he was delighted by the bitter chocolate
I took from our stocks as a present
and even more so by a pencil, for which he begged
and with which he then wrote a series of syllables
on a pebble polished smooth by the river.

He threw the stone back into the water
so that the current would wash over the writing
and pray the mantra again and again,
and on and on, after he was long asleep
or had passed into another body.

Our caravan crept without stopping
past the monastery and its towers,
moving for over an hour
along the fields of flags and the scree slopes
of Bird Mountain, until longhouses and towers
lay like scattered toys far below
and the vultures had shrunk to the size of songbirds.
Not until far up the ascent to the next valley
did pastures lie that offered the herds
fresh forage for several days.

At last I no longer needed to cast
around for new questions and new reasons
to talk and get close to Nyema,

for now I had a reason
and material for countless questions—
a mountain that flew.

Even though the name of Phur-Ri had come up
once before at the camp by the Yangtze, it was only
when the fields of prayer flags appeared at the valley head
that Nyema alerted me to its significance,
stating that the name *Flying Mountain*
did not merely denote the sight of ridges
flaring with plumes of ice and snow,
nor the visible crystal veils of peaks
swept by monsoon winds and storms,
nor the ragged banks of fog and cloud
sailing over gorges and bluffs;
rather, this name
was a description of reality,
of a visible, palpable event.

For as every hoofbeat of the caravan in those days
carried us closer to the summer pastures
and to the blank spot on Liam's maps,
and I asked Nyema
whether she had ever seen, with her own eyes,
a mountain rising into the air,

she pointed to the peaks soaring above us,
to the next valley
guarded by *Te-Ri*, Cloud Mountain,
and translated for me for the first time the name
of the colossus that provided water and shelter

for the final and highest expanse of pasture
that lay beyond:

Phur-Ri, said Nyema, *a mountain that flies.*
This mountain, the most radiant and lofty of all,
reminded any creature that walked upright and could speak
that nothing—nothing!—
however mighty, however heavy,
ice-clad, inaccessible and invincible,
could endure for ever,
but that one day everything must leave,
fly away!, up and away;
and what vanished did not vanish for ever,
but even the most distant times stood still
and began afresh,
returning, albeit transformed,

shattered into a thousand new shapes and guises
and a wheel or a star
or simply a prayer wheel, a wool spindle,
would begin to turn again;

of that, of that alone, Phur-Ri was to be
an example and a memorial,
when it rose up, over and over—
sometimes only for a few hours or days—
rose up and disappeared, yes flew away
and yet always returned,

sometimes after a few breaths taken
by the one who had witnessed its flight,

sometimes only after weeks
of rain, storms, snow.

Yes yes, certainly, of course!
She too had seen this mountain,
flying high above the clouds,
dazzling, ephemeral, light;

everyone in the clan, provided they had a head
to raise to the sky, eyes and a mouth
to form words and names
and ears to hear those names, those syllables,
and not just the clamour of a landslide
not just the lowing of the animals and the wind;

everyone could see this mountain fly.

8.

At Bird Mountain.
The masked man. A parade in the snow.

It would be weeks before the pastures
within view of the red monastery were exhausted
and Nyema's clan struck their tents again
to move higher into the mountains.
During this time, Liam occasionally grew so restless
and even so irate that we argued.

Twice he tried to persuade me
to leave the clan. Without pack animals,
bearing all the weight of our equipment
and provisions on our own shoulders, we should
set out for the blank spot in the last and highest
of the three valleys and rely
on being able to claim the protection and aid
of the nomads on our way back.
On our way back!

As though it were child's play to haul
the load of a tent, ropes, climbing gear and food

for weeks to the debris at the glacier's snout,
set up a base camp there,
reconnoitre and secure a route,
scale one or two mountains of unknown height
and then warm ourselves up again
by the clan's fires and in their tents . . .
No, I didn't want to leave; I wanted to stay
and only move on with the clan,
with Nyema.

Again Liam had no idea
what I wanted or desired,
but he did acknowledge my objection
that his hastiness would turn the hike into an ordeal for me.
Weeks hauling packs
with my sore feet!
Reaching any goal, let alone a summit
in such gruelling conditions would be
a gamble and likely to fail.

Quite apart from the fact that the Khampas' pride
forbade them from selling
their services as porters and sherpas,
the clan suffered from a lack of herders,
protectors and fathers, and they were convinced
that the death of Nyema's husband,
Tashi Gyeltso, executed at Nangpa La,
was the fatal consequence
of forgetting one's dignity and squandering
one's strength as a dogsbody and porter—
for one should not seek

a better life at altitudes
reserved for the gods and the spirits.

Tashi's accident had cast a pall over his family
and only compounded the labour shortage.
No, if we wanted to count on the nomads' help,
then this could only be achieved by sticking
to the leisurely pace of their caravan
and by not suddenly *having* to get somewhere
ahead of the season.

Yaks?
Might we . . . might my brother buy some yaks
or at least borrow them and
take them along as pack animals?

Nyema not only translated for me a list of refusals
to these and other requests from Liam,
she also tried to explain the reasons behind them,
and I passed on what I heard
or thought I had understood
to Liam as persuasively
as if a clan member were addressing him:

Sell yaks to a buyer
who would only lead them into the clouds?
To heights where at this time of year the grass
sometimes lay under waist-high fresh snow?
The most precious thing in a land of snow—
life—depended on every wafting tuft of hair
of every animal in the herd;

and this life was not for sale or for loaning;
it was to be followed, never rushed.
What did we know of the ways of yaks?
The previous winter had been the most merciless
in years, reducing most herds
to a fraction of their former numbers,
turning some entirely to carrion,
making each surviving cow and bull
even more valuable than before.

Had we not seen the towers erected
from the bones and skulls of their corpses?
These sacrificial structures to the spirits
and warnings to herders?
Or did we wish to add to these towers
by striking out with pack animals
with which we were no more familiar
than a herder would be with our diode headlamps?

Liam fumed when I spoke to him
in the name of the clan, as he put it, and feared
that through our sloth we might miss
the gap in the clouds
that opened cyclically between winter's end
and the random turbulence
that signalled the approaching monsoon,
and, in the remaining time, would once more
find the heights of our goal utterly barred
by low pressure fronts and impassable.

But what was the *remaining time*?
If we had a goal capable of luring us from the sea
to here, to the foot of Bird Mountain
and higher still, why weren't we devoting *everything*,
all the time we thought we had, to this goal?

This question from Nyema I relayed to Liam
as if I had asked it myself, and began to comprehend
that my brother maybe wanted to continue on,
onwards as quickly as possible
and upwards, because his goal
was also a turning point, on which
(whatever he might find up there)
he could at last turn his back and return
whence he came, to the sea, to Horse Island,
back from the smoke and the snow
to his screens, on which the mountains
rose up and vanished again
at his sole command.
And I also began to comprehend
that added to our other differences was
the fact that I didn't want to go back—
I wanted to stay.

Nyema's father Tsering Dorje had offered
that I sleep in his tent with him and his daughter
when he saw me crawl out of our green dome tent
into the dewy grass one morning
after a loud altercation with Liam,
and crouch shivering
between some ruminating yaks.

Accepting his offer and eventually moving
not just my sleeping bag
but also part of my equipment
into Tsering Dorje's tent—from then on I spent
my nights with seven people
from three generations around a fire
whose smoke escaped through a tent opening
in which sparks and stars flickered
equally brightly on clear nights—
for some reason made me sleep more peacefully
and also calmed my dispute with Liam.

For even though my new berth
was often loud when Tsering Dorje snored
and his wife Dekyi Tsomo coughed,
when Tashi cried out for his mother
and in doing so also woke Nyema's sister
Yishi Lhamo's daughter, who added her groans to his
        complaints,
I sometimes felt so safe and so pleasantly tired
after each startled awakening
that I would sink back and fall asleep again
more easily than I had ever done in the dome tent.

The gulf between Liam and me
even seemed to foster the respect
of one for the other.
Liam knew as well as I did
that we could no longer convert each other:
each followed his own urges.
But we came to accommodations.

So I agreed during the days at this temporary camp
to attempt an ascent of Bird Mountain with him.
According to the altimeter's indications, our tents
lay 4,820 metres above sea level,
and Liam's estimates suggested
that it was little more than 900 metres
to the top of Cha-Ri.

Tsering Dorje promised us clear, calm weather,
and so we set out with light bags
shortly before dawn on a cloudless day,
soon leaving vegetation and the last yaks behind us,
climbed with difficulty across fields of scree
and, sooner than expected,
encountered compact, icy rock.

We had studied the route of our ascent in detail
through binoculars in the preceding days,
and a monk from the monastery
(he had twice before made a pilgrimage
to a sacred cave just below the summit)
had described the trip
up from the monastery
and back down as one
that could be done in a day
—and yet we were soon puzzled as to how
a pilgrim in monk's robes and ungainly skin shoes
could negotiate such terrain.
Even with our crampons
we had trouble crossing gullies,

and banging the ice from the rock
with our picks was taxing work.

Far below us I could still make out the clan's tents
and beyond them the buildings and red towers
of the monastery; once I even thought
I saw a figure gazing up at us from one
of the tents—Nyema!—until, amid the bubbling fog
and following our decision
to look for dry rock on the other side
of a corniced ridge, monastery, tents,
people and yaks disappeared from view
and for the first time since our arrival
we were truly alone in a glacier-capped
high mountain landscape,
which seemed to brook no further human life.

The rock on the leeward side of the ridge
had no icy cladding, but some passages
were so difficult that we would have been better
to rope up and secure ourselves,
especially as residual snow lay so deep in some gullies
that we occasionally sank in up to our hips.
Yet we stuck to *our* own route
and unbuckled our crampons on climbing sections,
but we didn't use a rope
and switched back onto the invisible path
reconnoitred by the monk
only when the ridge levelled off
into a series of flattened pre-summits.

Even here, though, no sign,
no prayer flag, no tracks suggested any previous walker,
although the mist parted again here
to reveal a glittering island landscape,
a sunlit archipelago of rocky pinnacles,
promontories, glacier snouts and soaring bastions
amid a sluggish sea of clouds,
billowing as if in slow motion.

Only to the north-east,
where, according to the Khampas' tales,
Te-Ri and Phur-Ri should stand
as higher steps in a chain of mountains
that skirted their pastures, there still hung
an impenetrable wall of cloud.

I recall a childish sense of triumph
as we climbed higher and higher,
each for himself
and at a variable distance from the other,
through this blinding landscape
which gradually relented
and decreased in difficulty
with every step I took.

Clouds sailed past
above our heads
and beneath our feet,
enveloping the fields of firn, crags
and icefalls in a fleeting halo
of airy lightness.

Granted, my breathing rattled
and when the wind dropped
I was sometimes startled in the silence
(the unforgettable silence of high altitude)
by the sound of breathing,
which seemed to come
not from my lungs, not from my throat
nor my open mouth,
but from somewhere up above, from the ice
or the deep-blue sky,
sometimes ringing back,
hissing back from ridges and cornices.

Sometimes the distance between me and Liam
(who, as always, went ahead) was so great
that I lost sight of him
among the rocks or against the sun.

Was he testing me? Did he want to know
how far I would follow him
until I called out and asked him
to wait for me?
Whereas Liam always offered me
a safety line on new routes
up the cliffs of Horse Island, here I felt
that the steadily increasing distance
was a demonstration, a warning
that I was dependent
on his experience and strength on every path,
whether it led up or down.

If that really was his intention
(he later denied it), then its effect on me
was the exact opposite—that strange triumphant sensation
one can only experience
when moving through the clouds by one's own efforts,
requiring no rope, no security,
no help, no encouragement
and no other consolation than one's own strength.

My breath rattled, but it sufficed;
my steps were slow but unwavering
and could take me still higher (I thought),
far higher.

But probably I possessed enough
of all the things this route required
and needed no companions because down below,
outside a tent somewhere beneath the clouds,
maybe now, in this one happy moment,
Nyema was raising her gaze to where I was;

that gaze linked the safety of the clan,
their proximity to the summit of Bird Mountain
like a vanishing line, an unbreakable thread
along which I might continue to climb
or find my way at any second
back down to her.

Liam?
I no longer needed Liam's help.
We reached the top of *Cha-Ri* in the early afternoon,

finding a wind-polished, rock-hard snowy knoll
the size of two horse's backs
studded with a bouquet of flagpoles.

But no pennants were tied to these poles,
only frosted strips of wood
with mantras carved or burnt into them—
wooden signposts
pointing off in all directions,
showing a path out of time.

When the frost crumbled at Liam's touch,
he bent down in a reflex movement
as if he wanted to pick up the braid of ice needles
and stick it back onto the silver-bleached wood,
and I repeated one of my father's threats:
he had lectured us at a wishing well in the Cahas
that he would beat us if we ever dared
to remove the wishing ribbons
pilgrims had tied to the rhododendrons
and attach them like trophies to our tent pole:
Whoever touches them cuts a thread
binding heaven and earth
and will be struck down by misfortune,
and Liam answered me, unsmiling:
Shut up, Daddy!

Liam above the clouds,
Liam in the blue of the sky, Liam on the peak
of Cha-Ri, 6,170 metres above the sea,
the highest point of our lives.

Protected from the icy wind
by his storm mask, a black balaclava
whose eye-slit fitted with glacier glasses
showed my reflection and the reflection
of the empty sky,
he again resembled our father,
our marching father in his woollen mask
on that unforgettable St Patrick's Day
when it had snowed in the streets
of Bearhaven.

It was in the same March
as our mother had disappeared
with Duffy to the North;
she had fled to the North, and from Belfast
had begun a series of vain attempts
to fetch Liam and me to her side.
But the courts in both the South
and the North agreed, for different reasons,
to refuse her custody of her sons, and though these sons
did not wish to stay with their father at all costs,
nor did they want to go somewhere
where everything was so different, so alien and,
as they heard at the kitchen table, Protestant,
Anglican, accursed and *hostile*.

What issued from our father's mouth
at the kitchen table
were not so much complaints about his loss
as curses and outbursts
about this *betrayal* of him and of Ireland.

This anger could send him berserk
for a moment and he would then,
for no particular reason, rain blows
on his dogs and sheep, sometimes
on his sons as well.
These outbursts were followed
with predictable regularity by muttered,
stammered requests for forgiveness
(once even with tears) and, above all,
by appeasing gestures and compensatory gifts
on which Liam and I
eventually began to count
when we tried to assess the consequences
of overstepping lines, breaking rules or making short forays
into territories of our own imagining.
These calculations included chocolate bars,
even illustrated books about sailing boats or sea fish,
a penknife, a compass or angling gear
from Finbarr O'Sullivan's Hardware Shop in Bantry,
as well as liberties such as being allowed
to play a shipwreck victim
in a Marine Rescue lifesaving practice
or simply stay up half the night
in the flickering light of the television—
the television installed by Duffy, woman-stealer,
traitor and mortal foe.

The St Patrick's Day parade
had been preceded by one of our father's
tantrums caused by some missing sheep
having fallen down the shaft of a Bronze Age

copper mine, into one of the deep holes
gaping between the gorse bushes on our field.

Liam and I hadn't mended the fence
as we'd been ordered to, spending
most of the time allotted for this task
hunting a wounded seal
on the beach instead.

Father had grabbed our hair so furiously
that he was left
with clumps of it in his fists.

Finally he stood helplessly before his mute,
completely mute sons,
and his still-clenched fists looked
as if monkey bristles were sprouting from his fingers,
bloodless fingers that had turned almost white
under the pressure of his rage.

I recall our embarrassment
and my shock
when he suddenly raised these monkey fists
to his eyes and began to sob.

His atonement that evening was generous—
Liam and I sat, each with a tin of chocolates
and toffees before him,
in front of the television far into the night
watching shoot-outs, battles,
even a kiss, and the next day Father drove us,

without much haggling
and armed not just with coins
but also with paper money,
in the Ford Galaxy to the St Patrick's Parade
in honour of Ireland's patron saint that was to march
through the streets of Bearhaven—
a brass band and fiddlers behind a company of soldiers
from the army of the Free Irish Republic.

In the car park by the beach
Father merely made us swear
that we would meet up to leave
in time for the afternoon service,
then left us alone with the possibilities of our riches
and a gang of friends eager for adventure.

The main thing that interested us about the soldiers
marching under their banners were their guns;
we had never seen so many guns before.
Like the bristles of a gigantic caterpillar
crawling through the streets of Bearhaven,
the barrels and mounted bayonets
pointed into the white-clouded March sky
from which the forecast said much sun
and only the occasional shower could be expected that day.
We—Liam, me
and three blood brothers from neighbouring farms—
were standing in the front row of spectators
so as to be as close as possible
to the dull lustre of the weapons, the uniforms
and the hypnotic lockstep marching.

And fully absorbed with this spectacle of invincibility
we did not at first notice the sudden quiet
that rippled out from the centre of the parade
like a wave, taking hold of marchers and spectators alike—
yes, the entire procession.

Yet even as we noticed this strange silence
and realized the reason
the brass music and the hubbub had died away,
pointing it out to one another with a nudge,
it seemed completely natural
to see those black-masked men
pouring, as if at a sign, from various lanes
and through the crowd into the parade,
lining up behind the soldiers
and falling into step with the army
as if their appearance had been agreed with the other
        participants
and merely completed the procession.

With their balaclavas rolled down to their necks,
their green combat fatigues and their camouflage jackets,
the new arrivals were familiar to us from the front pages
of the *Southern Star* or the *West Cork Examiner*,
not to mention the screen
of our new television set—
fighters from the Irish Republican Army!
Marksmen and planters of bombs
in the battle for Irish unity,
underground heroes battling
against overwhelming English odds.

Some of them had sewn the eye-slits
of their balaclavas together in the middle,
leaving only two black holes.
(Such woollen hats floated in the window
of Finbarr O'Sullivan's store, pinned
among flannel shirts, work overalls,
butcher's knives and fishing tackle.)
There was no better protection against the cold
at sea and during the stormy winter season.

The first to notice the masked men were the spectators
by the kerb, next the soldiers in the procession
and last of all the officer at the front, a captain,
and, in the same way, amazement, shock
and perplexity spread from the back
of the procession to its commander
so that everyone's attention was drawn
in the opposite direction to the march.

Everyone gazed, everyone stared
suddenly at the back of the parade,
at where the IRA was marching, masked,
silent, without flags and without standards.

In the baffled silence
the marching feet pounded like drum beats.
And amid these blows first questioning
and protesting, then approving cries rang out,
fists were raised, people stretched out arms,
fingers formed victory signs.

And as if pushed and jostled
by the intractable question of whether this parade
under the banner of Ireland's holiest man
should now be broken off and the masked men
pushed back into the lanes and chased away (by whom?
and with what forces?) and whether the march
would descend into a street fight, a battle
—on St Patrick's Day—!
the parade continued to advance
with backward-turned faces.

And then as if in a delayed
but all-the-more-sudden reaction
to the appearance of the black-masked men,
my heart began to pound after all, violently,
as if to the beat of the unsynchronized
marchers' lockstep—
in the middle of the IRA men,
despite his mask,
I recognized our father.

He too had pulled his balaclava over his neck
but wasn't wearing fatigues, merely one
of those decommissioned American army jackets
that dangled in their dozens from wire hangers
in the secondhand section of O'Sullivan's store
each time the tanker U.S.S. *Missouri*
dropped anchor in Bantry Bay
and its Irish quartermaster
struck deals with O'Sullivan.

Father wore this jacket on our manoeuvre days too,
but I would have recognized him in any disguise
by his sturdy frame, that heavy, rolling gait
which was all the more conspicuous when he marched.
Only the hat, the black woollen hat seemed new.
Father wore similar watch caps in the mountains
and when setting lobster pots,
but they were all blue, navy blue.

Liam too had recognized this unmistakable fighter
(although only after me)
but he punched me in the side
and put his index finger to his lips.
As if I might give away a secret!
But then Liam took my hand,
took the hand of a brother three years his younger
and held it in his as if it were that of an equal,
a companion, as if he were witnessing something
that was too big for any single person to bear.

I recall a sense of triumph,
even if I didn't really know whether this elation
was due to the sight of our masked father
or the secret I now shared with Liam
and which so far exceeded
any previous confidence we'd kept—
yes, even exceeded the sight
that had presented itself to Liam
during one of his illicit games at the wheel of the Ford
        Galaxy
when he saw Duffy the electrician and our mother

as lovers—
Duffy and Shona, lovers!

On that October day, when the blue light
of the television was to shine on us
for the first time, the two of them
had disappeared for a while
to look for an extension cable
and had kissed in the garage.

And now our cheated father was marching with the IRA.
Daddy! That was our father marching there.
Daddy was marching with the IRA.
Daddy, the man Shona had once defied her family
to follow from Belfast to the South,
for whose love she had forsworn Protestantism
and become a Catholic

and whom she had then cursed as a diehard,
a savage and a candle-swallower,
and dumped for a 'souper'
('far too late' as she would write to her sons from Belfast);
Daddy, who could run his boat into the cliffs
even in a flat calm and sunny weather
because he lived more in the clouds than on this coast
and on his farm, which he struggled to keep
but still could not leave; Daddy
an underground fighter, an avenger, a planter of bombs,
whom even the British royal family had reason to fear!

Now we knew his secret, Liam and I,
and it was our choice whether to continue
to obey his orders, fight with him,
hand him over or shield him.
We had been his recruits.
Now we were his allies.

But then it was our father's name of all things
that ended the baffled silence on St Patrick's Day—
his name followed first by laughter
and then by the disintegration of the black-masked march,

for in the heart of that silence
and at the height of my triumph
we suddenly heard
the high, shrill voice of Dermot O'Brien,
a fisherman from a hamlet near Adrigole
who was notorious for using dynamite
and banned fine-meshed nets to catch fish.
And that voice, which dominated
the church choir during every Mass
suddenly called *Fergus! Hey, Fergus!*
and repeated my father's name
louder and louder: *Fergus, your hat's
still got the price tag on.
You didn't take the price tag off.
Hey, Fergus! The price tag!*

And amid the laughter,
hesitant at first, then gradually swelling,
I saw, Liam saw, everyone—spectators,

soldiers, marchers, every person in and outside
that St Patrick's Day parade—suddenly saw
the white label dangling at the back of my father's neck,
the price tag on a white thread.

Daddy must have missed it
when he rolled down his new hat for the first time
to cover his face.
Liam, who, in his balaclava on the summit of Cha-Ri,
looked so like our masked father
that I thought I saw my reflection in Daddy's manoeuvre
     sunglasses,
not in my brother's glacier glasses,
my own distorted figure
in front of a curving, semi-circular ridge
and beyond it emptiness, falling away—Liam
told me only many years after that St Patrick's Day parade
(during a radio conversation after Father's death)
that it was primarily his recollection of Daddy's reaction
to Dermot O'Brien's shouting
that had induced him to have the word *Gentleman*
engraved on his gravestone in Glengarriff.

For our father seemed unruffled,
didn't glance round at the shouter,
but without breaking step pulled
the black balaclava off his head—
and carried on marching;
blushing with shame or red with anger maybe,
he carried on marching,
while the other black-masked men—

there were only fifteen or so of them, perhaps fewer—
fell away from him; one by one they fell away
and vanished once more into the lanes of Bearhaven.

And as the brass band struck up again
and everyone lining the streets rediscovered their voices
and laughed or shouted over Dermot's mockery,
and with every step it became clearer
that this was not the real IRA
but merely some of its loud-mouthed supporters
who must have gone to war directly from the bar,

and as out of the sky above Bearhaven
the forecast showers cross-hatched the picture
of the parade, first with grain-sized hail but then
with horizontal, driving snow,
just as the electronic flurries did to the fleeting pictures
on our Duffy-installed window on the world,

our father fell back in step with the marching army
and followed the parade at the rear, the very rear.

9.

The heavenly bride. Happy return. Warnings.

If the cave the monk in the red monastery
had told us about existed
below the summit of Cha-Ri, then
its entrance must have been obscured by snowdrifts.

At the highest point of our lives thus far,
Liam and I found, apart from
a bunch of prayer flags in the iron snow,
no other trace of pilgrims
or of a sacred site.
The peak of Bird Mountain
was clad in spotless white armour.
It might have been tiredness, indeed exhaustion,
and not simply the sight of the sea of clouds
at our feet with so many foam-ringed islands in it,
that caused us to linger (almost for too long).
When we finally turned to descend

there were only a few hours
left before nightfall.
We had to hurry.

But the descent seemed
only to confirm Bird Mountain's
unexpected indulgence and benevolence,
for even in the gathering gloom
the air remained so calm and clear
that the moonlight would surely have sufficed
to guide us safely back to the Khampas' tents.

We had scaled our first six-thousander
and our triumph was such that we felt
beyond danger, invincible even,
attributing the almost playful ease
of the ascent not to that day's extremely favourable
weather conditions as forecast
by Tsering Dorje, but purely
to our own ability and our own strength.
We believed we were equal to the mountain chain
at whose end Phur-Ri awaited us,
and our gasping merely convinced us
that we still had air and enough breath left
to soon make it higher still.

We no longer switched to the leeward side
of the ridge but kept during the entire descent
to the pilgrim trail and found all the rocky sections
ice-free and dripping with meltwater,
though even on such mild spring days

most trickles froze again
after sundown and with them
all watery gurgling fell silent.

Seeing nothing more in this
than the confirmation of a rule
that we followed even in a trance,
we experienced then
what Liam had presented on the cliffs of Horse Island
as one of climbing's imponderables—

descents sometimes require greater skill,
greater concentration than any ascent
because on the way down steps
that are visible or at eye level
and testable for someone climbing up, now lie invisible
as he gropes for a hold,
and it is also not possible for him to tell
whether that traverse down below
or that outcrop there
does lead on to safety
further down—or merely to the edge
of an insurmountable overhang
so that he must adjust his route, climb back up!
and only then turn down, further into the valley.

When the Khampas' tents and the far-flung
black dots of yaks on the steep slopes
at last came into view again
in the deep shadow below us,
the crescent moon rose over snowy domes and ridges
bathed in the final pinkly reflected light of the sun.

And as if on the cusp of night
we saw above the tents
one of those gigantic swarms of Apollo moths
that were to appear over and over again
in the coming days—a rippling filigree ribbon
fluttering over the snowless saddle
into the fold of the next valley
and onwards, further to the west, as if
the sole purpose of a swarm of butterflies
were to reel in the fading light
and haul it back over the boundaries of night.

The dogs had not yet
been unleashed from their pegs
and strained furiously at their chains and ropes
when we reached the camp
and Nyema was the first to greet us
after our triumph and say,
We were waiting for you.
Tsering Dorje was about to come looking for you.

The small indent on the bridge of her nose,
visible only at second glance,
a reminder of hours of interrogation
and a punch by a Chinese border policeman,
cast a tiny shadow on her face,
a black flake of darkness that seemed to tumble
out of the night, melting
and vanishing into a smile,
a sign of relief at our,
at my return.

This fleeting little shadow on the face of a woman
who had not been comforted but beaten
after her husband's death and hasty burial,
and who had fretted about me
and my brother as we were gloating
above the clouds, touched me,
moved me, attracted me to Nyema so much
that I almost took her in my arms,
held her face in my hands
and kissed her in front of my brother,
in front of her clan,
but I merely laid my hand
on her arm as if to soothe her,
said something about how beautiful Cha-Ri was,
something about the risk-free, playful ease
of scaling it or about our happy return
or something I can no longer remember
because it was neither what I really wanted to say
nor what I really wanted to do.

What I felt at that instant
but withheld from Nyema was not the joy
of having reached a summit
or having been somewhere
among the clouds, somewhere *up high*—
I withheld and denied my joy
at having made it back from up there
to this camp, to her.

Yet it wasn't the eyes and ears of the clan
that kept me from making this confession;
it was my brother's presence.

I wished then that Liam was not standing where he stood;
I wished that my brother was not where he actually was.
I wished him away
so I might be alone with this woman.

Nyema was a *heavenly bride*,
one of those women to whom her clan gave that title
as a defence and an honour.
For if a community suffered from a lack of men
due to adversity or due to death,
and due to the unfavourable gender ratio a woman
could not find a companion and yet
did not want to remain alone,
night after night, or childless,
then it was also common practice in Nyema's clan
to wed her in a solemn ceremony to the heavens,
to the spirits that produced and protected life.

If a heavenly bride so wished
she was allowed to beget with the man of her choosing
a child that was entitled to the same affection
from the clan as any other offspring
begotten in exclusive intimacy.

The child of a heavenly bride was the child of all,
and Nyema's son Tashi, whose eponymous father
had been killed and buried at Nangpa La,
belonged to his mother alone and yet to all,
could count on the protection and help
of every man who lived his life with the clan
and on the care and love of every woman.

Nyema offered to take my rucksack,
and only now, with the release of tension
and my own relief at our return
and our reclaimed freedom
to place one foot in front of the other
without a climber's tunnel vision,
did I feel how exhausted I was.

The path leading back
from the peak to the safety of the camp
had come to a fork: Liam, presumably
as tired as I was, turned wordlessly
towards our green dome tent;
I walked beside Nyema (without accepting her offer)
towards a point
further up the slope next to a stream—
to Tsering Dorje's tent, Nyema's tent, our tent.

Despite the mildness of that evening,
which, even in the advanced twilight, retained the warmth
of spring or early summer, I gave an involuntary shudder.
I was soaked with sweat and now that
I had no exertions and their combustive heat
to raise this moisture to my body temperature,
even a mild draught struck me like an icy breath.

At the end of a long descent from the Cahas
Captain Daddy had always forced
his two recruits to take an almost ritual bath
or at least wash themselves with bared torso
before they changed out of clothes

sodden with sweat or rain,
because he believed that the cold shock
of the chill water of a beck or peaty mountain lake
was a welcome boost to the circulation
and fostered a toughness
that could only benefit us in the inevitable battles to come
and might even save our lives.

So I let the rucksack slide from my shoulder
outside the tent
and resisting the temptation to sink onto my bed
and stretch out on top of my sleeping bag,
pulled a towel and dry clothing from my luggage
and set off on the short walk to a rock ledge
over which a narrow stream cascaded
two metres into a natural pool
from which we scooped water for cooking
and in which, behind a screen of bushes
shielding us from the eyes of the camp,
we could also wash.

The regular roar of this cataract
seemed night after night to drown out
all the voices in our camp and was audible
in every tent until the noises of the following day
once more overpowered it, forcing the torrent
and its thundering into the background
and back into the mountains.

My willingness to obey Captain Daddy's washing
	instructions

like the most obedient son—no, as if under hypnosis—
might have stemmed from the fact
that I was assailed by fits of shivering and suddenly felt
a terrible need for the blissful warmth
that skinny-dipping in the Cahas had always sparked,

but maybe also, once again, simply from the fact
that I have always perceived the smell
of bodily odours, even the watery aroma of pure sweat,
to be unclean, a stench
that only running water can absolve.

I had trouble removing my clothes,
because the damp and the sweat
turned them into snares
that sent me stumbling into the bushes.
I waded naked through the freezing
knee-deep water towards the cascade
and couldn't suppress a yelp
when the torrent hit me,
wrapping me in an exploding cloud
of icy needles, white-hot sparks and snow crystals.

I yelped and simultaneously started
at this voice from so deep inside me
without the slightest volition on my part.
Under the pounding water I made a noise
as involuntary as the spitting and hissing of a droplet
falling on a hot stone
and instantly evaporating.

But after this spontaneous scream,
which probably owed to the shock of the water
than to the fatigue
that sapped my self-control,
I had to laugh. I froze. I burned. I screamed.
I laughed
and suddenly heard amid this laughter
and through the roar of the water
another voice,
a second, higher-pitched laugh—Nyema.

A mere shadow in the darkness,
in which the only trace of the now-faded daylight
was visible over the mountains to the west,
she knelt on the dry moss beside the pool
dipped a ladle into the water and laughed
without averting her gaze from me
(I sensed this gaze in the darkness
rather than feeling it).
Then she began to speak
in a strangely familiar, laughing lilt.
And, as if at her bidding, I stepped out of the spray,
naked, without a thought for my nakedness,
and, suddenly reminded of our outdoor baths
in the Cahas, reached back into the waterfall
for a bouquet of droplets to hurl
at this witness of my frightful vulnerability.
She didn't fend off the water,
simply let go of her ladle
and rose up and raised her arms
as if she were trying to catch the bouquet
and, laughing, continued to sing.

When Shona bathed me in a tub in our laundry room,
(while big brother Liam inherited
my water and, unsupervised, could unleash
hurricanes, tsunamis and shipwrecks),
she would run her sponge over my body
to a nursery rhyme that sounded like Nyema's humming,
lovingly naming every stage of its progress,

and I thought I heard from Nyema's lips
those old verses about a poor, dirty little man
who wanted a bath,
thought I heard the giggling lament
about a willy all shrivelled with cold
that needed warming and covering with white soapflakes,
about a bottom that needed patting and a tummy
that needed kissing before at last it sank,
along with its fragrant, freshly washed fellow limbs,
into the bed's snowy cornices
and there, deep into dreams
of water-lily ponds, the man in the moon,
black swans and talking trees.

Captain Daddy had eavesdropped
on one of these bathtimes
and banned his wife
from ever singing such songs again.

At first she had laughed at him,
then furiously asked him
whether Daddy's Holy Father in Rome

proclaimed such bans
because the only water he and his crusaders
in their robes and galeros did not spurn
was holy water. Finger baths in holy water!

But after that bathtime
Shona never sang again.

Nyema made no move towards me,
simply standing there in her motionless mirth
as I came wading through the knee-deep water
and the deep darkness towards her.

When I stepped dripping out of the pool I was shivering
and virtually fell into her arms,
embraced her body to conceal this shivering,
clasped her to me, yes *clung* tightly to her
to appease this shivering
and instantly sensed that I could let go,
could let go because it was suddenly *she*
who was holding me.

And then something was cast off me
and something inside me shattered and allowed me too
to begin to speak and whisper and sing,
finally pant in her ear, verses
that transgressed Captain Daddy's bans like no word
I had ever dared utter before—
verses relating
that the little man was no longer poor
and his willy was no longer shrivelled

and his tummy would no longer go unkissed
and no part of him would be cold any more—
and I drew Nyema, who didn't understand a word
and yet understood everything, down onto the dry moss
        where,
in our interweaving arms and fingers,
she was soon as naked as me,
and my skin as dry and warm
as hers.

How often had I felt revulsion
at the smells of my own naked body
and even more at someone else's,
the smell of my own
and the stench of all skin, and now I smelt,
as if for ever cured of this revulsion,
only aromas of earth, yak's wool,
snow water and hay on Nyema's thighs,
at her breast, on which she tolerated
my hand, my mouth, my tongue
and smelt only smoke and night air
in her hair, which streamed down on me
as she swung herself up to be my rider
and let me clasp her breasts
so hard that her milk, meant for Tashi,
dripped onto my neck and face
and sent me into raptures
of which Captain Daddy
and his Holy Father in Rome
can only ever have dreamt
in fear of damnation.

But even when I too began to fear
at some points in my frenzy
if not hell, then at least
the punishment of disgust,
I now had a hiding-place—Nyema.

I sank into her, I hid in her
and in her I was protected from every threat
and beyond the reach of every law and gasped,
yes ultimately screamed my pleasure into the hand
she held over my mouth
while she muffled her own scream
against my chest, leaving
a pattern there with her teeth.

That night
we returned to Tsering Dorje's tent only
to fetch blankets, a pelt, my sleeping bag
and a roughly woven rug
and then stayed snuggled together
in our bed on the moss by the waterfall
until dawn, sleeping little,
barely speaking, occasionally ascribing
shapes and names to the clouds
that, after moondown, drifted like rafts
through the black, spark-showered
emptiness, sometimes knowing
only in our mother tongues
the words for the beetles, fish,
birds and predators whose shadows
we saw chasing the vanished moon

and christened cloud after cloud without knowing
whether we were whispering to each other
the names of one and the same animal in two different
     languages
or two names for two animals
from two different kingdoms:

A snow leopard and a seal? a yak?
a gull? a ram or a diving falcon?
A whale?

We whispered, laughed
and even in doubt did not check a single word;
each saw what he or she saw
and named the other a name
that meant first and foremost: I am here; I am with you.
I am with you.

The next morning Liam,
still seemingly intoxicated
by the ease of our path to the top of Cha-Ri,
immediately began to hatch further, grander plans,
but I slept through that windy day
in Tsering Dorje's tent and,
stirred by a voice or a sound,
would sometimes find Nyema sitting beside me,
now working, the next time absorbed in a game with Tashi.

Get up, said Liam, leaning over me,
they say it's Phur-Ri!
You have to see this wall of ice.

It's breaking through the clouds. You have to see it!
Get up. You'll rot in here. Come on, get up!

But I was tired, probably as tired
as I was last in Shona's arms
when scarlet fever pinned me to my pillow
and I listened to the stories she told me
as I gazed out of the window at the Caha mountainsides,
yellow with gorse.

It was only the next morning
that I got my first sighting of the still-distant ice walls
of Phur-Ri, which outshone the rearing bulwark of Te-Ri
like a palace ensconced behind castle walls,
for when I finally stirred myself to leave the tent,
hours after Liam's enthusiastic entreaties,
the cloud cover had closed again
and, beyond the soaring ridges of Te-Ri
above which my brother had seen dazzling cascades of ice,
lay only banks of fog—lead-grey, chrome,
zinc-white, iron-grey, snow-white.

I didn't want to climb another peak, not now;
I didn't want to go any higher with Liam.
The heights that I had scaled for myself,
the heights at which I could now fall asleep,
night after night, and wake every morning,
were close enough to these grey, these white,
these impenetrable heavens.

That day, I think, and the following days
were the beginning of what I only much later
understood to be my long farewell from my brother.
Liam wanted to approach Phur-Ri along a kind of stairway,
rising towards it, step by step, and so the logical
next stage was Te-Ri, or Cloud Mountain,
whose snow-light would illuminate the valley
each time its glacier-clad east face
broke through the banks of fog and cloud like a ship—
a ship that appeared in a welter of breakers and surf
before vanishing again.
Liam had already spotted several climbing routes
through his binoculars and thought that Te-Ri
would barely pose us any greater problems
than Bird Mountain, its already conquered neighbour.
Yet we had no information from pilgrims and monks
about routes or caves near the summit
of Cloud Mountain.

Was it treacherous of me to want
to accompany my brother no further,
to want to go no higher
into this impenetrable realm?
Traitor.
Liam actually used one of Captain Daddy's words
(even if he half-heartedly pretended he was only joking)
when I didn't react to his proposed routes
and told him that if he didn't grant me some rest days
he would have to set out on his own.
Rest days? he asked. *Honeymoon, you mean*
and named Nyema his *sister-in-law concerned*

about her groom, declaring that he could share my fears
no more than her superstitions.

In fact, it had not been Nyema
but, rather, Tsering Dorje
who had warned us off an ascent of Te-Ri's summit
in those days leading up to the full moon.
Less because of the variable weather that
might veer dramatically in these phases of the moon
than out of respect for a revered
and dreaded creature that had been sighted
by two women gathering wood in the gloaming
and which the clan called Dhjemo.

An indomitable two-legged demon
whose realm began where humans' pastures
and hunting grounds ended,
somewhere on the border between the yaks'
world of moss and grass and the eternal snows.
A creature of superhuman size and power
that would stand for no breach of its territorial borders.

In Nyema's clan there was a survivor,
Rabten Kungar, whose upper body
was marked by broad scars running from his collarbone
to his navel—traces of blows from Dhjemo's paws
which had nearly killed him years ago
and which even now, at every sudden weather change,
burned as an unforgettable warning
and raged like fresh wounds.

Like many travellers through eastern Tibet,
long before we set out, Liam and I had come across
reports of an inhabitant of the icy regions
of the Himalaya and Transhimalaya
that the fanciful European imagination had gradually
built up into a *snow man* figure.

As the bearer of dozens of names—from Dhjemo to Yeti—
this mystery had once appeared to be the missing link
between the primeval age and the prehistory of man,
later merely a bogeyman
of childish fantasies,
a creature of dreams, superstition
or fancy.

In a monastery decorated with Tantric frescos
near Drayak they had shown us
(we were still members of a delegation
heading from Lhasa to Sichuan
that had just clambered, exhausted, ill-tempered
and dusty, from their off-road vehicle)
a frayed pelt and the severed,
mummified paw of a Dhjemo—
enshrined relics
which were said still to possess
the magical power of their former body
and could both heal and harm
and indeed kill.

Of course at the time
the other members of our delegation had

not seen much more in these rotting remains
than the scientific investigators
of these and similar finds before them—
a moth-eaten pelt and the paw
of a type of bear long regarded as extinct
which due to its upright stance had,
like every other variety of its species,
repeatedly (and in many of the world's high mountains)
been taken for a kind of human. A bear!
Only a bear, believe me! A beast!

But even hunters and herders
from Nyema's clan had never contested
such conclusions. A bear . . . Yes, of course.
What was appearance, anyway?
A hooded crow might look
like only a clever bird
and at the same time be a messenger from heaven—

just as the morning light pouring over a ridge
into the valley could indicate the sun's position
and the blink of a divine eyelid,
not to mention that to a sleepless herder a field of firn
reflecting the moonlight below the glaciers high above
looked like a silver gate in the rocks
or a patch of open sky!
and yet was *in fact*? only snow—
the previous year's snow.

In any case, *Dhjemo*, Tsering Dorje warned,
would not have been any less affected than humans

and their yak herds by the mercilessness
of the past winter, and now, as every spring,
he would be guarding his children in the caves
on Cloud Mountain and would therefore,
out of love for his clumsy offspring,
see every intruder as a foe;
for Dhjemo had not merely scored the deep wounds
into Rabten Kungar's chest all those years ago
out of rage at the healer's curiosity,
but had chased him back into the valley as a bleeding
    envoy
with one message only: *Stay away from me.*

He will kill you or he will leave you alive,
said Nyema, but up there you are in his power.

A stray bear would never attack him,
said Liam. Not him and not anybody else.

Although I must confess that the black paw
(shrivelled in the dry mountain air)
I'd seen at the monastery was still fresh in my mind—
the finger-length claws, the tattered, blood-encrusted pelt—
and so Tsering Dorje's warning
made a greater impact on me than on my brother,
it was not fear of *Dhjemo*
that held me back from an ascent of Te-Ri
but happiness.

Even my persistent tiredness struck me
as the sign of a comfort that is only,

if at all, to be found in another's arms.
The days were now summery
and the morning sun was so strong
that I went bare-chested to the cascade
(even when laughing children bounded after me).
If I could spend such days by Nyema's side,
why should I go back up into the cold,
the drifting clouds and the ice?

Traitor. It was impossible
to explain to Nyema the reason for Liam's abuse,
though I did tell her that my brother
had not intended the word seriously.
Not seriously? she asked. Did I really think
that one could use such curses—
for curses was what they were!—lightly?
If anyone was a traitor, exploiting
another's trust, love or affection
or even trying to cause him harm,
wasn't it Liam,
my brother, who was betraying *me*?

If someone climbed into the clouds,
not to make a sacrifice or pray up there
or to search for a missing person or animal
but simply to be there, simply to be *up* there,
and if that climb was attended by mortal risks
or, worse, provoked a demon's fury,

might he suborn a friend, a relative,
a brother to go with him?

The path to the top of Te-Ri led astray!
It had a high price, maybe the highest,
and yet led only to a forbidden place.

There was no need for Nyema to convince me
but to my brother the words
my beloved spoke carried no weight
or they were (according to an entry in his travel diary,
which I read only after his death, back on Horse Island)
as feathery light as the mountain that flew.

10.

At the lake. The invention of writing. Lessons.

The mild air—heat discharged
by the monsoon raging in the deep south—
had brought rain.

Its soothing murmur
and the largely veiled peaks
averted any further arguments between Liam and me
about departure (for the time being).
My brother made no further attempt
to persuade me to make a trial ascent
of Te-Ri.
This final barrier separating us from the ice walls
of the Flying Mountain
was shrouded in dense fog and had become
a symbol of its name—Cloud Mountain.

Whenever the rain ceased for a few hours
we saw the ribbons of swarming butterflies

almost daily.
Broad and seemingly endless,
they fluttered and danced up into the clouds,
then sank back down into sight
or streamed serenely along the mountain chains—
spectral rivers on their way
to a delta of life.

Did Liam compare the soaring ridges, the walls,
the mountain ranges—everything that appeared and
then vanished again in the driving clouds, framed
by the doorway of his dome tent—
with the digital fragments
and pictures on his liquid crystal screens
(which had only been turned off the day we left home)?
Did he find concordance or contradiction?

Did Liam, my brother, the cartographer,
the surveyor, detect in the glaciated pillars
and precipices he saw ploughing
through the seething clouds like a fleet of stone,
fragments of the pictures he had received
via broadband and high-speed Internet
transmission, evidence
that somewhere in eastern Tibet, in the Transhimalaya,
in Kham, an untouched, nameless blank spot
might be waiting for us, for *him* to bestride it
and perhaps to christen it?

Or had we long since crossed over
the passes of Sichuan into a world

that offered no scope for fantasies, or buried
them under sediments of actual perception
because nothing—no memory, no whim,
no expectation—could withstand
the outrageous sight of reality,
a swirling mass of clouds, crags, pastures,
walls, high peaks and star clusters?

We spoke little, barely saw each other.
Some days I only caught sight of my brother
as a tiny moving dot in my binoculars
between the larger, almost static dots of yaks
high on the scarps, or as a dwindling dot
beyond that rise, on tongues of snow,
in scree slopes, chimneys and traverses
in the shadow of gloomy overhangs.

Even the rain did not deter Liam
from tracing short yet complicated routes
on the rock walls.
Each of these was an unroped solo outing
and every one equally a first ascent,
for both herders and animals avoided
the rocky labyrinths surrounding their pastures,
in which huge cave entrances could
be distinguished, even without binoculars.

Liam was always back long before the dogs
were released from their chains and ropes for the night
(sometimes with a warning of Dhjemo's proximity),
but was taciturn and unusually sullen

as he described the characteristics of his climbing routes—
their friability, the risk of their icing up
and their generally unpredictable nature,
which fluctuated between weak purchase
and sudden glassy impassibility.
When Nyema and I wished to be alone during this time
she would leave Tashi in the clan's care for a few hours
(something she otherwise only did when gathering
branches, herbs or dung on the slopes with other women)
or tied her son to her back with a carrying cloth.

Then we would climb up to a cirque
containing a deep-green lake,
its shoreline a mixture of boulders and sand,
which cast back the light of a hanging glacier into the sky
even when rain troubled its surface.
If Nyema took Tashi with her on this trip
she would always turn down my offers to shoulder
the burden on the steepest sections at least,
and at the lake would not allow me
to take her in my arms
or so much as touch her in front of her son.
That was only possible if we were completely alone
or if all the eyes around us
were closed in deep sleep
(though then it was often *she*
who pulled *me* into her embrace).

The lake became *our* place
and was to remain our refuge until the clan
moved on to the year's highest pastures.

But the silence beside the water,
where the only sound was of small, crystal-clear waves
lapping on the sandy shore and the rocks,
accompanied by some occasional birdsong,
was no more ours alone
than the silence of the night,
for we shared it with an invisible creature—

a former resident of the red monastery
whom Nyema said had sought
complete seclusion up here by the lake,
settling in a cave where he had spent his life
and was now an old man.

Though never having sighted the hermit,
pilgrims, monks and sometimes
members of the clan left him
offerings of provisions on a rocky ledge
over which the torrent that drained the cirque
leapt into the depths in vaporous cascades.

The caveman withdrew from us and from all
the (admittedly rare) visitors to the cirque
into an inaccessible realm,
never spoke, could not be spoken to
and could, if ever, only be heard
from afar as he worked on the rock walls
and on gigantic, ice-polished blocks of stone.

Faintly, almost like the strains of a music box barrel,
the clang of his hammers, wedges and chisels

resounded across the lake's surface
as he carved the flourishes
of the Tibetan alphabet into the rocks,
sometimes in metre-high,
sometimes in palm-wide strips,
as if imitating the swirling words on prayer wheels.

He had spent his life engraving the cirque
and the entire lake shore with prayers
and Buddha's many names, but above all
(as I would only discover many months later
at Trinity College Dublin as I decoded a photograph
I had taken by the lake) with the syllables of the mantra
Om mani padme hum

in which, according to believers, the primal sound
of the universe had become word and text
and thereby effable, and every repetition of its wording
was a step—a tiny, graceful step—
towards liberation from all the mistakes, misery
and errors of the tangible world.

As if cocooned by these ribbons of script
which ran around the shore in rising and sinking spirals,
and which we could both study
but neither read nor copy,
the hours by the waterside enveloped
Nyema and me in a world of tales.

We told stories and listened to each other,
speaking less and less often about people

and matters that, while part of the childhood
and homeland of the teller, remained
necessarily alien and often mysterious to the listener;
we talked increasingly
and then exclusively of something
we had definitely and personally experienced and seen,
yet which was not unfamiliar to the other—
our journey from Lhasa to Kham.

It was as if this most recent and short passage
of our life stories made up for all those years
we had spent in an impossibly distant world
that was perhaps unimaginable to the listener,
because the settings for *these* memories were alike
(even if we often checked in a roundabout way whether
a name we each pronounced completely differently
really did refer to one and the same place,
riverbank, pass or lake).

Although Nyema, having been released
in an act of clemency after her husband's death,
had undertaken the journey
from Lhasa to Kham all alone and on foot
to rejoin her clan, and had given birth
to her son Tashi by the side of the same road
I had later *driven* along in a convoy of off-road vehicles—
as a member of a delegation furnished with documents
from Beijing, as a guest of Kham's enemies!—
we were nevertheless able to assume
that the other knew which river, which pass,
which bridge we meant;

the chain bridge at Qamdo, for example,
guarded only by prayer flags;
the bare, deforested hills near Kangding,
a razed desert, studded to the horizon
with tree stumps,
a dazzling, empty land
that had once been shaded
by Himalayan cedars and huge pines;

or the burrows of the Kandze gold prospectors
who had scoured a waterless riverbed
for their fortune and ultimately—
seconds before the shaft that was meant
to lead to a better life
closed over their heads, sometimes for ever,
amid abrupt, thundering torrents of rain—
unearthed only the realization
that for weeks, months and years
they had been digging their own graves.

We lined our route from Lhasa to Kham
with memory after memory, tale after tale,
as if by conjuring up the names
of the places we shared
and had only just left behind
each might gradually penetrate further
into the depths of those mysterious, fabulous spaces
from which the other came—
the other who was one minute a storyteller,
the next just an attentive, speechless listener.

Yet in all these stories, which were no longer
about times that lay somewhere before or behind us
but revisited only what was most familiar,
the most recent past—tales which, perhaps for that very
       reason,
bridged the seas, mountains and chasms
between our two lives—

what emerged again and again, with growing clarity,
were written characters—carved or engraved
in word or stone, painted on paper,
swirling in prayer wheels—characters.

And so by the lakeside we resurrected
the endless walls hugging the folds of long slopes
that we had seen on our way here to Kham,
to this shore—
walls built purely of inscribed stones
that presented their words to the rain and the wind
so that they might be washed into the sea
and blown into the sky.
And we remembered a ford across the Yangtze Jiang
where Nyema and I (and Liam and our convoy)
had taken a break on a bank
that was so untouched and deserted
that it seemed as if we were the first humans to stop there—
and yet, as we waded
through the smooth, strong current,
we saw that the bottom of the river
was paved across its entire width
with stones inscribed or engraved with characters.

Thousands, hundreds of thousands of stones
the size of pebbles, of a fist, sometimes of a head,
that pilgrims on their way
to the Jokhang Temple in Lhasa,
or returning from there,
had dropped into the shallow water

so that the river might carry to the sea
the prayers entrusted to the stones,
and every word might be kept moving and praying
and once more turn to vapour in the sun,
and the billowing steam would again become clouds,
from which sign after sign would fall
as rain or snow or even as hail
onto land that belonged to the gods alone.

And on a reed-choked bank along the upper reaches
of the Mekong (which, like the Yangtze,
rose exclusively from springs in Kham),
we had both—Nyema during a white-hot
summer whipped by dust storms,
I during repairs to a broken-down engine
in the convoy—seen the *printers*
who beat the water with wooden and clay tablets,
with wooden and clay stamps
carved with the negatives of letters
that were to mark and print the river itself
so that it might carry away everything
there was to say and everything
there was to read and write—
a flowing testament to the fact
that existence was in permanent flux.

I remember
a stormy afternoon
when we climbed up to the lake without Tashi
and were lying entwined on the sandy shore
onto which delicate waves, like miniature breakers,
cast up a flat piece of driftwood.

As Nyema rose from my arms
to drink some lake water from her cupped hand,
I picked up the piece of wood and used
my knife to engrave on it
the sound of her name in Roman letters,
and later, as she threw her clothes
over an uncarved rock
and swam shrieking and laughing in the icy lake,

I beat the water with this driftwood mould
as the printers along the Mekong had,
and called out to the bather
that the lake now bore her name.

For Nyema had spoken before in my arms
of how letters and writing
were a form of medicine,
a remedy for mortality,
which could not cure illness
but could certainly relieve it.
According to her, a person
who was able to read and write
could leave his time and his home like a god
if he converted thoughts, names
and his every word into writing,

marking a piece of wood, stone
or paper in the belief
that he was leaving a message that would be legible
long after he himself had disappeared
or was trapped in another form of life.

For wasn't writing, she asked, a means
for this man to speak across chasms and decades
to his loved ones as if he were among them?
So Tashi's father, she said,
could still address his wife
and his son,
even if his body lay long buried
under stones and snow at Nangpa La.

The art of writing, the art of reading,
said Nyema, was surely the greatest gift
that humans could offer one another
because this ability at last allowed them
to rise not only above seas and summits,
but above time itself
and to soar into the sky like Phur-Ri.

Although a thunderstorm that broke
that afternoon on the lakeshore was so violent
that, in our haste to take
shelter under a rocky outcrop,
I lost the piece of driftwood
on which I had carved for Nyema
the letters of her name
(as the first act of her training

in the Roman alphabet),
it was nevertheless this tablet—
which the cloudburst presumably
washed back out onto the water
where it has rocked ever since
in one of the countless stony inlets
above the green depths of the lake—
that marked the start of a period of learning for us both,
the beginning of a process of mutual instruction
during which Nyema eventually learnt
to write letters and to read letters,
while I began to parrot word after word
of her language and,

once our pronunciations
had become recognizably similar,
transposed the sounds into letters from *our* alphabet
that Nyema repeatedly practised
by running her index finger along my arm
and the back of my hand.
(Thus, little by little, during our nights
under canvas, often without a sound,
she painted my whole body with delicate,
increasingly legible capital letters.)

And when she revealed
her progress for the first time
by writing my name on a rock
with a piece of charcoal
in letters the same size
as the invisible hermit had used to carve his prayers

and we brought the sound captured
by that sooty motif back to life
and, spelling it out together in singsong voices,
read it aloud, then repeated it
several times, syllable by syllable, for practice

before falling into each other's arms
at the end of the exercise, laughing, triumphant,
as if we were the true inventors of writing.

11.

Constellations. A giant's demise.

This sensual game of learning to speak, read and write
kept Nyema and me so busy
after our first lesson by the lake
that I didn't notice how Liam was in the meantime
preparing to scale Cloud Mountain on his own
and Tsering Dorje had to tell me one morning
that my brother had disappeared.

It was the morning the clan
began to strike camp to move on
to the highest pastures of the year,
a day when both Cha-Ri, Bird Mountain,
and, beyond it, Cloud Mountain, Te-Ri,
towered dazzlingly above the stepped valley
and in the distance too one shimmering,
icy flank of Phur-Ri became visible
with such clarity that it seemed this peak
was not merely part of a mighty massif
but was also within our grasp
and reachable within a few days' march.

Even if there could only have been a difference
of about 500 metres in the altitudes
of the three colossi, their arrangement
along the gently rising valley bottom
gave the impression that they led like gigantic stairs
of rock, glaciers and ridges into the blue of the sky,
higher and higher into the void.

Liam, said Tsering Dorje,
had hit the trail before sunrise
(in that cold blue silence in which no menacing
sound of meltwater yet announced a risk of avalanches
and collapsing ice, in a quietness
into which we had so often set out together,
sometimes by the light of our headlamps;
I knew that silence well).

My brother had turned a deaf ear to all warnings
about entering Dhjemo's kingdom, said Tsering Dorje,
and had intimated that he would reach the summit
of Te-Ri by daylight and then rejoin the clan
farther up the valley, maybe tomorrow, maybe
at the last and highest camp.
There were no objections. The weather was fine.

She had noticed Liam's preparations,
said Nyema, for Liam had asked her
to suggest a deal whereby Tsering Dorje
would look after the rest of his equipment
and have it transported to the next camp
by yak in exchange

for a folding knife containing
various tools—a rarity.
She hadn't mentioned it to me
because my brother should follow his path
and we ours.

Liam! If he couldn't wait
then he would have to go it alone—
were those not the furious words with which
I had ended the argument about our departure?
But now he really had vanished
and for the first time a reproach disturbed our lessons,
an unease that lasted the whole day
and prevented me from sleeping that night,
keeping me awake for hours by Nyema's side
without our touching each other.

Why, damn it, had she told me nothing
of Liam's preparations for a solo climb?
Why didn't you notice? she asked.

The day had ended amid the jangling of bells
on the lead animals' collars
that rang far and wide with every step
our long caravan took towards the heights
and, with the same glow as that morning, it bathed
the ice fields of a west-facing rock wall
(bounding the plateau of another temporary camp)
in crimson light.

Despite its easy pace, the day's travel
had transported us into bizarre surroundings
dominated by huge stone blocks from a landslide.
Of Liam there had been no sign the whole way,
even through binoculars.

Nor did my brother return as, one by one,
the mountains fell dark in order of size,
and the ridges gradually blurred
into the edges of a black moonless sky.

When, after midnight, I could no longer bear
my sleeplessness, Nyema's sadness,
her mute proximity and the old man's breathing
and coughing in the dark tent
and crept carefully out into the cold night
so as not to enrage the dogs, broad bands
of cloud were starting to block out a sky
in whose swiftly shrinking openings
I thought, after several errors that Liam would
surely have mocked, I could make out parts
of the constellations of Virgo, Boötes and Scorpio.

Misled by the stinging cold,
I had automatically tried to assemble the stars
that kept appearing in the windows in the clouds
into the winter constellations Orion, Taurus and Canis
    Major
and had confused flickering red Antares
in Scorpio with Betelgeuse,
the alpha star in Orion—confused

two of those gigantic red suns
which were the object of Liam's astronomical interests.

When during his nights at the telescope
he had not been absorbed with observations
and measurements that my limited mathematical
and astrophysical knowledge prevented me from grasping,
he had sometimes shown me the boundaries
of the heavenly vault and the light phenomena it
         contained—
planetary fog, star clusters, globular and spiral galaxies—

and had even occasionally checked
the efficacy of his teaching by pointing
at the pinhead of a sun hundreds of light years away
with the laser aimer of a reflecting telescope
and asking me to select the correct answer
from three multiple-choice star names.

The particularity of this list of alternatives
was that it was impossible
for the bearers of all three names
to rise on the same night, because
they rode the skies in different seasons.

Given the real relations in space
(as Liam would sometimes scoff before returning
to his eyepieces or the star charts flickering
on his screens) the mistakes I made
in these tests were even more stupid
than mixing up the sun and the moon.

To think one saw a star from Orion in a summer's sky
was to his mind a sign of ignorance equivalent
to believing that the earth was a flat disc
or that the world had an edge over which
impious surveyors and helmsmen
would sail—or fall—straight into the devil's clutches.

For Liam it was a sign of incomprehensible
and unforgivable narrowmindedness for a person
to so apathetically ignore the riches of a cloudless night
that enchanted and overwhelmed the eye.

Although I was sometimes revolted by the scorn
with which my brother talked not only of dunces
whom the firmament struck as, at best, a kind
of heart-warming swarm of fireflies
but also of almost anyone
who didn't share his passions and opinions
(or even contradicted them), I still tried
to impress him with newly gleaned
astronomical knowledge, and began, like him,
to take an interest (as I had in climbing routes
up rock faces) in the celestial globe
and its brilliant phenomena,

cursing, as he did, the ship's spotlights
that marred my contemplation of the firmament,
even wishing sometimes that the bright fingers
of the lighthouses would go out, and rhapsodizing
(using similar words to his, in fact) about the

loss of the velvety-black darkness of night
over the course of civilization.

Initially it might not have been much more
than a gesture of gratitude for his hospitality
and for the security of life on Horse Island
that I showed myself so eager to be converted
not only to dry land, animal husbandry, a sedentary life
and climbing, and ultimately shared his passion for the
    night sky,
developing a special interest
in the giant red stars to which Liam devoted
so many of his nights at the telescope.

My brother could spend an entire night
following the red giant Betelgeuse
in Orion across the winter sky
until it disappeared below the western horizon—
secretly hoping, no doubt,
that one night he might witness
Armageddon.
For Betelgeuse, or *Alpha Orionis*, his favourite
(over four hundred light years from the Earth,
some seven hundred times bigger
and fourteen thousand times brighter than
our Sun)—a leviathan with a diameter so large
that the entire inner solar system could fit inside it—
was seen by contemporary astronomers as one of the next
and most likely examples of the transformation
of a fixed star into a supernova.

Swept by a hurricane-force stellar wind (arising
from its irradiating and dramatic loss of mass)
Betelgeuse was, according to Liam's nightly lectures,
in the final stages of its glowing existence
and might blaze overnight
into a supernova
in a cosmic catastrophe
during which the dying star
would swell to many times its original size
and become visible with the naked eye,
even in the daytime sky from Earth—
a hundred times brighter than the full moon.

At the end of their story, however,
even such giants would shrink back,
shrink back at great speed to a neutron star
of extreme density and ultimately (maybe)
to one of those impenetrable black holes
that could become the origin of a fresh start
eons after the extinction of all light.

But—and saying this Liam sometimes
earned not only my attention but also that of
inveterate drinkers at the counter of Eamon's Bar—
maybe Betelgeuse had already exploded
four hundred years ago
and we, Eamon's guests and also
guests on the cooling blue satellite
of a dim, medium-sized sun,

might the next night or maybe in one or two years
be the lucky ones whose lives
coincided with the instant
in which the news of Betelgeuse's demise
reached the Earth after a journey of four hundred light-years
and, like the reflected splendour of a firework display,
demonstrate what awaited our own solar system one day.

Huddled in my down jacket,
shivering occasionally in the gusty wind,
I crouched outside Tsering Dorje's tent,
listening through the yak-hair canvas
to the breathing of people sleeping
inside and Nyema's breathing too,
and scoured the night surrounding Te-Ri
for a spark, a tiny light
that might be a sign, a signal, from Liam,
maybe the glow of a fire,
a flame or a gas canister
or the dancing light of his headlamp.
But the darkness remained impenetrable
around Cloud Mountain.

Exhausted from staring into the unbroken blackness,
my eyes began to water,
and I recalled spending entire nights
awake at the telescope with Liam
at the end of which my eyes were as red as the light
from Liam's dying favourite in the area of Orion.

During one of those nights we had begun
(a game which we later occasionally continued
on night-time fishing trips) to rechristen constellations,
as we had the cloud formations
of our childhood air battles,
giving them any names that occurred to us
and which always seemed more obvious—
after a few glasses of whiskey or red wine—
than the whims of ancient Greek,
Babylonian or Arabian star baptizers
recorded in the star atlases.

We joined up suns rotating three hundred, five hundred,
a thousand light years and farther in space
to form new shapes every bit
as arbitrary as our predecessors'.
The constellation of Scorpio with its red super giant
Antares, for example, no longer looked
like the alert insect of astral charts
but like a paw swiping at the darkness—
stretching out from the red dot of Antares,
clawing at *our* night.

And the constellation of Orion with its brilliant belt of stars
morphed before our eyes
from a mythical hunter straining his bow
into a twisting, sailing moth,
into a butterfly whose edges were marked
by the four corner stars of our disarmed hunter—
Rigel, Saiph, Bellatrix and Betelgeuse—
and around its torso (which we had produced

from the former belt stars of Mintaka, Alnilam and Alnitak)
appeared the iridescent cloud of the Orion Nebula
like a halo of coloured scales
brushed from a butterfly's wings.

I never asked Liam
whether his passion for our moth's alpha star
might have something
to do with the name of the French tanker
that cropped up as regularly
in Father's stories
as the names of fallen IRA fighters.

For *Betelgeuse* was written
in man-sized red letters on the prow
of that enormous ship
that caught fire off the oil terminal
on Whiddy Island in Bantry Bay and exploded
with fifty-two dead, whose corpses
floated through the blazing waters of the bay
or were burnt beyond recognition
on the dock or trapped below decks
in a roaring rush of heat.

The disaster had led to the deployment
of the Marine Rescue, and Captain Daddy,
one of its volunteers, had singlehandedly
fished seven bodies out of the bay and heard
the screams and vain cries for help of those
in the flaming ocean
who could no longer be helped.

The many hours of this exhausting
and ultimately unsuccessful rescue attempt
had for years caused our father nightmares
from which no one—after Shona's betrayal
and her escape to the North, prepared
by Duffy the souper—woke him any more.

In his stories and dreams, Captain Daddy
saw the night sky over Bantry Bay
catch fire again and again—
the narrow bands of cloud,
the outline of the Caha Mountains,
the Atlantic, all in flames,
the water blistering and boiling in places,
and in this inferno a floating corpse, then another!
and more and more—acquaintances, even friends
with whom he had recently sat at the bar in Bantry
and drunk to his fifty-first birthday.

The sky above the bay flared as red
as hell, a cosmic abyss
into which towering flames plunged
as if striving to devour, consume and choke
the stars glinting in the depths of the sea
with clouds of soot, oil fumes
and a thundering vacuum.

When, by the campfire on a manoeuvre,
Captain Daddy invoked the war against England
and Liam and I (who both loved English football clubs
and English rock music) wished

to redirect his anecdotes,
read our comics in peace
or simply go to sleep
without his noticing our boredom,
we only had to mention the red sky
over Whiddy Island and ask, for example,
whether it had been seven or eight bodies
he had pulled from the burning waters that night,

ask him whether the flames really
had reared up so high that the updraught
had churned parts of the sea like a hurricane,
or ask him if such a flickering red sky would threaten
our garden, our sheep and our pastures

if, in its war against Irish heroes, England
were to send out bomber pilots or simply fire
the cannons of an artillery position in Ulster
across the border between the Free Republic
and the oppressed North of Ireland—
at the freedom fighters' safe houses,
machine-gun nests, foxholes and battle-lines.

Captain Daddy would invariably reach
for the hip flask in his jacket
when the fiery columns of Whiddy Island
were rekindled in his memory, and draining
the metal bottle wrapped in grey felt
with quick, short-spaced swigs,
he spoke (if he did continue speaking)
only of what had happened

and ceased at last to talk about a distant, heroic future,
mumbling perhaps that the fire on Whiddy Island
had been a glimpse of the whole of Ireland ablaze,
falling deeper and deeper into his memories,
into a snare, not once realizing
that his ensnarers were his own sons
who placed bets as to whether
in this latest version of his nightmare he would
recover seven or eight bodies from the flaming sea
and get so dirty in the process that he burnt
the red jacket emblazoned with *Marine Rescue*
(the one he wore that night) in the fire pit in our garden
as soon as he got home in the grey light of morning.

Betelgeuse. I hadn't heard the name of the red giant
in our butterfly constellation
since the days of Captain Daddy's anecdotes
and in all those years of forgetting I had believed
that the star's name was merely a reference
to a burning French tanker.

Like our father, I walked straight into the memory trap
when Liam pointed for the first time
to the blazing red sun on Horse Island
and told me of its (potentially imminent)
fiery decline.

As the grunt of a yak startled me
from the momentary nap that had overcome me
on my haunches outside Tsering Dorje's tent,
I thought I saw on the walls of Te-Ri, which were

barely distinguishable from the darkness,
at last!
that tiny, wavering light
for which I had kept watch for so long—
a sign from Liam!

I tried to jump up and hold the binoculars
to my eyes, but sank back groaning
because my legs, numb from lack of blood,
gave way beneath me.
Crouching, my head tilted far back
because the angle of the light signal was too steep
in my painful position, I realized
that what I had mistakenly taken for Liam's headlamp
or the glow of a bivouac
was in fact a star—a star
so dim that it can't have been
any of the great names of the sky

and it took me a long time and I was twice wrong
until finally I thought I recognized the area of the sky
to which it belonged. I had so far only ever seen
this constellation on Liam's computer screens,
on astronomical charts and presumably
(though I could not remember)
in the night sky in the southern hemisphere
during my years at sea—in the harbours of Santos,
Montevideo or Buenos Aires—but never
in the darkness over Ireland, because the constellation
appeared in the sky too far south of the theatres
of our childhood . . . Yes, yes!

What I saw above the mountains of Kham,
in my present sky and at the time
of mistaking a faint star in the depths of space
for a sign of life from Liam,
must be . . . was without doubt
Lupus, the constellation of the Wolf.

My cry of pain as I tried to stand up
must have startled Nyema from sleep.
I heard the slap of opening canvas,
felt a warm draught from the cosy interior
and the next instant Nyema's arms
closing around me from behind, felt her breath,
felt her voice, her whispering, so close to my ear
that I shuddered and, giving in to her gentle pressure,
let myself sink back,
sink further and further back until her hair
brushed my forehead, covered my face,
and the sky and its stars went out.

In a placating, soothing tone
that I otherwise heard only
when she wanted to calm Tashi's fear,
his anger or his fright
she whispered something to me, something
that I didn't understand in my frozen stiffness
or my sleepiness,

guiding me softly back
into the tented dark, into the shelter,
into the warmth of the darkness,

into the breath of the sleepers, and rocked me
as she always rocked her son to sleep,
in time to the breathing of one already dreaming,
and I murmured into her hair, murmured into the hand
she laid over my mouth, because I wasn't
to wake Tashi or any of the sleepers in the tent,
that I would set out at first light
in search of my lost brother.

12.

Going it alone. His brother's keeper.

I asked neither Tsering Dorje
nor any other clan member
for help or for company.

The answer to the question
of which herder would be willing
to endanger himself and his flock
and provoke Dhjemo's rage
by infringing the boundaries of its realm
was a foregone conclusion.

Neither could I divide up my gear.
I was equipped with an ice-pick and a pair of crampons;
the second pair was hopefully on Liam's feet,
producing somewhere up there, in the maze of glaciers,
that screeching noise that he had told me
was the sound of practicable ice.

Nyema urged me to postpone my search
for at least one more day.

But I could not wait
nor could I accept her offer
to accompany me at least to the foot of the glaciers.
(Although I had to admit to myself
that it would have been easier to cope with my fear
of the ice-clad walls rearing up between our camp
and the sky if she had been by my side.)

Horizontal plumes of snow above the mountain crests
and cirrostratus to the south-west did not bode well,
but Tsering Dorje said
that the bad weather was approaching
more slowly than a storm would.

With a promise (similar to the one
that Liam had given upon departing)
that I would rejoin the herd or the camp
somewhere farther up the valley
or perhaps even within a few hours,
maybe before nightfall,
and that I would bring my brother
back to the clan, I set out without a tent
but with three days' worth of provisions.

For one or, in the worst scenario, two nights
(which I hoped that my search
would not require) I would have to make do
with a snow hole, with my sleeping bag
and a bivvy sack pulled over it.
It was bad enough that the weight of this gear
(reduced to the minimum for survival)

seemed heavier than any pack
I had ever previously carried into high mountains,
especially as from the short rope
(and a single titanium ice screw
I took with me for an emergency)
hung the excruciating burden of solitude.

I set off at the same time as the clan
and only parted from their train when we
passed a scree slope that tumbled out of the clouds
which Liam had crossed on his reconnaissance trips
as he climbed towards the walls of Te-Ri.
The remainder of my gear swayed
on up the path on a yak's back
alongside the load he had left behind,
as I stepped out of Nyema's embrace
beside a block of stone the size of a house
that a landslide had prised from the rock face.
She did not breathe a word as I left.

Although (as I hoped, and as I twice
whispered with no great conviction into her ear)
this farewell might be only for a matter of hours,
I felt that Tashi was crying for us both
when he burst into tears because Nyema
wouldn't let him help her build the knee-high cairn
she erected at the forking of our paths.

I heard his sobs for some time in the still air
and when, having dwindled to a distant, faint noise,
they suddenly died away, as if Nyema had put

a mollifying hand over her son's mouth,
the herd, the clan,
every sign of human presence
seemed to disappear for ever.

The river of boulders—the flotsam
of a glacier that had retreated farther into the mountains—
poured over the threshold of a side valley
and hid the clan's progress from sight,
all its voices, all its sounds, inaudible,
and led me into such unexpected desolation
that it seemed as if the world of men
had collapsed behind me and fallen back
into the silence of an empty, bottomless pit.
Like a fugitive cast out of his sanctuary
into the wilderness and outlawry,
all of a sudden I was alone.

And then this river of stones
and polished rocks seemed to reverse its flow,
as if coming to a watershed or
in a mysterious changing of the tide,
and began to draw me deeper into the mountains.

As if scized by a current, I floated away,
losing weight—even my rucksack, my breathing,
everything became lighter with each step (whereas
the scree slope had merely flattened out),
yet stone after stone still stretched out to the clouds,
an endless stream of boulders.

From the camp, between the tents
and even through binoculars it had appeared
that the scree ended just beyond the valley threshold,
beating against the rock faces there
like breakers, a petrified sea
against the cliffs of Cloud Mountain.
But now, after over one and a half hours of walking,
the river flowed on sluggishly and level to the horizon,
as if Te-Ri were floating away
and dragging behind it in its flight
a trail of boulders, glittering here and there with crystals,
like a comet its fiery train.
My objective was receding before me.

What a relief when the blustery wind
intermittently tore open the blanket of clouds
and the ridges of Te-Ri,
once even its summit,
appeared in restless blue windows—
proof that I was on the right path.

I had only to follow the river of scree until it
vanished under the fallen ice of a glacier's snout
and, up on the western edge of the glacier,
would meet an obviously practicable ridge
whose virtually unbroken line ran
directly to the summit region. My route!

This is the path that Liam must have taken too,
for the terrain left almost no alternative.
Yet however slowly

I let my binocular-assisted gaze roam,
I discovered no tracks to confirm
that I was not the first person to pass this point.

When I lowered the binoculars, I called to Liam,
over and over again, but the sole response
was my own voice echoing from the crevices;
my voice—with which I had yelled at the sea
and its breaking waves, over the loud drone
on the machine decks and against the wind
on the cliffs of Horse Island—came back
feebly, plaintively, almost inaudible amid the gusts
and those gigantic mountainsides;
no more than the keening of a defenceless prey,
just loud enough to attract, if not
my brother's attention, then at least
that of a hunter hidden in a cleft
or the greed, anger and hunger of a demon
that tolerated no visitors to his realm.

Like a swimmer caught in an eddy,
I felt that the tide
that had carried me this far
was now starting to draw back, ebb away
whence I came, back to humans,
into the depths, and it took me a while
to assert myself against a force
that compelled me for a few breaths
to turn my back on the path
and take a few steps downhill.
But then the force abated

and I climbed farther, though
I no longer called to my brother.

Above me yawned the portals of those caves
to which the clan children had pointed,
giggling *Dhjemo! Dhjemo!* and erupting
into snorts of laughter each time,
as they had expected, I raised my binoculars
to my eyes and pointed them
at one of the far-flung cave entrances
which from down in the camp looked no bigger
than bullet holes in a peeling wall.

Yet now I passed so close to one of those maws
(it was the size of a church portal)
that I felt the icy breath from its depths
on my forehead and saw left-over snow shimmering
deep in its craw, as if its jaws had devoured
a snow crest or an avalanche and choked on it.
I felt hairs, like some residual fur,
stand up on the back of my neck.

If you want to go up, step forward.
If you've shit your pants, step back!
My ears rang with one of the stupid sayings
with which Captain Daddy
had sometimes tried to buck me up
(as the weaker of his two recruits)
when, tired, sullen or apprehensive
at the narrowness of a grassy strip
or the height of a ledge,

I had paused to catch my breath
during a climbing manoeuvre or sought
an easier route or a way around the obstacle.

Liam, who knew no such fears or denied them,
would sometimes even parody this nonsense
(though this was rarely directed at me
and far more often at the Captain,
when the latter's portliness prevented him
from keeping up with my brother
when Liam occasionally led the way).
Not only had Captain Daddy tolerated Liam's mockery,
he was obviously proud
of his first-born's supremacy.

If you've shit your pants, step back! Was that
my own voice I heard? Was I talking to myself?
Did I raise my voice like someone
who starts to hum, speak or
sing to ward off the dark?
Scaredyblubbing was what our father
called seeking consolation in one's own voice.
Once the maw lay far behind me
I pretended I had to prove to an observer
or a hidden witness of my weakness
that I had not talked to myself from fear
but from fun and exuberance
and continued my mutterings,
counted my steps under my breath,
praised the bold outline of a rock,
comforted a shrivelling lichen

but I soon fell silent once more.
The path grew steeper and harder,
and my breathing was now too short for speech.

The farther I climbed,
the safer I felt.
No bear or Dhjemo was likely
to chase after its prey
along a steep, crumbling ridge like this.
Whatever might lurk below,
predator or demon,
I could escape by climbing
into the heights, into the clouds.

Being the only person, being alone
on a rock face that led up and up,
gradually shedding all life,
into a tilted, upended world of stone
that did not end when it reached the sky
but pierced the blanket of cloud
and petered out only somewhere invisibly high,
perhaps unreachably high,
had occasionally triggered something in me
back in the mountains of Ireland for which,
even then, I knew no other word but terror.

It was not the silence of the heights,
which seemed almost to *ring* in my ears
like a blast from inside me, nor the loss
of all that was familiar in the valley and the deep,
but first and foremost this shifting,

rising and sinking hem of the sky
that simultaneously bound a rock face to,
and separated it from, the cloud layer—
this flying frontier
between an intelligible here
and a rain- and nimbus-shrouded
there.

This terror—a fear
fundamentally inspired, then as now, by death—
both deterred me and attracted me,
for I knew
that I only had to climb on, climb higher,
continue my route into the unknown
and cross this border, gasping,
screaming, singing!
if I wanted to discover within the clouds,
in the driving fog, rain or snow,
the calmness
that might even turn to enthusiasm
if my decision to carry on and on
through a dense bank of fog
brought me back out into a sunny, or at least clear,
wide and white endlessness—
into the naked heights.
Yet sometimes this terror gripped me
even on my way down, back into the valley,
into the deep, when the horizon had
once more to be overcome, the frontier
that made everything behind, above and below it
uncertain and invisible,

as if what awaited me beneath the clouds
and at the end of my journey back to humankind
was no longer familiar—a pasture,
a campsite in the valley—but only emptiness
and impenetrable desolation,
a lifeless land where one needed
a shovel to continue,
into which one had to dig a shaft, a tunnel
or a pit if one did not wish to stop
and accept that one had *arrived*.

The northern flank of Te-Ri
resembled a giant paw
with glacier ice between its splayed rocky claws,
and it was late afternoon
by the time my path reached
the ledge, traversed by two chimneys,
that had looked passable through the binoculars
but whose ice-encased overhang now proved
unavoidable and unclimbable—

an insurmountable obstacle, at least for me.
(Even Liam would not have risked passages
of this difficulty without being roped to a companion.)
In any case, there were no tracks
on a snow-covered traverse
that represented the only approach to the chimneys.
Damn it, Liam! Liam, my brother and better,
might in an emergency
have tackled even this barrier,
but had obviously opted for a better route

from the outset—over the claw-like ridge
on the opposite side of the glacier's snout.

Only now, from my present vantage point,
did I see that there were
no comparable threats over on that side.
Liam, my better, had not been led astray
by the initial enticements of the terrain,
probably spotting an easier route
from the valley and finding
that increasing elevation confirmed his judgement.

If I wanted to continue, if I wanted to find him
I'd have to seek a different route, somewhere over there,
somewhere in his footsteps,
but before that I would have to surrender
all my hard-won altitude and climb back
down to the maws of the caves
and somewhere down below, damn it,
where my claw came to an end,
switch to the other ridge or . . .

or risk the direct descent to the glacier
and cross the crevasse-riven ice
to that ridge I was already calling Liam's Staircase,
in the firm belief that I was wrong
and that he had chosen the better path.
But however much time a direct descent
onto the ice might spare me,
what if I happened upon a new,
as yet invisible obstacle—

an icy ramp or an overhang
too high to abseil down?
Liam! I yelled. *Liam*! As if his name
yelled into the up-rushing scraps of mist
might turn into a kedge, a chockstone
lodged in a cleft in this insurmountable ledge
that might bear a rope and allow me to clamber up.
Liam! No path would take me any higher.
I had to go back, I had to go down
and I opted for the direct descent.

The glacier lay beneath me, blue and alluringly
close, already plunged into deep shadow.
Bivvy lottery, Liam would have said—
if I came upon another barrier
I risked spending a night on the rockface.

Well done! *Great*! *Fantastic achievement*!
I repeated Captain Daddy's sarcastic comments
which Liam would still sometimes use
when a route or manoeuvre went wrong,
and I resumed my soliloquy,
talking, indeed screaming to myself,
not out of fear this time but out of disgust
and anger at myself and my brother.

If that fool had to set off without a word,
then why did he not at least leave,
somewhere along the way, a clue, a cairn . . .
running away, forcing me into this search,
luring me out of the camp into this trap,

and I, damn it, was stupid enough
to scramble around on these rocks, on this shit mountain!
Prick! Arsehole! Stupid git! *Liam*!

I would have loved to pull him
out of this labyrinth by the hair,
I would have liked to hit him, slap him,
wipe that arrogant grin off his puss
with a handful of ice splinters!

It was strange how safely I found my way
down onto the glacier, although
a descent across steep, unknown terrain
was always an escape route, and Liam had
specifically warned me: *Only in an emergency*!
For small steps and holds
that lay directly before your eyes when climbing up
were hidden under your feet when climbing down,
and the rock didn't always allow you
to glance back over your shoulder or grope
for a hold between your spraddled legs.

And yet I stood sooner, far sooner
than I had expected, on the ice.
The snout might have been 300 metres across,
maybe 350—
a short distance, in any case, if the ice was compact,
an endless distance
if the firn concealed crevasses.

On the far side—this much I thought
I could be sure of—a steep ramp
led back up to the next ridge, to my bridge
into Te-Ri's summit region.
Up there I would . . . up there I must
find a sign of Liam at the very least.

But could I manage the trail up there
and back again in daylight?
Captain Daddy had taught us
to quote altitudes and paths
not only in feet and miles, but more importantly
in metres and kilometres.
Yes sir! Vital distances,
ranges, heights and even gaps in hand-to-hand combat
were to be measured using the decimal system,
for miles and feet were English units,
and an Irishman should use a different gauge
for every path, every rise
and even for his distance from death.
Three hundred and fifty metres across the glacier . . .

I had already seen ice of this and greater thickness
from the railing in Antarctic waters,
but I'd only ever *set foot* on it in Western Europe, in the Alps,
and then only when roped to my brother.

But it was already afternoon, behind me lay a ridge
that exceeded my climbing abilities,
and before me a mere ice field
and beyond it a practicable ramp

and maybe the end of my isolation,
for maybe I would find . . .
maybe I would see Liam somewhere over there.
I had to make it across the river of ice.
But what did I know of the pitfalls of a glacier
that was like an ancient suit of icy armour,
smashed by the paw of Cloud Mountain,
streaming down into a chasm from which
snatches of fog were starting to ascend.
The high valleys below me, the clan's trails
and pastures and herds
lay as if forever obscured
below the smoky sky at my feet.

As I crouched and attached the crampons
to my boots by the glacial river's steep bank,
scanning as I did so the clouds at my feet
in vain for an opening
through which some sign of the human world
might wink up at me,
a cirrus-wreathed sun warmed my back
as if in consolation.

But when I stepped onto the ice, it slung long, spearing
shadows from the crown of a western ridge at me,
took cover behind the battlements of the crest
after this assault, leaving only its feathery red adornments
on the bulwarks as a mocking sign
that my new and sole companion on the path
across the river would be the chill of evening.

I had traversed over half the glacier,
the twelve-pronged steel claws
on each of my cup boots affording me
a secure, screeching grip,
even on passages of sheer turquoise ice
that glinted between broad firn-covered strips,
when I discovered the first—
and then three, four, five! more butterflies
lying in what looked like glass coffins.

Apollo butterflies. They lay with outspread wings
in cup-shaped dips
under a wafer-thin layer of transparent ice.

They must already have been dead
when, from a freezing sky hostile to all life,
they had snowed down onto the glacier.
Their wing scales alone had continued
to soak up warmth and light, melting
around their fallen bodies the hollows
in which they now lay as if under glass.

The silence over these shimmering graves revealed
how the cold of the advancing afternoon
was once more solidifying the streams
of water that had flowed during the day.

For a long time, for too long, I knelt
in that glass cemetery, attempting
with a digital camera the size of a lighter
(a gift from Liam) to capture memories

of my path across the ice,
for when I made to stand up again
from that crouching observer's position
a lancing pain in my back forced me
to my knees and I continued on my way
as tentatively as an invalid
(although this particular one recovered
step by step from his pains).

The life-saving bank on the other side
of the glacier river was so close now
that I could make out colourful patches
of lichen on snowless rocks

when I saw something claw-like
leap up out of the blue shadow
at me—a jet-black,
flash silently darting across the ice—
and the firn bed I was crossing
gave way beneath me.

The suddenly yawning crevasse,
spanned by drifting snow and firn,
had opened on the fringes of my vision
and from there had raced towards me,
devouring its white camouflage,
snatching at my clawed feet
and reducing my path to a dark void
into which I now fell.

I recall
that the abrupt lightness of my body
wrenched no scream from me, merely a groan,
a gasp, which the ice smothered
as it took me in.

I did not fall the full depth of the chasm,
but found myself lying on a surface
that crushed the breath from me.
My mouth, I recall, was gaping so wide
that my jawbones hurt,
but there was no breath,
no sound, no scream.
Had I really fallen
or had something dark and overpowering
struck out at me
from the pitch-black abyss
and hurled me with one terrible blow
against a hard surface, against a rock
or an ice wall?

Only some minutes after my fall did I begin to realize
that I had landed on a narrow ledge
covered with trickling firn—
a twilit ice balcony below which all light
was sucked into a bottomless pit.
The glacier that was to be my bridge
to the summit ridge of Cloud Mountain
had swallowed me up without a sound.

The saving ledge separating me from the chasm

measured barely a metre at its widest point
and ran in a gently rising line some six
or seven metres below the jagged edge of the crevasse,
above which I now saw a fleet
of graceful cirrus clouds sailing past
against the cold, deep blue of the high mountain sky beyond.

But those cloud-ships and that blue,
everything that lay beyond the fractured edge
and shone down on me below,
was *above*, unreachably high above.

Carefully—careful!—so as not to unsettle
my last support, my ice bed,
and, together with this bed, fall
into the menacing night beneath me,
I stood up.

My back hurt, my right knee
and my right shoulder hurt,
a warm trickle ran from my forehead
along my nose, over mouth and chin
and dripped onto my chest
with a ticking that divided
the deep silence into intervals.
But I could move my legs and arms—
bruises, grazes,
but no breaks.

My rucksack too
had not been torn from my body
and the ice axe still hung
by its leash from my wrist.
The pick must have stabbed
my forehead as I fell, but the cut was not deep
and I was able to staunch the blood
by applying persistent pressure
with a splinter of ice.

Even my crampons' razor-sharp claws
had only slashed out in play,
shredding one trouser leg
and cutting—as if to remind me that they could
easily sever tendons, muscles and veins—
a red exclamation mark in my thigh,
a weeping line and, below it,
a gaping dot in my kneecap,
a hole through which even in the twilight
I saw a glimpse of gleaming, unscathed skin.
Lucky escape,
I heard Liam say,
the Liam of one August afternoon
on the cliffs of Horse Island when
a startled gull dislodged a stone
that whizzed down
with a strange hum and shattered
the nail bed and top phalanx of his ring finger.
Lucky escape.
Liam?

Liam! I yelled up at the unattainable edge
of my chasm and at my sliver of sky
in which cloud-ships were beginning
to compact, a white fleet
wedged up against a darker one
as if the tropospheric wind were cajoling them
into battle formation.
Liam! I'm here,
I'm down here, Liam. Here!

But *lucky* was just a word,
a voice in my roaring skull,
even my brother's breath, sucked
through teeth clenched in pain—
a mere memory. No Liam. No brother.

Completely alone and in a silence
in which even the ticking blood clock on my brow
had stopped, I cowered
in my depths and froze,
as if for ever separated from my brother
and from everything *above*.

13.

In the deep. The comfort of one's own strength.

The sky, I recall,
the cloud-ships and their battle ranks,
went dark first, followed by
the crevasse's gleaming edges
and lastly its glimmering walls,

as if my fateful day lived on in the reflection
in my dungeon's mirror walls
until finally, after some hours, everything,
high and low, the chasm as well as
the narrow wedge of remaining firmament,
faded into an uncaring, echoing darkness.
I hesitated for a long time
before pulling my headlamp
from the top pocket of my rucksack
as carefully as if it were woven from the finest glass
and would smash irrevocably into shards

and vanish for ever into the pit
should it slip through my clammy fingers;

I hesitated also because the battery-powered
diode light would run out
more quickly in this black cold
than in the warmth of a tent
and every second of light was precious;

I hesitated above all, though,
because using the light of this lamp
would be an admission
that night had truly come.

I had naturally tried, in panic
and to the point of exhaustion, like a trapped animal,
to free myself before nightfall
and had crawled to and fro on my ice balcony,
slowly, infinitely slowly,
constantly fearing that my movements
might deepen a fault line hidden
under ice crystals and consign me
and my last support to the abyss.

I had naturally stood up, with the caution
that now governed my every movement,
felt the wall and also tried
to stamp the front prongs of my crampons
into this crumbly glass;
maybe I could find a point along my fall line where,
step by step, I might climb back into the world above.

Yet not only was the wall brittle,
spitting a shower of ice splinters
onto my claws at every blow from my pick,
it was also slanted, braced
against me in an overhang, threatening
to cast me out
as I tried to cling to it with claws and pick,
to push me over backwards
and brush me off like an irritating burr.

The titanium ice screw
I tried to twist into this overhanging, brittle wall
so as to fasten my short rope to it
and approach, arm's length by arm's length,
the edge of the cleft and safety,
broke free of the ice at the first stress test,
escaped my damp fingers
and fell, tinkling, into the night below.

I don't remember how long I listened
to the receding jingle
of my one remaining hope,
an eternity, a dreadful tolling of seconds,
each of which did not measure time
but only the bottomless depths.

Crawling on my knees
and on my bare palms,
which I left unprotected
to sense even the smallest crack in the ice,
I measured the length and breadth of my ice balcony

and found that although on one side
it curved gently upwards,
in the process it became narrower
and narrower until it was merely a sill
which finally slid into the smooth,
mirror-like ice face and disappeared.

In the despairing breaks between exploring
and measuring my dungeon
and in the diminishing light, I called
and roared Liam's name over and over,
always trying to shout in the direction
that produced the greatest echo and turned
my crevasse into a funnel or a megaphone,
a mouthpiece of ice to channel a single message
up and out: Help!
I'm here, Liam, down here!

Again and again I used this ice mouthpiece
to adjure my brother's presence
and kept on trying, after periods
of breathlessness, exhaustion and silence,
until my shouts became hoarser and fainter
in the advancing twilight and finally died out . . .

How much of this wailing
made it up
and over the glacier ice
to the ridges of Cloud Mountain?
Had I not myself experienced before my fall
how the rising wind, with gusts

lashing out from every direction,
crammed every syllable of a cry back down your throat,
choking every call for help, every name?

But down here in this silence
there was not the slightest breeze,
down here I heard the loud,
reassuring ring of my own voice,
and I yelled, breathed and listened.

It was odd how long it took
for me to realize that I was calling
the wrong name—Liam. Liam was unattainable.
Liam was deaf to my cries,
was perhaps caught in his own trap
or, after a safe and entertaining solo ascent,
well on his triumphant way down
from the peak of the accursed mountain
that had devoured me,
and was now trotting along a secure path
back to the clan's summer pastures;
no, no help would come from my brother.
Liam himself had never needed help,
at best a little admiration
for feats he could achieve without me.

Ah, why had I bellowed myself hoarse,
as if dazed by the wrong name!
Whereas there was no need to shout
nor even to raise my voice
if I called to mind the only name

that still mattered down here—Nyema.

Nyema would not give up:
she would wait for me and miss me,
maybe dream of me and in her sleep see me
crouching at the bottom of an ice well
and set out.

Tsering Dorje would accompany her
or else that herder whose name
I could only pronounce with difficulty
(a long name I had forgotten
although a laughing Nyema had repeated it to me);
that herder would surely accompany her,
one of the clan's strongest men, strong enough
to lift someone like me out of the depths
and indeed to carry someone like me.
Nyema, my girl,
would climb down from the high summer pastures
to where she had built a cairn at the fork
in our paths and, setting out from this marker,
would seek and find my tracks
in the scree, my footsteps in the snow
and in the sand amid the debris
ground up by the glacier.

No imprint on the soft ground,
no scratch or nick in the rock
would escape her attention;
she would read every unwitting sign
from me like writing

and, following the clues
testifying that I had passed here,
climbed here, fallen here,
would follow them to the edge of my abyss

and peering over the edge into the twilight
and the darkness
she would need no calls for help
to find me
but instead hear my breathing in the depths
if I happened to fall asleep from fatigue,
waiting and trusting
in my salvation, in my beloved.

Tracks?
Nyema would follow my tracks?
Over the ridge? Across the cracked ice?
To the edge of my crevasse? In her yak-skin boots?
She would follow me without the claws and prongs
of crampons and pick
over rocks and glacier ice
to the place where a snow bridge had collapsed?
Some time during the night, as I tilted my head
up towards the invisible black edge
of my well, a star twinkled in my torch beam,
then another!
A star cluster, the Milky Way,
spanning my chasm,
began to trickle
down onto me below—

snow.
It was only snow.

In the world above, on a cloudy
lightless night, it had begun to snow;
it was only flakes twirling
and tumbling down into the open
silent mouth of my crevasse,
a flurry that grew thicker and thicker,
quietening in the still air of my pit
and thickening to a uniform veil
that brushed the smooth icy wall
with a gentle, melodic tinkle,

sending me samples
of the flawless crystalline covering
that was now erasing every one of my tracks above
and which would hide, even in broad daylight,
the clear outlines of steps carved,
as if by a knife, in the fine sandy debris,
as if no man had ever gone
where I had gone—
where I still was, hoping for help.

When the dark and the falling snow
had tormented me to the point where I began
to realize that I was lost down here
and that this place would be my last
if I did not make it out by myself,
that no bridges would be built for me,
no steps cut into the ice

and no hands stretched down to me, ever!
I was seized with panic and despair and I wept

as I had that afternoon on the cliffs of Horse Island
when I had sought to reach
the edge of our pastures, the sky's limit,
in the angry teeth of a summer storm,
when the gusts threatened to sweep me from the precipice
and salvoes of hail and stones rained down on me,
cutting off all routes back to the raging sea
and leaving me no other path to safety
than to climb.

When my sobbing let me breathe again,
I swaddled myself in my sleeping bag
and, crouching in the darkness
with my arms wrapped around my knees,
began to speak to Nyema, whispering pet names
with my head pressed against my knees,
as if I were hugging my girl
and not my blood-encrusted leg.

Nyema was so close that I took my warm breath
rebounding from the taut synthetic material
of the bivouac shell for the warmth
of *her* breath and kept talking
to her until it was her breath alone
that warmed my face and I could say, *Be patient,*
I know, could say *You're waiting, my girl,*
have no fear, be patient, wait for me,
wait for me . . .

and as I raised my head
after this long communion with my beloved
because the first grey light of dawn
was filtering down from the world above to me
and into my embrace,
I spotted a path—the only one
that had remained hidden from my eyes
in the shock after my fall
in my despair, in the twilight and then
in the darkness of night:

my bivouac, my ice gallery
did indeed become narrower and narrower
as it curved gently upwards
and disappeared into the reflecting wall

but it re-emerged at a distance that the beam
of my headlamp had been unable to span
in the black of night—it re-appeared!
There it grew like an icy wave out of the glassy smoothness,
widening into a sill and, completing the arc,
eventually once more became a gallery
that met the horizon
at the jagged edge of my crevasse!

In the void
left by the arc's missing middle section
shimmered a strip of wall that seemed free
of cracks, free of watery shadows and brittleness,
glinting lead-grey and silver in the early light.

Solid ice! a band of glass—reliable support
for the front prongs of my crampons.

If I stabbed my clawed feet like beaks
into this band, I could move sideways
across the vertical wall
and so, step by step, bridge
the broken arc of this gallery.
The ice axe, punched into the glassy surface
an arm's length above my head,
would act as an anchor
that steadied my weight
and could bear me even
if my foothold collapsed.

If the overhanging, crumbling wall of my crevasse
could not be negotiated vertically,
then a way out lay open across this reflective strip
—across a saving, solid band of ice
on the far side of a bridge rising up
out of the deep . . .

I only had to follow the lessons
Liam had given me on the cliffs of Horse Island
and on glaciers in the Western Alps,
something he had called *vertical walking,*
walking on ice.

I remembered well his rebukes
when, after initial interest, I attempted to mask
with facetious questions the fear
that this vertical motion inspired in me.

Why, I asked my brother during those days,
why follow the (ever-unattainable) example
of a lizard, a gecko, an ant, a fly or
any non-flying beetle?

Even a cockroach had no trouble
mastering vertical or overhanging larder walls
and, turning its elytra
with inherent nonchalance to the ground,
could run diagonally across the larder ceiling
without once pausing
to look for the next hold or resting place.

Why copy something
any dung beetle could do so much more skilfully
than even a world-champion rock climber?

Scaredyblubbing, Liam had answered,
we're bipeds, and when we climb
we are simply continuing on a path
that would be barred to us if we did not use
our hands, but it is, nevertheless, a footpath—
a variation on walking.

You lift up your weight,
you walk vertically, you simply walk on
into a perpendicular landscape
that separates you from a higher plain,
a terrace, a saddle, a more level ridge.
But even if a wall
or an overhang forces you to dangle

from your fingertips above the void
and swing to the next grip,
ultimately it is always
your heels, toes and feet
that carry you the decisive step up
to a ledge that is simply a section of a longer route,
of a path that does not necessarily
lead to a peak.

The true goal always lies beyond
all vertical barriers, either in your head
or somewhere far out in the plain,
a sand or asphalt desert
in which you can at last turn around
and recognize that although it is necessary
to climb now and then, it is never more
than a transitional part of one's progress.
The walker overcomes vertical obstacles
by climbing whereas he clears others
by swimming or jumping,
yet he always remains a walking biped.

When Liam spoke this insistently to me,
teaching me his lessons, dispelling my fears
and waking an explorer's curiosity and ambition,
I often had the feeling
that he was really talking about times
when climbing had been an opportunity
for him to put an insuperable distance
between himself and our father's world,
for during some of our manoeuvres in the Cahas

Liam had climbed up to heights
where neither Captain Daddy
nor I could follow him,
withdrawing into unattainable places
where no whining requests
or orders could reach him, all of them
carried off unheard on the wind.

But as I strapped my rucksack
as tightly as possible to my body
on the morning of my escape,
then from the last spur of my ice gallery
took my first step onto the perpendicular,
digging in both my ice-axe and my crampons,
all of those lessons were forgotten, Liam's voice
faded for good and all I heard was Nyema:
I'm waiting for you. I'm waiting for you.

As I paused for breath and looked down
past my claws into the bottomless pit,
I heard her confident voice
protecting me from the emptiness
and darkness below my heels, accompanying
my every step through a tilted world.

Once I even thought I saw *her* eyes
and her mouth in that fleeting shadow
that stayed as close to me throughout
my vertical traverse as her face—
her face—when we embraced,
when we kissed, so close

that I seemed to cling not to the ice face
but to her—and the cold sting startled me
as I instinctively leant my forehead on her forehead.

I leant against my own reflection,
I kissed my own reflection,
which appeared as a blur in the clear ice,
then faded again on milkier surfaces
and yet kept returning

until I reached the far side of the gallery,
and crouching there on all fours
so as not to overburden a single inch
of my escape route, I scrambled back into daylight
and, with a pounding heart,
across the glacier to the first rocks on the summit ridge.

There—safe at last!—
after taking a first step on firm ground
I was overcome by a curious rage.

Liam! I did what my brother would have done,
taking this first step not *down* the ridge,
not back to Nyema, not into the valley,
but climbing, as if in a trance,
like a puppet on a string,
farther *upwards*!

It was not enough that I had fallen while searching
for Liam and that only Nyema's voice had been capable
of calling and accompanying me back into the world
        above . . .

Barely out, I was once more crawling after *him*,
my brother, who had abandoned me,
beguiled me into following him into a world of ice
that had never been mine.
Liam! Again I roared his name,
this time in rage. Then
I set my back to the summit of Te-Ri
and turned to descend.

While my brother's heights
remained untrodden (but maybe this time
it was *I*—I—who had got higher than him)
and I climbed towards the valley along a ridge
that although less steep, was just as trackless
and bare of his presence as the one I saw,
still threatening, on the other side
of the glacier, I ceased to imagine
that Liam might still be imprisoned somewhere up there,
hoping I would persevere until I rescued him,
close to the peak or in an ice trap similar to the one
I had escaped from without his aid.

For had Liam not done without me
from the very beginning, and even
when he slipped out of the camp
unnoticed for his solo ascent?
Without me and any assistance?

Had he not, on leaving the camp,
bade farewell to me and all other companions
and signalled that wherever he might go

I was, as always, incapable of following him?
Shown that in the end
I was merely a hindrance, a burden?
My brother's wish to reach the summit on his own
meant first and foremost:
Leave me alone.

As if the cold of the hole continued to pursue me,
as the winter's air does a home-comer
who steps into a house out of a snow flurry
on a clear, frosty night,
a chill breath followed me on my way
down to the valley bottom where I hoped
to rejoin the clan and Nyema.

The change in weather that Tsering Dorje
had predicted at full moon
had taken hold of the summer pastures.

The temperature had dropped.
The wind blew intermittently from all sides
and grew constantly stronger.

Even the very foreground of my return trip
occasionally disappeared in lashing snow showers
and even when the gusts and precipitation briefly abated,
they revealed only slopes falling abruptly into the valley
whose vegetation so longed for and prized in the clan's tents
—interspersed with herbs and stemless flowers—
vanished again into the snowy whiteness.
Woe betide anyone left alone and exposed
in the peaks behind me.

Instinctively, without the least intention,
yes, without even having caught my breath,
I began, after hours of descending,
during which I had followed only Nyema's voice,
to whoop,
began to whoop with excitement
as, still far below, the black dots
of grazing yaks appeared,
through a hail of icy grains—
tiny, far-flung,
charcoal stars in a dazzling white sky.

My whooping sounded like a croaky imitation
of that alpine cheering and yodelling
that carries exuberant emotions
across gorges, bouncing off rock faces
into the populous lowlands,
which is ultimately only playful variations
on a single triumphant statement:
I'm still alive, I'm here,
here I am, here!
The black dots of the herd were so far away
(and even farther and even deeper in the fog
lay the clan's tents) that I could only have told
through binoculars if my whooping
stirred the animals on the snowy slopes
from their reverent grazing and chewing
and if they raised their skulls for a moment—
or whether my jubilation and my faint voice
died unheard on the blustery wind,
just as all my cries for help had died in my ice hole,
all my cries to Liam.

Only now, within sight of salvation,
did I feel my exhaustion;
I was suddenly numb with tiredness,
far too tired to stop,
open my rucksack and lift
the binoculars to my eyes, far too tired,
and I stumbled automatically on, downhill, onwards!
downhill to where I might at last
sink down, rest and sleep
but above all drink, drink,
as for hours now handfuls of snow
had been unable to slake
the thirst burning inside me.

And this time too,
though completely unlike the day
Liam and I returned together from Bird Mountain,
it was Nyema who came towards me, Nyema—

a figure, the ribbons and folds of a yak-skin coat
fluttering around it, detached itself from a snow shower
and climbed uphill, quietly, unswervingly
amid the turmoil, but as she drew closer
did not stretch out her arms as I did,
did not wave as I did, did not laugh
but stayed still, stayed very straight,
as if all her attention were on the bowl
she carried before her,
a steaming bowl of yak-butter tea
which she at last held out to me without releasing it
because my frozen fingers could not

grip anything small and certainly no receptacle—
my fingers, battered from clawing and gripping
and clutching, which I could now warm
on the unscathed hands
moulded to the curve of the dish.

And I drank, drank
and felt Nyema's warmth passing into me,
permeating me, drank until the thirst subsided
and the bowl was suddenly gone,
fallen into the snow or emptied, rolled away,
and no longer having a bowl to hold
we held on to each other

and my head rested at last on her shoulder
and, embraced and rocked by my beloved,
almost asleep, I opened my eyes again
after a blind kiss and saw some of the clan's tents
on the banks of a pool—snow-dusted,
inhabited, heavenly shelters,

some adorned with prayer flags
as if to celebrate survival in this icy wilderness,
yet all bedecked with even more beautiful,
fluttering flags—
signs of life,
smoke!
And in the midst of those homesteads
of warmth and light that seemed so strangely noble to me,
there, crouching between those magnificent pavilions
—small, ridiculously small, kennel-like—a dome

fastened to the ground with guy-lines
that were all that kept it from flying away.

The snow found no purchase
on its dully gleaming surface
and from its guy-lines fluttered something
that was unrecognizable from this distance.
Pennants? A balaclava?
Socks plaited together to dry in the wind?
Down there, as if guarded and protected
by the nomads' dwellings,
stood my brother's tent.

14.

On high. Heavenly apparitions.

Liam had seen Te-Ri's paws very differently from me
and *read* the ice fields, walls, ridges and bands of rock
very differently too, charting his route
on a flank far from where I had gone astray,
yet still he had not reached
the summit of Cloud Mountain.

He too had been forced by the unpredictable length of the
    hike
to bivouac for a night and finally to turn back
due to the impending bad weather. The same evening
I had set out to look for him
he had (as he had predicted) rejoined the nomads' train
and had set up camp with them on the banks of the pool
around which the tents now described a wide arc.
Drogsang was what Nyema called this place,
from which cold rain was beginning
to wash away the fresh snow—*Beautiful Pasture*.

When Nyema saw my brother descending
from the clouds, for several minutes
she had hoped against all the evidence
that this still-distant figure was me returning.
(In the eyes of the clan, this kind of hesitation
was in itself a bad omen, for if a man appeared
to be what he was not, the edges of his life
became visible like the warp of threadbare fabric.)

He spared you . . . your brother,
said Nyema before she released herself from my embrace
and, my hand in hers,
I began to stumble down over the last stretch of scree
to the camp beside the pool.

She strode ahead so nimbly that she had
to pull and support more than guide me.
I had difficulty keeping up with her,
but our interwoven hands
did not part.

Spared? I asked.
Dhjemo, she said, spared you both.

The fact that we had only come across deserted caves
in Dhjemo's kingdom and no paw prints,
the fact that only one goat had vanished
on the way to Drogsang and
(to judge by the trail of blood children had discovered)
been dragged off to one of those caves
while Liam and I had been able to return unharmed

might be related to the fact that neither of us
had set foot on the peak of Cloud Mountain
and defiled its purity
and perhaps to the fact that Dhjemo's wrath
about our intrusion
had been appeased with a lost goat,
or simply that Tsering Dorje
had prayed with an incense offering
for forbearance towards his guests from the sea.

These in any case were the explanations that Nyema
translated for me that evening in her father's tent,
to which my brother and the healer
Rabten Kungar were invited for a feast.
We ate yak meat and fried bread,
drank salted butter tea and rice liquor.

Reminded by the alcohol of a long-gone
spring evening, Rabten Kungar began
to sing a monotonous ballad
about his encounter with Dhjemo, rocking
his upper body back and forth
in the glow of the cooking fire as if in prayer,
opened his fur-lined jacket
and displayed his chest, furrowed by slashing claws,
to the women in the tent, then the children
so that they might touch the prominent scars.

But the women simply laughed, shoving him away,
and the children—Tashi and Yishi Lhamo's daughter,
who lay awake in a cot rocker—were scared.

After his return the previous evening
and hearing from Nyema
that I was searching for him,
Liam had been so sure
that there was no path up to the summit
and that I would have no option but to turn around
and, like him, immediately rejoin the clan
that although surprised by my long absence,
he had not been worried.

I would surely return on my own,
for the many reconnaissance walks before his own departure
had shown him that there was no danger of avalanches
        up there,
that the caves offered
enough shelter from the weather
and that the rock made for easy walking
before it became in any case
insurmountable for one of my climbing ability.

Would my brother have searched for me?
Searched? In this weather? Yes, of course,
at some point, certainly—at some point
he would certainly have set out.
Nobody could have guessed
that I would be reckless or stupid enough
to hike across a glacier
that was obviously fractured with crevasses.
Had Liam not told me,
told me twice or three times, that the ice up there
was one big trap in waiting?

When late that night my brother left
the company gathered around the fire
and Rabten Kungar tottered after him,
the wind was plucking at the canvas
but the rain and snow had ceased.

The moon seemed to chase through cloud fronts
that looked like surf-spattered, smoking ramparts,
ruins in which it went dark
and shone forth again,
girdling the rubble of the sky with a halo one moment
and delicate silver linings the next
in a series of furious moonrises and moonsets.

Nothing but fragments of terra firma,
fragments of ridges, ice fields and peaks,
were to be seen in this shifting light.
Snow-covered rock and clouds
became indistinguishable.

Hours later I started from my sleep
because I thought I was falling, thought I felt
the pulpit of ice on which I was trapped
give way beneath me
and tip towards the abyss—and awoke
and in my stupor realized
only gradually that it was Nyema's hand
that had stopped me from plummeting
and pulled me back from my dream

into the warm, smoky dark of our tent
in which I then lay awake,

listening to the sleepers' breathing
and listening to the muffled sound of the wind
billowing and slackening the canvas—
the sails of a stranded ship.

Exhausted by vain hopes of falling sleep,
I brushed aside Nyema's hand,
which lay as lightly as a bird on my chest,
and crawled out of the tent without waking
my beloved—or the other sleepers.
I recall that the phenomenal night sky
that greeted—no, assailed—me outside,
crashing together above my head,
forced a sound or a groan of stunned disbelief,
indeed horror from my lips.

Cloud fronts, walls of fog, wraiths of mist,
every variety of water vapour seemed
to be caught up in a slow-motion explosion,

sailing and swirling past one another or plunging
silently into each other, binding themselves
into constantly changing, bursting forms
that afforded the odd glimpse of ridges, rock faces
or drifting peaks above which
chocks of star-sprinkled sky
were pulverized into sprays of sparks.

Although at ground level the wind
had softened to irregular gusts,
moonlit storm clouds rushed through the high air,

revealing and immediately concealing precipices
and rows of snow-clad cliffs that eventually
melted away into veils of mist or flapped like seaweed
in the swirling eddies of the tides.

All this movement, though, with barely a noise,
over everything a silence in whose deepest recesses
the occasional wind-blown singing, whistling, piping
could be heard, a symphonic wailing that sounded
like the mechanical workings of the firmament,
filtered through layers of atmosphere.

And amid all these slivers and fragments
of one permanent stone and one ephemeral world
there suddenly opened a cleft, a window
showing a peculiarly peaceful image—
all of a sudden a razor ridge reared great
and menacing and irrefutable in the distance,
detached from these explosive dynamics,
frozen, brought to a standstill by a cold snap.
It led from a glacier-covered saddle
high up into the night, almost to the zenith,
and ran as sharp as a paper cut-out
over pinnacles and crenels that I . . . recognized . . .
Pinnacles I recognized!

For as if this apparition had detached itself
from one of Liam's liquid crystal screens
and now shone like a monstrous projection
from this tattered sky,
I suddenly saw the saddle and saw the ridge

that swept upwards, more and more steeply,
from an icy col,
and whose picture I had seen before—
one stormy night on Horse Island.

Soaked and swearing, Liam and I
had returned home across scourged pastures
after a failed attempt to retrieve
a sheet of metal that was beating in the storm
and I saw a digitized photograph flickering
on three screens in his study
(Liam had only just discovered it in the data stream
when the metallic thunder interrupted his contemplation).

No doubt about it: what was visible
through the widening cleft in the clouds,
so clear and yet as distant
as if observed through an inverted telescope,
was the reality
behind the picture on Liam's screens;
it was a detail, part of a mighty
massif, wrapped in weather fronts,
which a Chinese bomber pilot had hailed
in a triumphant radio transmission to his ground control
before vanishing into a snowstorm over Chamdo
as *the highest pillar of the revolutionary world*.

Wreathed with bands of cirrus and icy plumes
(or simply my own breath?),
I saw the ridge, towering up into the night
through clouds the moon had turned the colour of chrome,

the enigma that had led us up from sea level
to these snowy summer pastures.
Only now—here!—at the clan's highest camp
did its shape reveal itself as identical
(or almost indistinguishably similar) to
its image on Liam's screens
that stormy night.

Phur-Ri,
I suddenly heard Nyema's voice say behind me.

I must have woken her after all as I crept outside.
She was squatting by the tent door, and the moon
at her back grew so dazzling
in a gap in the clouds (which closed seconds later)
that I could not make out her facial expression
as she repeated either for me or in a soliloquy
in my language: *the Flying Mountain.*

Then Tashi, awaking from a scary dream
or a feeling of abandonment, called out for his mother
from inside the dark tent
and Nyema disappeared.
And as though the night sky
would only entrust the sight of this ridge,
its secret, to a woman
and not to any old inquisitive insomniac seaman
who had wandered into the mountains,
all the clefts and gaps in the clouds closed again
to form an impenetrable,
intermittently lit, scudding mass,
from which ice needles now fell.

The next morning,
there was nothing but the pattering of rain
from clouds that had descended on the camp,
and the day began with the questions I shouted
to my brother through the rivulet-veined green
of his closed dome tent.
Had Liam at least seen the ridge,
seen the same one, exactly the same, as back then
on his computer screens—and had he recognized it?

The summit ridge of Phur-Ri? Yeah, of course.
What was so special about that? Here in this camp
we were closer than ever to our goal
and my brother had only yesterday,
as the sky brightened after his return,
seen the reflection of Phur-Ri
rippling on the surface of the pool
between the tents, and thrown
stones at the shimmering watery peak—
yes, he had even spotted the peak
in the pool and, later, through binoculars,
a path also, a route
that had to be practicable, a path
that definitely didn't end in the nearest crevasse
but would lead us to the very top
and back down again.

Liam opened the tent door
without leaving his sleeping bag,
and for the first time since Tsering Dorje
had offered me a calmer bed,

I crawled, dripping, into the dome.

Where my berth had once been
lay a Chinese map of the mountains of Kham,
spread out over the pile of equipment.
The progress of Nyema's clan
and our path to the foot of Phur-Ri
were marked in the same fine pencil
with which Liam made his sparse diary entries,
often consisting of no more than dates and times,
notes about temperature and height differences.

He didn't want, he said, to waste any more time
on a second attempt at Cloud Mountain,
but, rather, as soon as the weather got better
or, to be precise, more stable,
the last and highest level of this massif—

We'd scale it? I asked, conquer it?
Or apply the same strategy to our *area of operations*
as Captain Daddy had followed on his moors
(which sometimes had to be stormed, sometimes
simply occupied and held
until the end of the manoeuvre).
Storm it? Liam took no notice
of my nostalgic olive branch
about our wars in the bogs.
Were our old man's barked orders
still ringing in my ears?
Was it not enough to walk on and on,
all the way to the top?

And all this for the sole reason
that the top, the peak, existed,

because the mountain was there, just there,
maybe there for us alone, for the two of us,
who had now learnt its true name
and knew more about it
than any cartographer or surveyor alive.

Up to the top and back down again,
no more, that was it—
or had I perhaps lost the desire to continue
our journey from the sea to the heights
after my night in the icy crevasse
and would prefer to wait by the stove with wife and child,
with yaks' grunting me to sleep at night,
for my brother to swiftly return
with a series of dazzling photos
of the summit and his tale
of a successful solo ascent?

This much was certain: when the weather improved
Liam would set out with or without me
for a summit whose altitude lay
just under the seven-thousand-metre mark
(and, who knew, a re-measurement might even
raise its height slightly above that).
Seven thousand metres above sea level!
Not too bad for a sailor
who'd spent years clambering up and down
between engine rooms and decks below the water line

like a hamster in an exercise wheel . . .
And if, said Liam, even if
it wasn't the highest mountain of all
that awaited us, it was at any rate one
that bore no tracks, an unconquered colossus.
And however much it flew,
we would catch up with it
and climb up onto its head.
By God, it was ours already!
For the route he had followed yesterday
through his binoculars—a ridge walk
with some teeth but no special bite—
was, incidentally, easier than our route
to the top of Cha-Ri, and that route, said Liam,
did after all lead you
to your sweetheart, right?
So which heaven might the ascent
of a mountain that flew offer me?

Be quiet, Liam, be quiet.

After having seen the summit ridge of Phur-Ri
(or what I took for it)
among the night-time clouds—
the fulfilment of a prophecy
that had appeared on my brother's screens—
it took no further powers of persuasion
to rekindle my curiosity.
I was bewitched by that night-time vision,
as if one of the virtual landscapes
that arose and unfurled into tectonic waves

in Liam's digital atlases
had become *real*
by an act of electronic creation.

Guided by a magical magnetic force,
I would even have been willing
(like Liam) to strike out alone
at least to set foot on this ridge
and this mountain that had been conjured
from pure imagination into reality.

But when Liam's words spilled over
into zealous rants about subjects
on which I had no desire to hear
or tolerate his opinion,
whenever he spoke about Nyema
or about my life with her or about
what I should do and what I should not do,
he became an intruder, an enemy
who stirred only one emotion in me—defiance.
None of this stubborn bigmouth's beliefs
could I believe in, nothing that
made sense to him made sense to me,
and nor would I follow him anywhere.
My brother would have to not talk if I were
to accompany him; he had simply to be quiet.

I never discussed passions with Liam,
never talked about relationships,
never about women, never about his men,
and even what he thought he knew about me

was never more than the little
he could observe and deduce.
Nyema might even have been the first woman
with whom he saw me in public,
and she had influenced not only the course of our travels
but also our . . . brotherliness (was brotherliness the
    right word?)
perhaps more profoundly than our mother had.
To Liam it must have seemed that
I had completely forgotten why *we*
had come here from Horse Island
in my joy at being here with Nyema,
at being alive and in these high valleys—
and above all forgotten
who had brought me to these mountains
and who would guide me back again
from this beautiful mountain pasture,
from Drogsang,
to Horse Island and the sea.
Although I'd played only a bit part in Liam's plans,
I had veered off during this journey
(for no compelling reason he could see)
into an inaccessible world
in which I was alone with a woman, this woman,
and unattainable for him.

My brother could move virtual mountains,
could make me angry, sleepless, anxious,
but on our journey to Phur-Ri
he had lost the power to *coax* me
from the sea to the mountains
or simply from one place to another.

But then what did I know
of my brother's intentions?

Virtually everything I know now,
I only really learnt after his disappearance—
from digital records before I deleted them,
from his letters before I burnt them—
for Liam protected his emotions, passions and inclinations
like a secret that he wished to conceal
not only from others (even his own family)
but for many years from himself.

Did Liam ever feel attracted to any
of the men in Nyema's clan?
No record or memory
provides an answer to that question.
The clan contained not only old men
like Tsering Dorje or the scarred and disfigured
Rabten Kungar, but also youngsters,
tall child-men
who, with their artfully woven, waist-length hair,
their laughter and their dark, alert eyes,
certainly fulfilled as many of the criteria of beauty
as Nyema (to whom Liam spoke only when necessary).

It was Nyema who made me aware
that the only source of tenderness or joy
between Liam and me were memories—
childhood memories of the Cahas—
and that nothing could bring us
to talk at length and even make us laugh

apart from our manoeuvres, our wars in the bogs,
our captain and many things
that lay gone
and buried in Ireland.

As for the present—
a time when we still had to make
our decisions, when we had to act
and live *now*, and would eventually die—
we were more accidental companions than brothers,
living together, housemates, yet grown foreign
to each other in foreign parts.

What did Liam know of my years at sea
and of my homesickness, not just for places
but for people too, their voices, their embraces,
the pet names Shona had invented for us,
the lilt of her Gaelic lullabies
and that eternal childhood
in which death was something
that only ever happened to others?

And me? What did I know of Liam?
What of his years in cities which
I saw at best from the harbour,
what of his decision to return home
from air-conditioned offices to a house
(strangely similar to our parents' farm)
on a wave-beaten rock
where many of his wishes, his desires,
must surely remain even more unfulfilled

than in places to which he had once
fled from the *moor* (as he called it)?
We continued our kinship
in name only,
just as Horse Island itself bore a name
hollowed of its meaning—an island
where horses had long since ceased to graze.

Only with the Dunlough rescue service,
Liam had declared, had he rediscovered
his passion for climbing among a group of volunteers—
farmers, fishermen, mussel producers—who
came to the aid of the crews of run-aground freighters
or yachts that had split on the cliffs
in an uncapsizable Marine Rescue speedboat,
occasionally towing a trawler with engine damage
out of the storm into the lee;
above all, however, it gave my brother
virtually free access
to the coastal villages
when he returned from elsewhere.
A member of the Marine Rescue did after all
become as familiar with the inhabitants
of these villages (and their pubs)
as with their cliff faces,
the pounding of the surf
and the reefs submerged at high tide,
but he had also to be capable of floating
down from the jagged edge of this coastline
on a rope and climbing harness
into a howling abyss.

Sometimes this was the only way to retrieve
the dead from a shipwreck or injured people
trapped in rocky clefts, in shafts
into which the sea boiled up like a geyser
and sank seething back.

I remember Liam mentioning
in one letter the victims of an accident
who had been stripped by the breakers, maimed
and then dragged by the current into the deep
and down into underwater caverns
where the Marine Rescue divers had found some
only weeks later and others not at all . . .

Only once had Liam written to me
about this and about his fear
of being delivered up, helpless, to the sea,
but we had never spoken of this fear
(and what might have been at its root).

For two years my brother had repeatedly
obeyed the sea-rescue calls
until the house that he had built
on the ruined foundation walls was ready
and he moved from Dunlough lighthouse
(which had stood empty since the automation
of all beacons and which he had rented thus far)
to Horse Island.

But on his—on our—island
he himself was now unreachable

during a hurricane or an emergency,
a rescuer cut off from his comrades
and their lifeboat until the storm abated,
who could only follow the happy outcome
of the drama or the end of the tragedy
on his radio set
and who eventually—in good weather—
would take part in practice rescues,
a simulation of reality.

Harnesses, ropes and jumars, pitons,
bolts, titanium carabiners, abseil figure-of-eights,
nuts—anything that might brake one's fall down a cliff
and might hold or help a rescuer back to the top
with his unconscious, moaning or dead weight—
gradually became props for a rediscovered passion,
independent of the sea and maritime emergencies,
and hung in the house on Horse Island next to axes,
fishing rods and lobster pots in an equipment room
smelling of salt and seaweed
with a broad view of the Atlantic Ocean.

One of the unsolvable mysteries
that remain after Liam's death on Phur-Ri
is the question of whether his membership
of the Dunlough marine rescue was merely a bridge
connecting him to our father's past—an extension
of Captain Daddy's failed attempts
to salvage what could no longer be salvaged
from the burning oil
after the tanker *Betelgeuze*'s explosion.

For just as the sky-licking blaze on the sea
and the dead bodies rocking in the flames
had become an inexhaustible subject
that pursued our captain into his dreams,
so Liam's outings in the Marine Rescue speedboat
had been part of the many experiences
that followed him to the foot of the Flying Mountain.

The only story my brother
ever told beside Tsering Dorje's fire and
asked Nyema to translate so that it could
be passed on to the clan as *his* story
was a description of a sinking ship
and the subsequent tale
of a burning sea.

It was only when Liam told
the Khampas about the catastrophe off Whiddy Island
that I remembered
that the orange oilskin that our father
had bought in O'Sullivan's shop
after burning his stained jacket
and inscribed with his own hands
with the words *Marine Rescue*

was the only item of Captain Daddy's clothing
that my brother adopted,
and I also remember
that Liam was wearing that jacket that stormy night
when the corrugated iron came loose from his observatory
and Phur-Ri's summit ridge

first appeared on a computer screen.

That ridge, its truly
awe-inspiring steepness, framed by clouds
and adorned with moonlit ice plumes,
a fleeting image in the night sky
above the clan's highest and last campsite,
was to be the sight
that restored a shared emotion between us
and a harmony
we had believed lost.

No, I truly did not need
to be persuaded;
I needed none of the diatribes, none of the arguments
that Liam called out to me the next morning
from his tent streaming with mazy rivulets of rain.

I was by then long primed
to depart, as was my brother,
and was determined, despite Nyema's objections,
despite her sadness, despite my own residual fear
of height, crevasses, cold and falling,
to follow that ridge, that flying mountain—and a trail
that led from Liam's dim virtual worlds
into reality.

15.

Drogsang or the Beautiful Pasture. At base camp.

Although Nyema did not share her father's belief,
she translated his misgivings for me:
anyone who set foot on the tip of a flying mountain
ran the risk of being hurled
out of the world before his time
or sent spinning out into space.

Nyema did not want me
to follow Liam onto Phur-Ri—
but badger me, implore me to stay?
Hold me back? She didn't want that either.

The clansmen
(with the exception of Tsering Dorje)
would invariably laugh as they warned
that my brother and I would reach the goal of our travels
and then, like passengers on a cloud-ship,
fly up and away.
Up and away! Fly away!

But their giggling and laughing
sometimes made scaling Phur-Ri
seem only a harmless folly,
no more dangerous than one of our childhood
manoeuvres in the Caha Mountains, a mere game
that only a father, an eccentric old man,
be his name Fergus or Tsering Dorje,
could still take seriously.

Even if my liberation from the crevasse
struck Liam as an improbable,
outrageous stroke of fortune
and Nyema's clan
as the work of merciful gods,
since I had managed to haul myself
out of the depths and back into the daylight,
without a rope, without my brother's advice,
without any help from the clan, I felt,
in a strangely buoyant burst of confidence
based entirely on having survived,
my brother's equals in areas
in which I had hitherto always
followed in his footsteps.

For whether it was a route to the summit
or simply reading an ice wall,
confident in my own powers,
I now felt experienced enough
to agree with my brother
or contradict him, indeed strong enough
to judge entirely on my own

whether to take a step onto a vertical face
or to leave it be.

And thus the blazing ridge
which after four rainy days loomed at last
into a clearing sky was more inviting
than challenging; it appeared enticingly near,
its peak more accessible than ever.
And yet it was precisely this nearness
that hid more of the true form and shape
of Phur-Ri than it revealed.

The mountain towered so steeply, so close above us
that we had to throw back our heads
to point our binoculars at the summit.
But whether it really was the highest peak
that we saw or only part of a closer wall,
buried under drifts of snow,
remained a mystery, even with binoculars.

My confidence in my powers
was further swelled by the fact
that Liam (perhaps deflated
by his failure on Te-Ri)
no longer seemed so determined
to attain his goal by any means,
solo if necessary,
but talked instead once more of *our* mountain,
our route, *our* project.

Tsering believes, said Nyema, that you were spared
by Dhjemo and the gods of Cloud Mountain
because you come from the sea, have no family,
no herd and no experience of the snow
and you therefore deserve some leniency;
but no one should test
that clemency twice.

And you? I asked. What do you believe?

I believe, said Nyema, that you should stay here.
I believe that you have both gone
high enough and far enough,
but I know that you want to continue.
Then she smiled, and I,

I thought I detected even on her face
a touch of the same insouciance
I had seen in the men's expressions each time
they laughed at the seamen's plans,
their craving for the peak of Phur-Ri
and the titillation
of perhaps being swept away
together with the mountain.

During our approach,
Phur-Ri
had shown itself only in fragments,
framed by narrow valley entrances
and constantly encircled by nearby mountain chains,
changing with every new valley,
every new viewpoint—indeed, it seemed

to twist before us in a slow ballet
as if the full spectrum of shapes
on the Earth's crust must still be paraded
before ignorant island-dwellers like us;

one moment it seemed to us a pyramid,
the next a towering wedge-like colossus,
a craggy block, even a blazing dune
and then gradually outgrew its shifting guises
to form one immense, unbroken barrier, a wall
that appeared to hold back the rest of the massif,
the clouds, all space and the very heavens.

They approached, sta-anding tall
a ballad about Macgillicuddy's Reeks
that Captain Daddy would always begin
to sing or simply whistle when I
complained about the steep path or the weight
of my rucksack on our way to a manoeuvre.
They approached, sta-anding tall as the sky
as we gaze at them from below.
Do not despair! Do not rest! We climb
and push the mountains back into the sand,
for each peak disappears when we set
foot on its head. Forward, comrades!
Only up top, up top, does every path lead down
and Ireland lie-hies,
all Ireland lie-hies at our feet . . .

Were the ridges, ledges, chimneys
and arêtes which Liam and I scanned
through the binoculars for traps, insurmountable

obstacles and apertures, really
part of that terrifying Jacob's ladder
I had seen one stormy night through a gap in the clouds?

We sat together
for hours in the fine grass
on a hillock above the pool
(the best place for guarding
the scattered livestock), holding our binoculars
to our eyes as if in prayer, and yet we saw
nothing but variants of the same route,
a path that needed only
to be adorned with our tracks.
I recall
leaning shoulder to shoulder
in the sun during these observations
as we checked various sections of the looming wall
before us through the binoculars,
each of us absorbed with a different part of the route
when I began to feel the warmth of Liam's body
through the insulating layers of windcheater and fleece
and tried to move away from him;
for me this position was too near, too close.

But my brother involuntarily
followed my sideways sway
and I responded to the light pressure of his shoulder
so as not to disturb our equilibrium,
achieving a hovering balance
that caused the trembling image of a snow-covered step
in the ridge just below the peak I thought was the summit,
to suddenly freeze.

Nyema did not oppose the new harmony
between Liam and me, a rapprochement
that seemed to lead only over the peak of Phur-Ri
—no remonstrations, no questions,
no warnings—yet I tried
to explain this unity to her
(and probably to myself too)
by saying that I couldn't let my brother
go on his own; not now
that he was dependent on my companionship
for perhaps the first time in our lives; not now
that the goal that had been barely more
than an illusion or a mirage on Horse Island
lay attainable, within reach, before our eyes.

It was only when I saw her amazement
at my justifications that I realized
I must be discharging a duty
that still bound me to the *true* Ireland,
to my parents' house.
There too, accompanying someone had
usually meant moving away
from someone else who stayed behind.
For as our father laid down deeper
and deeper roots at his home,
growing more immobile, more unswerving,
yes, immovable, going *away* became
synonymous with another word—betrayal.
In the preceding weeks
the thought that I was leaving my brother behind
sometimes oppressed me when I sought

to be close to Nyema, but now
the preparations for our summit ascent
made me feel that I was cheating on her.
But what she showed me
when she hugged me was, shortly and simply,
Go and come back again.

Anyone who crosses this boundary
has left my house and
—I swear!—will never,
may never come back!
Captain Daddy had yelled
when after a long, secret affair,
Shona finally decided to follow her Duffy
to Belfast, and Liam and I
carried our mother's luggage (boxes, bags,
crates, but only one suitcase)
as far as the gate in the dry stone wall
that divided our garden and a sloping field
from the road to Glengarriff.

Tackling the heavy items together, we hauled
Shona's belongings one by one out of the house
and along the winding gravel path towards this *boundary*
between wilted hydrangeas
and badly pruned fuchsia hedges;

we hauled everything so close to this line
that we had to drag crates and boxes
back a few steps
when Shona went to open the gate
(which swung towards this side of the boundary)

and left us for ever.

The captain was crouching
on the asphalted flat roof of our henhouse,
a shotgun he had borrowed
from O'Sullivan's store
to defend our rose bushes
from wild rabbits at the ready.
And although he had never let off
a deliberate shot from this gun,
and even at the height of his anger
(it was one Sunday evening)
and after wild curses and warnings,
had only fired one shot into the clouds
through the open kitchen window
as a deterrent,
the whole time all of us—Liam, me,
even the waiting Duffy—obeyed his order:
This far and not one step further!
Duffy's delivery van was parked on the other side
of the road opposite the gate, a Ford Transit
whose windowless sides were painted
to look like television screens—on the driver's side
a crude view of the Cahas with the moon riding high,
on the passenger's side, a night scene
of the twinkling sea from one of the mountains.
Below the pictures on both sides
stood the stencilled words: *Duffy's Window on the World.*

So the Ford Transit resembled a huge television,
the cabin a panel painted
with control knobs, and inside this fake television

with which, during peacetime, Duffy
had also delivered our window on the world,
our mother's abductor sat motionless,
kept at bay by the shotgun,
one elbow resting on the steering wheel,
the other propped uncomfortably on the rim
of the wound-down window.

Not one step further!

Shona opened the gate and stepped over the boundary
without looking back at the captain,
but Liam and I did not dare
to carry her things across the road
to Duffy's delivery van,
but watched, arms dangling,
as our mother struggled with her effects.
She could only drag
a large box full of books, tied together
with a washing line, that Liam and I
had lugged to the boundary.

Stay in your van! shouted the Captain
when Duffy made a move to get out
and help Shona. *Stay in your van,
you fucking souper*! and fired
—fired!—a round of lead shot
into the canopy of the arbutus
that shaded the henhouse.
In the breathless silence that followed
one could hear the sound of delicate leaves

fluttering down out of the treetop.
The same Captain Daddy who had
to get his wife to slaughter the hens,
because his hands and his heart, everything in him,
was too soft for killing
had actually fired a shot.

Shona wrote letters from Belfast and greetings cards
which when we opened them
or pressed them tightly to our hearts
played a few bars of ballads, stored on microchips,
such as *Danny Boy* or *Road to Castlehaven*.

Shona sent woollen sweaters, hats
and scarves she had knitted for Liam and me,
and three weekends a year she came alone
or with Duffy to Glengarriff
to eat mussels and apple cake
with us in Eccles Hotel
and then visit the seal colony off Garinish Island
or the waterfall on Hungry Hill—
but, as the captain had sworn,
Shona never again crossed
the threshold of our house.

Although I occasionally dreamt
in the nights before our departure
by Nyema's side in Tsering Dorje's tent
of crevasses and dark well shafts
in which I was held captive,
and although for a long time after I awoke

I was haunted by visions that were all
related to the dangers of our ascent
although Nyema did indeed sometimes have
to hold, restrain and calm me when I hit out
in my dreams and tried in vain to find a grip
on protruding crags and crumbling rocks
and then saw the chasm rushing up at me,

and although the mere thought
of being separated from Nyema
(even if only for the two or three
days we had calculated for our summit climb)
pained me as much as
those melancholy days when Shona
had begun to pack
for her escape at Duffy's side,
and I felt loss and an insatiable longing
before the separation,
before the farewells by the gate,

I had to admit to myself
that I was overwhelmed and, despite all my trepidation,
sometimes almost intoxicated
by the sight of the high mountains
and the blooming meadows flowing down
from the snowy light and turquoise glaciers,
across which the shadows of clouds drifted, shadows

that had been presented as rafts
in the bedtime stories with which Shona
had rewarded Liam and me for our obedience

when we were boys
—as silvery elfin rafts
on which the meadow flowers and the summer
rode inland over the slopes of the Cahas.

Here, outside the Khampas' tents,
those shadows were even capable
of flying up the glacier-walled pastures
and climbing up the rows of rock faces
until they were lost in a blue-black sky
scattered with cumulus clouds.
Here, from the Khampas' highest camp,
one's gaze could only ever rise higher—

from the resplendent vegetation
with its profusion of fragrances
and flowers of many colours and shapes amid the green,
soaring away over this organic splendour
and on through silky, shimmering bars of haze
to the blinding, all-overpowering blaze of ice
that preserved within its crystals the oxygen,
aroma and breath of past millennia.

In the days leading up to our departure
I sometimes felt an excitement
similar to that which had gripped me
when I had first accompanied Liam
to the Alps in the second year after my arrival
on Horse Island, and stared up from the meadows near
        Chamonix
(beneath a sky exactly like this one)

at the icy armour of Mont Blanc.
Back then, I had trouble imagining
what would happen (and happened)
the following day, that a person—that *I*—
could climb *back* by my own strength
from the spring, through climatic zones
and seasons—yes, through time itself—
into the past, into the winter,
up to the glaciers and into
the unique blaze of a world of ice
that cast the light back into the sky
rather than keeping it for itself, not absorbing it
like the light-converting,
light-devouring organic world.

Ice, Shona had told us, ice was the stuff
from which the coat, the jewellery,
the crown and even the heart
of that haughty king were made
who scornfully turned away the sun
when it requested a handful of soil and water
in exchange for the colours of the rainbow,
the gold of the gorse and flaming bouquets
of rays of light.

But the haughty monarch simply snapped these bouquets
and hurled the splinters in the petitioner's face.
For this he was punished with a scorching summer
which thawed the king's magnificent snow-spun robes,
the ice flowers in his gardens
and even his throne, encrusted

with crystals and garlands of hoarfrost,
transforming them into gushing rivers
and cascades of meltwater

where sparkling flights of stairs, ice palaces,
colonnades and beds of ice orchids had once been . . .
Water! Water in such abundance
that the torrents softened even
the blackness of night into peat and earth,
in which starlight and gorse gold,
grass green and the colours of the rainbow
lay buried and preserved
for warmer, more propitious times.

From the tears of the king, however,
whom the sun sentenced to mourn
his coldheartedness for millennia,
from his never-ending grief
were born the seas and the ocean
from which mist and rainclouds evaporated
in memory of that ephemeral ice world
so that, fed by their precipitation,
the springs of the new water-world
might never run dry.

On those pastures near Chamonix
I had recalled Shona's tale
as if it were a prophecy,
and in my mind the ice and water worlds
merged into a single, dazzling landscape
every bit as real

as the cold, flickering electric fire
in the *fireside room* of our parents' home,
beside which Shona would reward us
with stories long before Duffy's window
on the world began to glow.

That summer's day below Mont Blanc
was the first time the vertical path
into the mountains struck me
as a path through time.
For the world had not only once been
as luminous, as empty
and as bare of life
as in the ice region *up* there,
but it would revert again, after the end
of all measurable time, to being a world without us,

which I could nonetheless scale
with my brother—
from the fertile lowlands up into the icy light,
and from that lifeless silence
back down to the sea.
It was only then during that progress
that the short timespan and the narrow,
contour-hatched stratum of human life
began to seem as fabulously precious
as in Shona's tales
or the passionate sermons
Liam and I heard alongside our parents
in Glengarriff church every Sunday.

It was not only our father's trips, but all trips
that seemed in truth to lead not out and away
but only ever up or down—
even as Shona drove off towards Belfast
in Duffy's van, thus betraying her family
and the Irish cause,
she was fleeing from the arbutus-,
cordyline-palm- and rhododendron-dotted
coasts of West Cork, a paradise in which,
in the words of our captain,
she had had everything—everything!—
not *over* to Belfast
but *up* to Belfast.
The day before we set out for the summit
the weather became so windless and clear
that the Flying Mountain began to tilt towards us
and move irresistibly closer.

Liam considered taking the lightest of bags
and only three days of food with us.
The route from the Khampas' summer camp
(which he now simply referred to as our *base camp*)
up to a curving saddle
and the ridge beyond it,
to the peak and then back
to the safety of the clan,
must be *feasible* in three or four days at most.

Tsering Dorje, who had climbed
to the saddle once (but never higher)
warned us that even this section

was long and arduous, but it was above all
the isolated thunder clouds, which
(from a reassuring distance) we sometimes
saw rise to the dome of the troposphere
and morph into white anvils there,
that led us to the realization that,
despite the current stable air pressure,
a sudden weather change
might force us to add some rest days.

And since we wanted something that was impossible
both on land or at sea, let alone in the mountains—
to be prepared for anything—we increased
our load of equipment and food
(which, in our exhaustion in the coming days
when we were already high, very high up,
seemed like the boulder of Sisyphus
and ultimately lured us
into leaving much of it, including
the saving tent, behind in the snow).

Above the first entry in that thin notebook
barely a breast-pocket wide,
in which I intended to record
the first ascent of a mountain that flew,
I wrote the date and, as a link
between our calendar back home
and the one that governed our life at altitude:

Drogsang, Kham. First of May in the Year of the Horse.

16.

Leader, follower. A rope team.

Liam had set out alone.
Had simply walked away! and was suddenly
high up on the slopes. *Wait! Wait, will you!*
Hey! had simply walked off
without any warning
during that one fleeting instant
when I had fallen into Nyema's eyes one last time
and rested there for a heartbeat—
secure, invulnerable, shielded
from everything that might threaten us
above the morning fog patches and sky-high
above the clan's summer pastures . . .

Just walked off! And already shrunk
to a tiny figure, barely visible
in his light-blue down jacket,
climbing upwards in the shadow of a huge
boulder: *Liam!* What an idiot. *Wait, will you!*
Had he gone mad?

When I resurfaced from Nyema's eyes and saw
that Liam had almost vanished,
when I turned, calling his name,
towards the blinding heights
and tried to follow him
as fast as the weight of my gear
and the incline would permit,
I heard the herders
laughing again behind me
(were they not watching
one madman run after another?)
but I didn't want to turn and face their scorn,
and so I didn't turn either to face
Nyema, whom I only much later
saw standing outside our tent,
so far below that I could no longer make out
her face, her eyes, but only her outline.
Liam! Wait, will you!

I was out of breath when I finally caught up
with my brother on the edge of a scree slope
stretching far up above the boulder
in the morning sun.
As if what the glacier cast on us
was not dazzling snow light
but unadulterated darkness,
for a moment everything went black
before my eyes as I looked up.
Liam! Are you nuts.
Running off like that.

Once the blackness had passed as quickly
as it had come, and the pounding of the blood
in my head quietened,
I found my brother in the best of moods.
He had trained on me the lens
of the battered black Leica
he had brought along on the summit walk
instead of his digital camera (due to
the anticipated cold and damp
he didn't trust the electronic-memory technology,
and the evidence of our triumphant ascent
must not be lost under any circumstances)
—and he pressed the shutter release.

The picture, which captured the instant
of my arrival, the instant of my anger,
would only emerge from the developing tray
several months after Liam's death.
It showed me breathless, panting,
mouth wide open, furious,
the valley behind me
and in it Drogsang's pool—
a mirror clouded by rasping waves,
in front of it the tents, in front of them the laughing herders,
and Nyema's figure,
and all of them, all of it already so far away . . .

It was the first picture of two rolls of colour film
from our *summit day*, and the only reason
it wasn't lost along with other pictures
of me, several portraits of my brother

(for whom I pressed the shutter release),
some dim views of the valley bottom
and a blurred, out-of-focus memento
of our victorious pose on the summit,
taken on self-timer,
was because Liam packed all the heavy items—
the rope, the carabiners,
pitons, jumars, ice screws—
into his rucksack during our first break
on our panicked flight from the summit,
leaving me, the bone-tired one,
with only a few small objects—
the camera, the gas cooker, the pouch
containing the altitude-sickness pills.

It took me a long, long time
to have these films developed in the drugstore
next to Eamon's Bar in Dunlough.
By that time the house on Horse Island
and Liam's study had been completely emptied,
and I was standing in the bare space when I finally dared
to take the envelope of negatives and prints
from my jacket pocket and open it.
The very first picture forced me to my knees.

I recall that I was suddenly
kneeling on the bare floorboards,
which had once been as soft as moss
with the deep pile of a Tibetan rug,
and began
to cover this bare space with photos,

laying them down in consecutive rows
as in Patience—a card game against death.

In doing so I tried desperately to follow my instinct
to maintain the silence in the house at all costs,
stifling my sobs with clenched lips,
hearing in Liam's house, from whose windows
one could see veils of spray surging
soundlessly up cliffs and rocky islands,
only the impact of my tears
on the matt surface of the photos.

All in all, there were seventy-two pictures
that I ordered and rearranged over and over again,
shuffling about on my knees
as if in the hope that this would make
picture after picture arise from memory,
arise from their flatness
and rail at the irreversible flow of time.

Again and again, in my brother's empty house, I returned
to the first pictures in this gallery of remembrance,
to our path to the summit,
again and again to those moments
when I had at last managed to close the gap
on Liam, my mouth wide, panting:
Are you nuts? . . . Running off like that.

These—that much and that little
I can say now—
were the final moments of our life together

in which I felt something like rancour
or rage for Liam, for this masked person
who was waiting for me,
pointing his Leica at me, shrouded in breathy vapour,
high above the camp at Drogsang.

For my arrival at the point where he stood
was followed by hours, days, *our* last days,
in any case a period steeped
in completely different emotions, which,
however diverse and contradictory
they might have been,
could be contained by no other term
than the all-describing,
all-obscuring word *love*.

Love.
As if the accusations I had levelled at Liam,
Master Coldheart, up to that day
and over the course of our travels,
had also invalidated all my doubts about my decision
to accompany him to the contour line
where he awaited me.

He pressed the shutter release, lowered the camera,
looked at me and smiled, said
that he had just gone ahead for a few steps
to photograph the camp, our start for the summit
from up here, which offered the best view
of our base camp; said
I must have been too busy to hear him,

asked with disbelief if I hadn't felt his hand
on my shoulder as a signal
that he was setting out so that he might
capture, as the first picture of our path
to the peak, my farewells with Nyema—
a pair of lovers, minuscule in front of the tents,
a beautiful picture . . .

Only gradually did it dawn on me
that my brother had not started out without me,
not this time, not to the summit of all places
of which we had dreamt, sometimes together
and sometimes each on his own,
since a stormy night on Horse Island,
but rather that Liam had wanted to make me
a gift of a photo taken in the first hour
of our path to the summit.

No, I hadn't felt Liam's hand,
I hadn't heard his words.
I remember only that he had slung on his rucksack
with the crampons fastened to the sides, ready to hand,
tightened his shoulder straps and then
taken a few almost playful, bouncing steps
to check that the load sat well.
Still hopping, he had spun away
quite casually, as if in practice,
towards the Flying Mountain
and simply walked off unnoticed ahead of me
while I sank deeper and deeper

into Nyema's eyes, blind and deaf
to anything beyond our embrace.

The diminutive figures, almost merging
into one, beside Drogsang pool,
which I identified on the photo
that forced me to my knees months later—
that was my farewell from Nyema,
that was me, that was *us*, and I saw us,
saw our embrace for the first time
through the camera . . . through my brother's eyes.

In two days we'll be back,
said Liam reassuringly, consoling me
as he lowered the camera.
In two days you'll be with her again . . .
And I remember that his words,
his tone triggered in me an unfamiliar emotion
that was completely new between us—
I sensed with a sudden, overwhelming
intensity that Liam, my brother,
perhaps for the first time in our lives,
was by my side, fully with me,
that Liam understood
what held me back *and* what pulled me away
and thus kept me in a yearning limbo
between the camp at Drogsang
and Phur-Ri's still-distant white heights,
between the security of Nyema's
world, lit and warmed by open fires,
and the destination of a journey

leading from our shared fraternal origin
into the clouds and into the depths of the sky.

As we searched for something
that for me lay ultimately by Nyema's side
but only ever in the future for Liam,
perhaps in an unattainable sphere,
my brother and I had *strayed* into each other's lives,
without any false expectations and intentions,
but strayed nonetheless—and now I felt
that his consoling remark was a signal
by which he meant to tell me
that he no longer saw Nyema's presence
as an obstacle to his plans, but as my happiness—
the happiness of his brother
he had brought back from the sea onto dry land
and then high up into mountains
where he must now set him free.

And so I was transformed
in the lens of his Leica, before his eyes,
from a furious straggler
into a willing companion
who saw his path laid out like a tracer before him.
Over the peak! Over the peak of the Flying Mountain
and, by my brother Liam's side,
back into Nyema's arms.

For the highest, blinding heights of Phur-Ri
made our return, made everything
that awaited us beyond the peak

so precious, so obvious and radiant,
that the love I felt for my brother,
like my love for Nyema,
would only become clear and indisputable
at the point on our trail from which
every onward step led only into the void.

I sensed at that moment that Liam, my brother
Liam, knew that we must *accompany* each other
to the summit but from there

each must return to his own life. And maybe
it was truly and mainly for this reason
that we climbed higher and higher,
as only this vertical path
leading back in time and down to the sea
could lead us into our future.

In our weeks of travelling, so many divisive,
alienating and even hostile issues had become perceptible
and palpable between us as we realized
how deep a rift had grown between us since our
        manoeuvres
in the Cahas (and despite our years on Horse Island).
How many times during these weeks I had wished
to annul not only my brother's companionship
but also our *brotherliness*;
but now, up here, where he was waiting for me
at the start of the final section of our path
to the tip of a mountain that flew,

even Master Coldheart was finally able to show
also how close we were—we still were.

Perhaps surprised
by how much he was affected by his comforting words,
in two days you'll be with her again . . .
he somewhat clumsily (or embarrassedly) stowed
his camera in a side pocket of his down jacket
before we turned laughing towards Phur-Ri
and continued on our way, *laughing,*

for like two polite, slightly gauche gentlemen
in the doorway of a drawing room, we suddenly
tried to let the other go first, coyly,
signalling to the other to go first and go ahead,
Oh please . . . after you . . . oh no, after you!
and in the end we set off almost simultaneously
and with a tiny hesitation
so that we almost collided,
but then Liam went first after all—
and I followed him, but this time more easily,
more cheerfully and more naturally than ever before.

I have very few and faint memories
of the nature of the route
that led us up to the saddle
to which Tsering Dorje had once climbed,
but beyond which the clan had no experience,
only tales to tell,
myths about a flying mountain.

The fact that my memory holds almost no images
of steep slopes, rocky clefts and traverses
we had to negotiate on our way to that saddle
might be because the route was technically
        straightforward,
allowing us to climb for hours,
lost in our thoughts, across rivers of scree,
mossy slopes strewn with tiny flowers,
then the first firn fields,
but it might also have been an unprecedented
sense of fellowship with Liam
that captivated me and had me set one foot
in front of the other as if in a trance.

We barely spoke, so swathed were we
in our steamy breath and loud breathing,
and although Liam moved across the pathless terrain
without pausing and without once looking
around at me, I followed him
at a short but constant distance.
My brother determined the steepness
of our route by the number of hairpins,
but he took account of my strength
and my pace as he climbed ahead of me.

Only twice more did Drogsang emerge from the deep,
appearing on the edge of our field of vision
between ridges, then under jutting rock faces
and vanishing immediately again like an island
or like flotsam in the surging swell.
When we reached the saddle at early afternoon

without a single major break,
I could not have said whether
I had seen any evidence for Tsering Dorje's
warnings in the past hours—
our climb up here was no sooner negotiated
than practically forgotten.

Before us there opened now a glaciated cirque,
enclosed by a series of walls festooned
with cascades of ice, a glistening dam
that seemed to prevent the very firmament,
like a sea robbed of its beaches and cliffs,
from crashing together over the crevasse-riddled
valley bottom and the surrounding land.

Though we had examined and studied this barrier
many times from a distance, section by section,
through our binoculars, the sight
of its skyline still took our breath away.
Was it across this valley bottom, this ragged ice
and this immense wall that we must climb
to reach the ridge we had identified
through the eyepieces of our binoculars,
during our reconnaissance from Drogsang,
as the final, highest segment of our path to the summit?

Yes of course, said Liam, yes, not today,
obviously not today, but tomorrow, definitely tomorrow.
Today I am convinced
that we should have turned back, rethought our route,
established a second camp and

ventured from there up to the summit . . .
But on that glorious afternoon,
when I was, perhaps for the first time,
truly travelling *with* my brother,
neither Liam nor I considered that.

Although we were filled with a strange trepidation
at the sight of *our* mountain, whose menace
was not tempered by clouds and veils of mist,
nor by foothills or mere distance,
it was as if the magnetism of Phur-Ri
acted on us like a law of nature,
drawing us ever closer now that all possibility
to turn back had gone.
As if we were climbing, clambering
towards our destiny.

In my brother's footsteps I leapt
over icy cracks and walked, roped to him,
across snow bridges spanning the ice-blue depths
as though I had no memory of my night
in the hole on Bird Mountain nor of my intention
never again to cross scarred glaciers
such as those that now separated us
from the walls of Phur-Ri.
Unhesitatingly, I placed one foot in front of the other
as if not only my brother's safety cord
but his mere shadow might preserve me
from the hidden chasms
and from falling into the void below.

I obeyed Liam's instructions as naturally
as I had on our first trial runs on the cliffs
of Horse Island when he had finally got me—
a panic-stricken pupil who desperately rebelled at first—
to push off with both feet from the cliff face
and let myself fall backwards from the edge
of a rocky spur onto the rope and into the harness—
yes! let myself fall with my back to the void
purely so that he could show me

how securely, one-handed, he could hold me
on the belay device and how happily such a fall
might turn out—and falling,
falling and screaming, sobbing involuntarily
with relief or excitement, I suddenly felt,
presumably as a parachutist does,
the saving springiness
of the safety cord
and was the next moment swinging high
above the surf, an arm's length from the wall,
on the end of my brother's rope.

As Liam preceded me so decisively
through the maze of crevasses
as if he were simply following a secure path,
pausing only occasionally
to test the stability of a snow bridge,
I let the rope that bound us
run in a double loop
around the handle of my ice axe
so that I might ram the tip into the ice,

transforming it into an anchor,
should my brother suddenly be
swallowed up by a crack
splitting the spotless firn.

Yet Liam did not check once
that I was using the rope as he had instructed,
but now too, without glancing back,
trusting me completely, went ahead—
whichever of us stepped out into the void,
the other would rescue him from the abyss.

17.

In captivity. The gift.

The route we took to cross the glacier
seemed so protracted and exhausting
that I felt we were exploring
every curve and cul-de-sac of the maze
of crevasses that lay hidden
in the firn beneath our feet.

When we finally reached secure ice-covered
rocky ground, the sun disappeared
behind the crags and scarps of the ridge
that was meant to be our path to the summit,
plunging us into a blue twilight.
Shielded by an immense overhang
from any falling stones and ice,
we pegged our dome tent to the glassy ground.

The altimeter showed 6,400 metres.
By Liam's estimation that figure
was at least a hundred metres *above*

our true height.
The carefree tone of voice
in which Liam announced the erroneous reading
was in stark contrast to its cause:
such a large discrepancy signalled
a dramatic drop in air pressure.

But as we made our preparations
for a cold night, the first stars
appeared in a cloudless sky, undeterred
by these ill omens:
Regulus in the constellation of Leo, 77 light years away,
and Spica in Virgo, 262 light years from the Earth.
Liam had questioned me on the names and distances
of about two dozen stars during my years
on Horse Island—bright reference stars
by which to align his telescope.

Regulus and Spica were twinkling that evening
in unison with the light gusts of wind
that began to press against the tent's canvas, as if
their ancient light had stirred the wind itself.
We heaped a protective wall of snow
around the tent, secured the guy-lines,
removed the crampons from our boots
and crawled into our shelter.

After these final exertions I was suddenly
overcome with such exhaustion
that Liam had to start the gas cooker,

melt some snow, make tea and soup
and then even persuade me to drink.

From the very first sip
I had trouble controlling my nausea,
but Liam encouraged me to carry on drinking
with the same onomatopoeic calls
he used to direct his sheepdogs
on strenuous walks or during herding
to slake their thirst in a rivulet
or a puddle before urging them on again—

Flop-flop! Hey! Flop-flop!, calling
at the same time the derisive
and tender nickname
with which he had tried to help me
overcome my fear and weak muscles
on our first climbing tours: *Mousepad!*
Don't be scared, Mousepad!
Flop-flop; Mousepad.

Mousepad. Back then, high on the rocks,
Liam had named me after the synthetic surface
over which, before the invention
of simpler methods, every computer user
needed to move a device
the shape and size of a mouse
to make a hand, an arrow
or some other sign of his choosing
appear in the window on the screen.

And, with the gentle mockery
of this christening, Liam had managed
to associate the world of his computers
and liquid crystal screens with our father's patriotism,
by concealing within it the *Pádraic*
after whom Captain Daddy had christened me—
Pádraic, the Irish, the true, the only name
for Saint Patrick, who had freed Ireland from serpents
and led the redeemed country
to believe in the Holy Trinity:
Pádraic. Pad. Mousepad.

(Shona had, however, accused our father
in a letter from Belfast after her flight with Duffy
of having actually had in mind not Ireland's apostle
when he chose this name
but of Pádraic Henry Pearse
who had fought in the Easter Rising of 1916
against the British rulers and for Ireland's freedom
and as a result had been court-martialled
and executed in Kilmainham.)
Pad. Mousepad. Mousepádraicpearse. *Flop-flop*.
Was I named after a hero or a saint?

When I finally lay in my sleeping bag
I was so cold that I only gradually
realized, as if awaking from a druggy haze,
that the noise I heard was the chattering
of my own teeth, a continuous annoying sound
that I wished would cease, cease at last.

Every movement with which I tried
to wriggle into a warmer position
in my mummifying bag sent a fresh icy shiver trickling
through my joints, down my back, my chest,
as though it wasn't a down-filled bag
protecting me from the biting frost
but a bundle of threadbare rags.

But then it turned warm, snug and warm
and I felt a gentle pressure
moulding the down lining so tightly to my body
that there was no more space for the cold
and it receded with every breath.
This warmth began to transform
my exhaustion into the peaceful tiredness of a child,
and I thought Shona was rocking me to sleep,
thought that I could even hear her soothing whispers,
but then it was Liam who said, *Are you asleep, Pad?*

It was Liam warming me,
it was my brother holding me in his arms.
His open sleeping bag around his shoulders,
like a coronation mantle whose train
dangled over my desiccated husk,
lending me additional protection,
he was bending over me, holding me,
rocking me in his arms.

When I suddenly started from sleep
in the pitch darkness because a strong gust
was causing needles of our frosted breath

to slide down the flysheet onto my face,
and I felt Nyema by my side and pressed up against her,
wishing to dry my cheeks on her hair,
wanting to kiss her—and was fully woken
by Liam pushing me away
and whispering, giggling, *I'm the wrong bride,*
I'm the wrong bride.

Ashamed, as if I'd been caught behaving
unchastely, I struggled out of my shell,
wishing only in that instant that Liam
would carry on sleeping and forget my mistake,
and groped in the dark for my boots.
A spasmodic, piercing pain
in my bowels, which had perhaps
chased me from deep sleep
even before the sliding frost,
now forced me outside.

In the open air at last, I had just enough time
to crawl a few metres from the tent
and uncover myself,
then crouched shivering in the thick snow flurry
as watery diarrhoea shot out of me,
melting a black crater beneath me
and filling me with revulsion at myself.

Breathless from my haste in the thin air,
groaning with cramps, a shitting
infant lost in the dark heights,
I saw dense needle-thin snow crystals

criss-crossing the beam of my headlamp—
snow which began to smother the light; snow
which would wipe out the messy sinkhole
under me; snow that swallowed everything—
disgust, sky, mountains, the tips of the ridges,
even the tent's dome was barely perceptible
despite being mere metres away.

Twice I crawled awry, finding only emptiness
and darkness hatched with ice crystals
where a tent, warmth, a berth,
my brother, my shelter should have been,
and was about to shout for help
when finally one of the dome's guy-lines
became my guiding thread.

Was Liam really asleep—or did he merely want
to fulfil my wish and help me over my shame
by pretending to be asleep?
His breathing was regular and deep as I
was at last able to extinguish my headlamp and
crawl back from my wanderings into the rimy dark.
I never found out
whether Liam was asleep during that time
or just pretending, for neither the next morning
nor at any time during the remaining days
of our lives did he mention
that I had mistaken him for my beloved.

Morning came painfully slowly,
and I sat and waited for it with stomach cramps

in my sleeping bag because I feared I would choke
from the rarefied air and lack of breath if I lay down.
To me this damned air felt as icy,
as low in oxygen and as arid as the empty space
between the stars, and when I fell for a few minutes
into a gloomy half-sleep, it set me dreaming
of a wide-open mouth—
a mouth as big as a whale's maw,
yet still not big enough to satisfy
my thirst for air and for life.

The daylight turned a blackish green,
then deep green, baize green and, infinitely slowly, lighter
and lighter, as if the sun had to rise through every nuance
of the photosynthesis whose eventual result
would be a luminous leaf-green, the first colour of life.
Green.
Our closed tent dome tinted the snowy light,
tinted the daylight, tinted all light green,
and I entered a waking state
with a memory of the leaves of *Gunnera manicata*,
that giant plant known as Brazilian rhubarb
that adorned the gardens of Dunlough alongside camellias,
rhododendrons, acai palms, metre-high fuchsia hedges
and trees laden with bitter figs.

As big as beach parasols, their stems as thick as an arm,
the leaves of a *Gunnera* could make even adults
look like Tom Thumb—and still
the plant sank back into itself year after year
and rotted to form a blackish compost,

from which it would emerge again,
bigger than before, early the next summer.

I had shown Nyema a photo
I was using as a page-marker in a book about Kham.
In it Liam and I could be seen
under the gigantic umbrella of a *Gunnera* leaf.
We were posing in front of the great *Gunnera*
on the jetty at Dunlough with a conger eel
over 2 metres long in our arms,
two pride-swelled dwarves unrolling
an earthworm like a fire hose
—for Nyema had said, laughing, that to her the picture
looked like something from a dream, a fairy-tale image.

The garden (later gone wild)
outside our parents' house was shaded by a *Gunnera*,
but on Horse Island Liam had tried in vain
to raise a seedling against the westerly winds . . .

Homesickness? Was it homesickness
I felt that green morning?

Twice more my cramps drove me
out into the driving snow,
and I secured my return with a rope
that I laid from the tent door into limbo,
where I bent over

and struggled with my clothing
until I heard Liam's voice as if from a vast distance—

he was calling to me and waiting for me in the tent,
wide awake and already busily making tea;
he brushed the snow from my shoulders and back
as I crawled into safety again and asked me
in a voice as soft and caring
as Shona's had once been:
Are you ill, Mousepad?

My head was about to burst. I felt sick.
It was stormy. The snow, whose needles
now darted horizontally against the tent wall
and stung our cheeks and eyes every time
Liam opened the dome to look
for signs of improvement in the weather,
rose in uneasy waves outside our shelter
like briny surf—crystals everywhere, pricking,
stinging crystals, penetrating
every tiny opening.
We were captive.

Amid this chaotic, surging white,
the path leading back into the saving deep
had vanished, as had the path to the summit;
the ridges and cliffs of Phur-Ri,
which way was up and which down,
the whole mountain, which had a moment earlier
risen as mighty as a cathedral above us—
it was all gone, all flown.
All that remained
was this impenetrable, wailing whiteness,
a needle storm and, encased in it,

lost in it, was our tent
and, imprisoned in that,
Liam and I.

And yet I recall the sense
of sleepy, dazed happiness
that I felt repeatedly that morning
and throughout the whole day
and again during the following night
of our snowbound imprisonment.

Maybe it was due to my hot flushes,
maybe I merely dreamt
most of these blissful feelings,
but being ill meant even
in our isolation up here
that I was exempt from all duties, all toil,
exempt from the nuisance of departing,
from every step outside
and every further step
into the agonizing heights.

As on feverish days in my childhood
when Shona had cared for, protected and comforted me,
I floated, unhampered by any burden,
even the burden of my own weight,
in a limbo-like state that allowed me
to fall asleep without a care only to find,
upon every fresh awakening, that I was not alone.
If I was thirsty I got a drink,
if I was hungry Liam gave me food,

if sweat stood out on my brow
a slow hand would wipe it carefully away,
and when I sighed as I dozed
or in pleasant fatigue
and my brother thought I needed comforting
he spoke confidently of our avalanche-proof campsite,
of the slackening wind,
the rising air pressure and of weather conditions
that were improving by the hour—
but spoke mainly
of our imminent descent
and the ease of our return journey to Drogsang.
What was the medicine, the snow-white powder
Liam administered against my headaches
and against my cramps,
sprinkling and stirring it into a mug
which he then raised to my lips?
He held my head as he did so, because
I was falling sleep even as I drank.
Oh, I enjoyed a privilege greater
than any other up here—I could rest,
rest as long as I wanted, rest
as if I never had to go back out into the snow.

I can't remember how long it was
until the cramps finally left me in peace.
But they subsided.
The splitting headache abated and with every
new awakening, I became more acutely aware
of how my strength was gathering
because I did not immediately have to squander the gains.

I could rest, I could sleep
and hoard all my unspent strength.
Even the air seemed to grow more nutritious
and saturate my lungs with oxygen,
as if from an Atlantic breeze.
Was it all a dream—that the innermost core
of the surging crystalline chaos around us
was our tented dome? a green repose
in which we could remain until Phur-Ri
allowed us to return to the pastures of Drogsang.

Medicine? asked Liam. What medicine?
He had cooled the scalding tea with a handful
of snow—the white stuff was snow.

But even if my brother had stirred opium
or some other anti-diarrhoeal narcotic
into that mug (after all I would not be
the first fatigued person for whom a drug
made the high altitude, breathlessness
and internal and external terrors more bearable)—even if . . .

In truth it was mainly those words of solace
that filtered through sleep to my mind,
helped me back onto my feet
and perhaps even healed me:
We're going down. We're going back.

I don't know how often
—though certainly several times—
my brother said, We're going down.

We had, he said, only to wait
until the snow stopped, nonsense, we
only had to wait until the snow *abated* . . .
And wasn't it already getting brighter?
The wind was weakening, it was beginning to clear,
so we would soon
be on our way, back to Drogsang.
In two days, two days, you'll be with her again.
In two days you'll be with her again.
And the peak of Phur-Ri would have to fly after us!
That peak was of no concern to us now,
here in our green camp—of absolutely no concern.
We were as good as back in Drogsang.

I remember the day I was sick
and even the following night,
as if day, night, all the pain and revulsion,
had evaporated within a few hours;
I remember that time as a short sequel,
a mere coda to the instant
in which I had crawled back into the tent
out of the swirling snow, plagued by cramps,
and there had found Liam, my brother,
in whose protection I felt safer
than I would ever have dreamt
possible in the isolation
of a high-altitude camp.

Liam nursed me to health by evoking
the shore of Drogsang, the clan's tents
by calling to my mind, even in sleep,

the joy of our return, Nyema!
Nyema, who suddenly seemed so close
as though it were not the path across a glacier
riven with crevasses and hundreds of metres
of altitude that separated me from Drogsang,
but a few harmless steps.

Although I often reflected on this
during my long and arduous
return journey to Horse Island,
it remains a mystery to this day
why the next morning my brother and I,
when the time of our agreed
and promised descent finally arrived,
when the snow abated, then completely ceased
and above us a deep-blue sky
began to expand until there was no space
for fog banks and clouds . . .

why my brother and I, although everything
occurred exactly
as Liam had promised in soothing tones,
exactly and even better—
there was not a breath of wind in the luminous mountains,
the snow-capped peaks shimmered like porcelain,
the air was clear and mild, and the wind had pressed
even the fallen snow so firm in some spots
that it promised to bear our weight;
we would cross the snowy expanses
as if walking on a sandy beach pounded flat by breakers;

even the crests and waves had settled
and were now mere flourishes in the landscape . . .

why, when our improbable hopes were realized,
did we turn *not* downwards
to Drogsang, not towards the saving deep
but upwards, towards the summit,
the glittering ridges of Phur-Ri
on which even the ice banners had now faded
and disappeared—as if rolled up and stored away
after the stormy night-time parade.

Why.
I felt a deep gratitude.
I was grateful to Liam, indeed I loved him
for looking after and tending me,
for invoking Nyema's closeness,
mainly, though, for forgoing
his peak out of concern for me
and trying to console me with the promise
that as soon as the snow allowed,
he would descend by my side and bring me
safe and sound to the clan's tents and to Nyema.

I remember my heartfelt desire
to show Liam my gratitude
and pay him back for the security and strange bliss
of my hours of illness and exhaustion.
A gift! That's what I wanted to make him,
and I felt something like relief or satisfaction
when I realized even as I made my wish

what that gift should be—
the summit; it should be the summit.
I wanted to give him
the summit of the Flying Mountain.

Now that he had nursed me to health,
and the enchantingly beautiful heights
seemed no farther away
than the overhanging edges of Horse Island's pastures
over which, from our climbing routes,
we had seen gulls and clouds sail;
now that we were closer than ever before
to our goal—an empty space,
a white spot marked by no tracks,
the highest survey point of our lives—

now I was the one
who argued against a descent
and tried to persuade Liam to grasp a chance
that might arise only on this radiant day
and then be lost for the rest of the year
in the snow showers driven by monsoon fronts.

And was the summit
not in any case a modest gift?
Perhaps 300, 400 metres in altitude
lay between us and our goal. In this weather
we should be at the top in a few hours, right at the top,
and from there in even less time we would be back again.

The ridge—our route—basked in sunny serenity before us:
up there and then past a needle of rock
we had to go to reach the small snowy saddle
that already marked over half
of the remaining ascent—over half!—
and how close, how temptingly close did the saddle seem
already from the secure pitch of our tent.
And if this closeness was deceptive
and it did take us longer to get up there,
we could always turn around
and be back in Drogsang by afternoon.

If we left the tent and the majority of our gear
here, we would be fleeter,
faster and could either use our gear
again for a night's rest
on our return from the summit
or keep going straight down,
even long after sunset,
for the moonlit night to come
would be every bit as bright as this glorious day.
Had we not climbed down
from Mont Blanc the previous year
(and by a more difficult route than this)
in the moonlight?

Just as unbearable pain
or intoxicating happiness soon fade
when past, and may only be recalled
in their former clarity when they
next approach, I now have trouble

imagining the zeal with which
I tried to persuade Liam not to forego
the peak for my sake, *but* precisely
for my sake to continue our path to the top.

For in my excitement at my recovery
and my returning strength
I no longer saw any conflict between
the safety of Drogsang, my reunion with Nyema
and completing the ascent together—
under these felicitous circumstances both
were perhaps to be achieved in a single day
and I did not need to choose.
We had only to seize the opportunity.
And we seized it.

The fact that Liam agreed only reluctantly to my
        suggestion
and only half believed in my *resurrection*
(in his doubt he actually used Captain Daddy's word)
only reinforced my eagerness,
also because I sensed how the prospect of reaching
his already abandoned goal after all spurred him on,
but of one thing I am sure:
if I had stayed silent, my brother
would have breathed no further word of the summit
and set about preparing our descent
without another upward glance.

In the first weeks after Liam's death Nyema had
often disagreed with me, sometimes with a ferocity

I had never known in her; and yet
I could not shake off one thought
that crushed every other perspective
with the relentlessness of a millstone
and always left me thinking, mumbling and dreaming
the same identical words: *I killed my brother*.
Even now, during my long pointless
inspection rounds of the property and pastures
on Horse Island (there is nothing else to do),
I am tormented by the thought that by wishing
to make a gift of Phur-Ri to my brother
I did not care for him as he cared for me,
but killed him instead.

So we left behind the tent and many belongings
we would never see again
and initially found everything on the way
to the summit just as we had expected—
the ridge to the small saddle swept virtually clean
and easier to climb than binoculars had suggested.
It took us less than two hours
and we continued without a second thought.
We would soon be at the top.
The sky remained bright.

When I realized that my strength
might not be as great and as lasting
as I had perhaps
only imagined that morning,
and that I could lose it just as swiftly
as I had won it back with Liam's aid,

the distance to the top
seemed already shorter than the way back
to the tent and the valley below.

Moreover, as long as one deviated not a metre
—not one metre!—from it, the route
revealed no great difficulties; the chasms,
overhanging ledges and ice-clad chimneys
remained mere threats beside the actual path.
On more level snow-covered sections
the snow even bore our weight as we had hoped.

So I concealed from Liam my growing travails
and gradually returning pains,
for they would, they must come to an end;
concealed the tormenting breathlessness and the urge
to pause every few steps, then every step;
concealed the agonizing thirst that made me
guzzle down snow by the handful
and, even in these frozen wastes, hear
the occasional gurgle of streams, of impossible
        meltwater
whose rushing sometimes swelled to the roar
of surf, freshwater surf, beating somewhere
up above—against the peak? . . . Don't stop!
Anyway, this thirst could not be slaked
with a swig from the (almost-empty) thermos flask;
any moment we would reach the top,
there alone salvation awaited, up there
we would refill the empty bottles

with meltwater.
At the top a freshwater sea gurgled, roared, raged.

Which of us was carrying the gas cooker?
Was Liam carrying the gas cooker? Don't stop!
Every break for breath or rest, every swig
that could only moisten parched lips
not quench a burning thirst,
merely delayed the salvation
awaiting us up there at the summit.

How strange, the idea
that this trackless whiteness,
this empty space, our goal . . .
might already be occupied—
by enthroned gods, ice spirits, demons—
but whatever the being who ruled this peak
without having set foot on it
or left the slightest trace,
it was presumably laughing at us,
it was toying with us!

For sure! someone was toying
with me and my brother Liam,
someone was pulling strings, pulling the summit
away from us one moment, then letting go again
so that the peak drifted back towards us,
one moment in crystal clarity,
the next shrouded in scraps of fog,
in clouds and icy plumes.

Clouds . . .? Fog? Icy plumes?
Nonsense, those were not icy plumes.
Those were no scraps of fog, no clouds.
It was just mist! My own breath
was misting up my goggles, that was all.
My own panting!
The sky was black or blue, in any case clear
and still clement towards us—*Heaven have mercy*!
May God protect you! Merciful heavens!

And even when these merciful heavens
and this damned peak,
which once more darted away,
mocking us with its backward leap—
even if this damned sky-peak
danced up and down before our eyes,
appearing one moment like the Holy Virgin
and immediately vanishing again,

it would not escape us now,
we would haul it in, Liam and I,
this damned sky-peak would not escape us, not me!
After all, it was not only to be a gift
for my brother, but my last—
the last—peak I scaled,
the last I reeled in!
I had seen enough of heights.

Now I wanted, I would be able . . . I would soon
be able to turn back, back down to the sea,
down to the shore above. Don't stop!

The roar was deafening now,
thundering freshwater, drinkable surf.
Any moment we would reach the top.

I recall that my flaming,
then smouldering, glimmering confusion
sometimes subsided
and for a few moments would even disappear.
Then I thought I could see everything clearly
and definitely before me, and was sure
that Liam was rewarding me
for bravely hiding my returning pains
as he climbed ahead of me,
slowly and with infinite caution.

I was still able to follow him
(albeit at a growing distance).
Were we not attracted by one and the same force?
Or was it desire? Was it the same desire that I had
for so long thought a weakness of Liam's?
The desire for an infallible end to this path,
for the point at which every further step
could lead nowhere but into the void . . .
Had we drawn so close to the summit
that its magnetism prevented us from turning back?

Don't stand still. Don't put down roots
in this stone-hard snow . . . or was it ice?
An engraved icy tablet? A blackboard
made of marble, criss-crossed by the roots
we would necessarily put down

the moment we stopped. Roots
that snaked to the peak before us . . . Marble?
Liam, what a guy! He crawled along these roots,
reciting poems,
singing!

Should I sing too? We were brothers after all.
But how could anyone remember
verses and poems
when, 10 or 12 metres above him,
where my brother now stood, a hail of stones
suddenly broke loose—fist-sized hail-pebbles
two or three of which
struck me on the back of the hand.

Was Liam trying to kill me? Oh, a ledge
or foothold must have given way beneath his feet
and crumbled into this hail . . .
From where Liam was now, almost at the peak,
the poor guy couldn't see or know
what harm such hail could do, such hail
at this solemn moment just below the peak!
Liam, my poor brother
had no idea,
no idea of this hail's effect.

Now he called out to me.
What else could I shout back than
Everything's okay, no problem,
all's fine, I'll be right there!
My glove was not ripped

and inside it all I could feel was warm
drinkable water, not blood. What could I say?
We had to go on, now
that a white bandage for my battered hand
lay up there on the summit—everything,
everything awaited us up there, ready.

The summit.
So this was the summit,
which now began to rear above us—
a white fist clenching
and slowly rising into the sky?

Yes indeed, that must be the summit,
for behind it there was only a deep majestic blue
with stars twinkling in it.
That blue was the sky.

What a relief when I finally realized
that the summit lay not high up among those stars
but in fact much closer and lower,
and that the dazzling white, raised fist
was only water vapour, a snow cloud—
only the dome of a stack of cloud sprouting
slowly and exactly in time with our steps
from the edge of the actual summit ridge.
How delicately, so delicately, ran the line
dividing the summit ridge from this stack of cloud,
blurring all distinction
between mountain and cloud.

I couldn't help myself; I had to grin.
Not only because of my breathlessness but also
because such a delicate, unbelievably fine line,
a mere thread,
could divide the most awe-inspiring mountain
of my life from empty sky,
could sever it . . .

I grinned so broadly that I felt
scales of ice break free from my gaping mouth
and tumble down with an audible tinkle
onto my brother's tracks.

Grinning, clasping the ice axe
like a walking stick
with a hand bathed in warmth,
I stumbled towards that
delicate, glittering edge.

18.

Epilogue: Steps.

The grass on Horse Island stands tall
this February, but the pastures are empty.
The gusts pluck blood-red, white and pale-pink petals
from the crowns of the camellia trees,
send them swirling up in swarms, which float,
swarm after swarm, off into the void.
At night the beams
of Dunlough lighthouse
sometimes glide over curtains of spray that rise
high above the coastal reefs
and sink noiselessly back
into the darkness.

It's a mild spring. By Epiphany
the red camellias were in bloom
and after them the white ones flowered,
two weeks earlier than usual.
The wind does not allow what it tears from the trees
and scatters over the fields to lie for long,

but no sooner has it sown them
than it gathers twigs, leaves and blossom
and tosses them skywards again, before eventually
casting them over stone walls cluttered
with brambles and gorse into the abyss
out of which my brother and I
climbed so many routes named
after turbot, hake and codfish,
up again and again, to here, to this edge
which was for us the edge of the sky and—
until our departure for Kham—
a substitute for harsher heights.

Now black terns,
great black-backed gulls and shearwaters,
gliding on seemingly frozen wings,
rise high above the exits of our climbing routes,
test the pastures' grassy waves with their bobbing heads,
turn away and, with a shriek
(which I interpret as excitement),
let themselves fall back into the deep.

Sealed storm-proof cameras
no longer observe the island's
single short stretch of road leading
down from the house to the quay.
The screens have gone dark: sold
or packed for sale, they are stored
in the sheds behind Eamon's Bar
like the telescopes, like the remaining furniture,
like the boxes of books and the carpets

with their patterns knotted into endless loops—
snow-capped mountains, meandering rivers, yak caravans.
I walk through the empty house, day after day,
hour after hour, across the empty fields, over and over,
walk down to the thorn-barbed stone walls,
climb every day over the thicket,
stand at last on the edge of the abyss
and follow through the binoculars
the receding coastline of Ireland
until it fades into the breaking surf.

Sometimes the wind forces me
to put down my glasses to keep my balance,
forces me to turn my back on the sea
and thus shows me once more the house on the knoll—
my house, the camellia, myrtle and arbutus bushes
and all the shrubs planted by Liam
that grace my inheritance,
waving to me from there and bending
and bowing under the pressure of the wind,
even blowing me kisses,
as if their evergreen beauty, endangered
by the salty landward-blown spray,
needed displaying one last time to me
before I leave here for good.
I must be on my way.
I am going.

Still I must wait, however, wait,
as in the past few years Liam and I
waited time after time, sometimes for days,

until the sea between Horse Island and Dunlough
became navigable once more in the waning wind.
Leaning into the wind, I walk down to the quay,
then across the pastures and, again and again,
to the edge of the abyss and back to the house
in whose sliding glass doors I see
my reflection advancing towards me.
What happens
when a man who has taken his decisions
and made all the necessary arrangements,
goes to take the first step towards his goal,
and what happens when he finally
sets one foot before the other?

As we sought a description of the ailments
awaiting a lung-breathing creature who ventures
into the mountains and highlands,
Liam and I found in printed and digital
reference works, most of them online,
accounts of disorders
affecting the functioning of the brain,
of the risks of hypoxia
and a dangerously high heart rate,
a thickening of the blood—
and general descriptions of all paths
into the upper layers of the atmosphere
as gradual approaches
to the boiling point of our bodily fluids,

but we also came across
pictures of neurophysiological processes

that portrayed a single step
(whether upwards or down) as
a complex and mysterious drama
which even the most passionate researchers
were incapable of explaining in full.

For this one step, whose origins
lie hidden in the subcortical regions of our brain
in which the first manifestation of our *will*
creates an electrical impulse
(which whizzes through the associative cortices,
triggers readiness potential and
calls on patterns and exercise programmes
in the cerebellum's basal ganglia
that by way of supraspinal switch points
finally reach the locomotory outlets
governing muscle contraction . . .);

this one step seems to condense, in slow motion,
so many stages of the entire evolutionary process
that even the associated changes
at molecular level (such as an avalanche-like
increase in ionic conductivity in the cell membranes
or the miraculous conversion of an electrical signal
into a chemical process—measurable at the synapses
of the nerve cells—and its magical reversal
by neurotransmitters into a purely electrical event)
strike one as a digest of humans' elevation
from the animal kingdom.

Steps.
How primitive the binary sequences
in Liam's computers seemed in contrast to the drama
of a single step . . .
Stone Age technology, said Liam, *Stone Age*!
when he compared his programs
with the mysteries of the human organism
in the days we spent preparing
for the breathless highlands of Tibet.

Each of my steps across the fields of Horse Island
now brings me closer to the black tents of Nyema's clan.
I know that Nyema is waiting for me,
not in Drogsang—winter has beaten
life back again from clouded heights
to lower encampments—but at some other point
on the path the clan takes through the seasons
to follow the vegetation, moving higher and higher
towards the unattainable snowy peaks
and returning in the autumn to the valleys,
towards *depths* where, somewhere,
distant and inaccessible as the stars,
lies the sea.

Nyema is waiting for me.
I promised I would come back.
I would carry the news of Liam's death
down to the sea and in doing so
follow Nyema's example as she brought the news
of her husband's death at Nangpa La
back to the tents of the clan

so that Tashi's soul, no longer encased
in a spent and shed guise,
would not be trapped in hearts and memories,
but might continue its progress.
After fulfilling this last and greatest service
the living can do for the dead,
I would return.
To her.

This morning Eamon radioed me and offered
to send the Marine Rescue, Liam's old mates,
in their lifeboat to save me
from Horse Island
like a castaway.
But I can wait.
I have food. And I have time.
I lean into the wind,
pace my inheritance, the edge of the abyss,
the empty rooms, the short road to the quay,
the fields.

While clearing the house, things appeared
that I had thought long lost;
Liam had kept them without ever mentioning them—
the papier-mâché landscape we had given Captain Daddy
after many hours of secretive work
for the first Christmas
we had to spend without Shona.

This landscape, the scale model
of a valley on the road to Macroom, was meant

to represent the scene (shaded by bushes
and trees made of moss) of a heroic death,
the spot where Michael Collins,
the commander of the Irish Republican Army,
was shot the year of our father's birth—

by traitors from within his own ranks or
henchmen of the British crown.
Captain Daddy had a stock of conspiracy theories
regarding the life and death of his idol,
an ever-replenishing stock of murderers' names
he drew from a collection of books
and historical journals that grew from year to year.

The captain had been so touched by our gift
that our panorama replaced
a plaster nativity scene comprising
the Blessed Mother, Saint Joseph, the swaddled,
new-born saviour and praying shepherds
(arranged on the mantelpiece over Christmas
to remind us of God's incarnation).
Hence we were able to retrieve plaster sheep
from the now missing Bethlehem
to make our heroic site more life-like.

Even I could not bring myself
to throw away the papier-mâché landscape.
It was part of the first cargo
I shipped from Horse Island to the mainland.
Now it stands between whiskey bottles
on a shelf in Eamon's Bar.

I sometimes thought that one reason
my brother had built the house on Horse Island
was so that he could finally store
the many objects related to passions
meant to help him cope
with the empty spaces and his unrealizable longings—
the computers, the screens, the books,
the measuring instruments and equipment
for life by the sea and in the mountains,
the climbing ropes, harpoons, tents, bivouac bags,
his collection of old globes and maps . . .

Liam had even stored photographs and pictures
from our father's *true Ireland*
in the cardboard case
that Captain Daddy had kept handy
his whole life for his travel and escape plans,
without ever using them.

Liam must have inherited his collector's mania
from our captain. I remember my horror when,
on the day after Shona's elopement, my father,
a man who could hardly bare to discard
torn oilskins and junk,
stuffed Shona's clothes, shoes, blouses
and shawls, everything she had left behind
into an oil drum and set it on fire.

I saw the panels of a summer dress
with a yellow-diamond print fluttering in the fire.
Shona had fetched me from the hospital

in Bantry in this dress
after I had fallen from the gangway of the ferry
to Cape Clear onto the cobbled quayside,
and, with both arms in plaster,
had to spend my first ever nights
away from my parents' house,
convinced I was going to die of homesickness.

Now, when I lie awake on my island
or the fingers of light from Dunlough
draw me back out of the darkness and a dream
into my echoing room, scenes and places
from my past, both recent and distant,
appear to me in a disorderly sequence—
the overgrown garden of our parents' house;
the wreck of a Ford Galaxy
sinking into the thicket of our drive;
night manoeuvres in the Cahas—

and, time after time, stages of my journey
back from Drogsang to Chengdu,
of my return to the sea;
the trader from Ya'an who helped me
(and may well help me a second time);
the exorbitant demands of a Chinese border guard
to ignore the expiry date of my permit;
Eamon's black suit; his tears
when he welcomed me at Cork airport;
the wake in Dunlough church
after which all the mourners were invited to Eamon's Bar
and catered for until everyone raised

toasts to Liam's memory
and inserted his name into the verses
of a ballad from Galway and sang
and sang, on and on.

I sometimes have the feeling
that I must wake from another
and then another dream
to arrive at last where I really am.
And sometimes I'm not even sure
whether my brother and I actually reached
the tip of the Flying Mountain, or if we yielded
somewhere high up, very high, to the temptation
to declare our goal attained on a sub-summit,
    a sub-summit
from which the storm drove us back into the deep.

Only gradually are my doubts fading, and I realize
that everything was as it was and that it is I, I,
who lie safe in the dark on Horse Island—
in a sleeping bag because even my bed is already
in storage in the shed behind Eamon's Bar.

Then I hear the chorus of storm sounds,
hear the embattled, moaning house,
hear the thunderous surf in the deep
and sleep calmly on, relieved
that all is done on Horse Island
and I must only wait
for the wind to subside,
for a calmer sea.